Howard S.

D1500174

"FASTER! FASTER!"

"Faster! Faster!"

By

E. M. DELAFIELD ⸤pseud.⸥

De La Pasture, Edmée Elizabeth Monica, 1890–

> "The most curious part of the thing was, that the
> trees and the other things round them never changed
> their places at all: however fast they went they
> never seemed to pass anything."
>
> Lewis Carroll

HARPER & BROTHERS PUBLISHERS

NEW YORK AND LONDON

1 9 3 6

CONTENTS

*

*

PART ONE

August Week-end

*

𝟙

A slender, middle-aged lady stood with an air of mingled recklessness and timidity on the kerb and watched, in some despair, the stream of London traffic.

Twice she stepped into the roadway, and twice she stepped back again onto the pavement. There, for some little while, she appeared to take root, her head turning from side to side with quiet regularity, as she followed with surprised and reproachful eyes the endless procession of cars and taxicabs, omnibuses and vans.

At last the traffic signals altered. The watcher, as though unable to credit such a reversal in her fortunes, still hesitated, looking from right to left and back again. But other pedestrians were plunging: she plunged with them, scurried to a refuge, scurried again, and landed with a gasp of relief on the river side of the Strand.

As she went, she talked quietly to herself, commenting on the noise and the number of people in the street, and adjuring herself from time to time not to be ridiculous and absurd.

It was six years, since Frances Ladislaw had last been in London; and she had then only spent two nights there, in frantic preparations for a voyage that was to restore her husband's health. It had not restored it, but it had prolonged his life, to cause them both a good deal of misery. Eventually, Jack Ladislaw had died in Arizona.

She made no pretence to herself of regretting Jack's death. Through the ten years of their married life he had always shown himself selfish, unimaginative, slightly unkind whenever he lost his temper, and at all times contemptuous of his wife. Frances often wondered why he had ever married her. She also had the candour to wonder why she had ever married him, and to know that it was because nobody else had ever asked her. She had been the daughter of a widowed clergyman in a Yorkshire country parish.

"Like the Brontës," she muttered, thinking this over. But she immediately added, with characteristic honesty and common-sense: "Well, no. Not really in the least like the Brontës." And indeed she did not, in any way, resemble the gifted and unhappy Brontës.

Presently she turned down Norfolk Street and entered a doorway that bore a plate with the inscription: "C. Winsloe and S. Oliver: London Universal Services."

The stone stairs were dark and winding and led to a bright blue door on which was printed in black letters, Please Enter.

Mrs. Ladislaw entered, prefacing the entrance with a small knock that was unlikely to be heard by anybody but herself.

Inside the little office were two young girls, very decorative and brightly made-up, and an elderly woman with short, thick hair, dyed a disastrous canary colour, and a rather mauve face coated in white powder. In spite of these curious adjuncts she looked both pleasant and competent, and her manner reassured the visitor.

"Could I see Mrs. Winsloe? She is expecting me."

"Is it Mrs. Ladislaw?" enquired the canary graciously.

"Yes," said Frances, relieved. Although she had spoken to her old friend Claudia Winsloe over the telephone the previous evening, and had been assured of a warm welcome at the office, she still felt anxious and insecure.

"Would you be seated for a moment?" elegantly enquired the canary, sweeping several papers from a chair to the floor. She went through a door leading to an inner room.

The two young girls looked steadily at Frances. Then, by a simultaneous impulse, they turned away. Each had a typewriter in front of her. One of them was polishing her nails with a little buffer, and the other was stitching at a piece of pale-green silk. They spoke together low and earnestly. Frances Ladislaw could catch words and sentences here and there.

"And directly she came into the office, I got up and I said. . . . My dear, I nearly *died*. . . . It isn't, I said, as if I could afford to put on weight. . . . Oh, but you're *not*. . . . Oh, my dear, I *am* . . . honestly. . . . Look at my oyster jumper, if you don't believe me!"

The inner office door opened and silence fell.

"Mrs. Ladislaw, would you come in?"

The canary bowed Frances in, and closed the door discreetly behind her.

Mrs. Ladislaw started eagerly forward, but it was a stranger who sat at the desk in front of the window, not Claudia Winsloe. A slim, upright, good-looking woman of six or seven and thirty, with a beautifully-shaped head, shingled hair like carved and polished ebony, and a smile that showed perfect teeth. There was an air of finish about her appearance generally that struck awe, as well as admiration, to the mind of Mrs. Ladislaw, so conscious of her own lack of poise and total absence of finish.

"Mrs. Ladislaw? How do you do. I'm Sal Oliver, Mrs. Winsloe's partner. She's so very sorry, she had to go out on business unexpectedly, but she'll be back as soon as she possibly can. She hoped you'd wait."

"Thank you," said Frances, uncertainly. She thought that she must be in Miss Oliver's way.

"Please sit down," said Miss Oliver. Her voice, thought Frances, confusedly, was much gentler than one would have expected.

"Will you have a cup of tea? I'm going to."

"Are you really? If it isn't too early, I'd love one."

"It's never too early for tea in an office," said Sal Oliver. She twice pressed a little buzzer that stood on the table. "That means tea."

The tea was brought by a small girl in an overall, to whom Miss Oliver said, "Thank you, Edie." It was nice tea, not too strong.

"Do put down your parcels," said Miss Oliver, gently. Frances became aware that she was slung, like a Christmas tree, with small parcels. A pot of cold cream—a new sponge-bag—Lux—a little packet of milk chocolate for her landlady's baby. . . . She put them all on the floor with a sigh of relief and realized for the first time that her fingers ached from clutching them and that the string of the Lux parcel had been hurting her wrist.

Miss Oliver opened a box of expensive-looking cigarettes and handed it across the table.

"Will you smoke?"

"Thank you."

"Claudia," said Miss Oliver, informally, "was so sorry to have to go out. It was a very important client, and she didn't feel she could send anybody else. She knew you'd understand."

"Of course. I know she must be very busy. How are things going—the business, I mean?"

"Pretty well. Of course, nothing's too good just now. But we do quite a lot, one way and another."

"I'm not sure—I've been away from England for six years—I'm not sure if I quite know exactly what the business is?"

"Anything and everything, more or less. We find servants—when we can—and meet trains and escort children and invalids, and look for houses, and shop for people who live in the country. And Claudia's very anxious to develop the literary side—a sort of literary agency, though we have to be careful about the real literary agents. She does a certain amount of journalism herself—oh, and cross-word puzzles, and setting literary competitions in weekly papers, and all kinds of odds and ends."

"I'm sure she works terribly hard."

"She does work very hard," assented Miss Oliver.

"She was always wonderful," said Frances, respectfully. "We were at school together, you know. How does she manage to do it all, with her children and her home and everything?"

"Well, she goes home every night in the car—it's only thirty miles ——"

"Thirty miles!" ejaculated Mrs. Ladislaw.

"Sometimes she sleeps at my flat. And in the school holidays when the children are at home she doesn't come up every day. She does some of the work at home."

"But then, doesn't that fall rather heavily on you?"

Miss Oliver smiled.

"Well, you see, I'm not the mother of a family. I haven't got a house, or a husband—only three rooms in Bloomsbury that I share with a friend. Not that she's ever there."

"Never there?"

"No. She's a professional dance-hostess, and when she isn't in one of the big seaside hotels she's usually cruising. She's doing very well."

"How splendid!" said Mrs. Ladislaw, looking extremely startled. She paused, and then added: "I've been out of England so long. Six years. And before that I lived in Yorkshire, right away from things. I feel dreadfully out of touch."

"Six years? I suppose you see quite a lot of differences."

"Oh, quite a lot. Even if one doesn't count the traffic and Park Lane and things like that. Women—working so hard—and everybody talking all the time about expenses, and money—and having rather bad manners. I don't mean just very young people, but one's own contemporaries which is such a shock. I'm afraid I must seem terribly old-fashioned and stupid."

Miss Oliver shook her head, but said nothing.

"I don't at all want to be prejudiced. I think I shall

get used to it all quite quickly—in fact, I must, because I'm going to live here, I hope. Just now, I'm going down to Arling to stay—I dare say you know. Wasn't it wonderful, that they should have been able to buy Arling, Claudia's old home?"

"It was Claudia who bought it. Not her husband. He hasn't any money at all, of his own, has he? And no job."

"No job?" repeated Mrs. Ladislaw, half in dismay and half in hopeful enquiry. "He hasn't found anything, then?"

"No, he hasn't found anything."

They looked at one another rather solemnly.

"Then Copper just—just lives at home, I suppose?" hazarded Mrs. Ladislaw.

"Yes."

The telephone bell rang.

"Please forgive me." Miss Oliver picked up the receiver. "Yes? Yes, I'll speak to him. Put it through, please. Yes—Miss Oliver speaking." There was a long pause, while the telephone seemed to click and Miss Oliver listened and made notes on the blotting-pad.

"I see. Yes, I quite understand. You want me to inspect the school personally and make the position clear to the head mistress, and then write to you. And make all the arrangements, when you give the word. Certainly, Mr. Barradine. Either Mrs. Winsloe or myself will go down there. I'll ring up the school and try and fix it for tomorrow. We've got all the particulars. We'll write you. . . . Not at all, Mr. Barradine. Good-bye."

Still scribbling on the blotting-pad, Miss Oliver pressed the buzzer.

One of the very young girls appeared. Frances eyed her incredible slimness with honest admiration as she stood swaying in the doorway.

"Please bring me Mr. Barradine's file—Nursery Schools," said Miss Oliver.

"Right-oh," said the young girl.

Sal Oliver turned to the visitor.

"It's a man who's just divorced his wife. They've got one child—a boy of seven—and he's supposed to be very difficult and nervous. We've got the job of finding the right school for him. As a matter of fact, we have quite a lot to do with schools, and I think I know the very place. He'll be all right once he gets right away from his parents. These difficult children always are."

"If the father and mother have been unhappy together perhaps—" said Mrs. Ladislaw.

"Oh, always, I think. Whether they're unhappy together or not."

Mrs. Ladislaw, unlike most women of her generation, had a peculiar faculty for giving due consideration to ideas that were unfamiliar.

After looking at this one, and remembering spoilt children, neurotic children, and naughty children, of her acquaintance, she remarked thoughtfully that very likely Miss Oliver was quite right.

The girl from the outer office reappeared, put a file on the table, and said, in a drawling, expressionless voice:

"Look, could Edie go off now? It's nearly five, and Collier or I could take any telephone calls. We haven't got a thing to do. Collier's knitting a jumper."

"There'll be plenty tomorrow morning."

"Yeah, I know. Is it O.K. about Edie?"

"I suppose so. Yes."

"Right-oh."

She drifted out again.

"That's our Miss Frayle. She's actually a very efficient young woman, though I admit she doesn't look it."

"What does she do?"

"Secretarial. Takes all Claudia's letters, and acts as her secretary generally. Miss Collier does the general correspondence and the accounts. The one you saw—the older one—does most of the outside work—interviews, and shopping for clients, and finding houses and so on. Except what I do myself."

"You must work very hard."

"It comes in rushes. You heard what Frayle said. They're slack tonight, but tomorrow they'll probably be rushed off their feet. Especially if Claudia's in the office."

"I suppose she's still tremendously energetic."

"Oh, definitely. After all, one's got to remember that she supports her whole family—Copper and three children."

"It's marvellous!" said Frances, her eyes shining with admiration. "And when I think how they were brought up—she and Anna. Do you know Claudia's sister—Anna Zienszi, she is now?"

"I met her once, staying at Arling. She hasn't been there for at least three years, though."

"Not been there!" Frances echoed in ingenuous astonishment. "But I should have thought— They were always so devoted to one another ——"

A rapid footfall sounded outside, and almost simultaneously as it seemed Claudia Winsloe came in.

"Frances dear!"

"Claudia!"

They kissed affectionately, and then stood, looking at one another.

Sal Oliver slipped from the room.

"Oh, Claudia! you haven't changed a bit. Well—except perhaps your hair."

In Mrs. Winsloe's dark hair, the grey showed plentifully. But her clear-cut, intelligent face had retained its well-defined oval, there were not many lines round her eyes—big, and hazel—and her tall figure was slim and upright.

Impossible to say why she looked like a woman of forty-three—except that she was forty-three.

(2)

Sal Oliver from time to time went to Arling with her partner for the week-end, especially if there was any work that could be done away from the office.

She was going there now, and was pleased to think she would meet Mrs. Ladislaw again. She had found her, though faintly absurd, rather charming and, if certain aspects of present-day life eluded her, Sal felt as if they might be defective in significance, rather than Mrs. Ladislaw in perception.

She wondered how Mrs. Ladislaw would react to Arling.

Sal travelled down by train on the Friday afternoon before the August Bank Holiday.

Arling stood in a Kentish village, some miles from Canterbury. Sal, from the train window, looked with absent affection at the hop-fields, the glaring white patches of chalky ground, the cherry-orchards, dense with green, and the little black-and-white houses.

She was a Londoner born and bred, but she liked the Kentish countryside—though perhaps mostly, she admitted to herself, on account of its associations with David Copperfield.

A shabby, familiar old car, driven by Copper Winsloe, met her outside the station.

"Hullo, Copper!"

"Hullo, Sal! Nice to see you. It's going to be glorious weather for the week-end. How was London?"

"Very hot and very full, as far as I was concerned, of women screaming for impossibilities without delay."

"The whole world is full of *them*," remarked Winsloe, without rancour.

He was a tall, angular creature with thinning hair that had once been red and was now a faded rust-colour. The lines deeply-bitten into his tanned face, his slouching walk and listless movements always brought to Sal's mind the word *désœuvré*.

"Frances Ladislaw is staying with us. She's a good sort. I like her. And Claudia's mother."

"O God!"

"I know. And a chap of Claudia's—a fellow called Quarrendon."

"I know. I've met him at the office. An Oxford don, very clever."

"I dare say," said Copper without enthusiasm.

"He came in to ask us to fix up a journey to Esthonia

for him. It seems that he can't manage railway time-tables."

To this peculiarity Copper Winsloe paid no tribute beyond a brief ejaculation, expressive of scorn. He changed gear as the car approached a hill, and the noise that ensued made conversation temporarily impossible.

It was some little while before Sal spoke again. Then she asked:

"How's everything?"

"The situation," Copper said, deliberately, "is as usual—serious. The school bills are in—absolutely terrific—they've surpassed themselves—and Claudia's working overtime and all on edge."

"It's bad, but is it any worse than it's often been before?"

"No, it isn't. And she'll manage, of course. She always does. My God! though, it was a fool's trick ever to buy this house."

"How's the mortgage getting on?" asked Sal, as though enquiring after a familiar and long-standing ailment. Nor did the reply surprise her.

"It isn't getting on at all, so far as I know. I haven't asked Claudia, but if she'd done anything about it, she'd have said so. I suppose she's paying the interest."

"No hope of a job for you, I suppose."

"I haven't looked for one. What's the use? Nobody wants a man of my age, not trained for anything in particular. The next war will give me my job. The whole world's in a funny sort of mess, isn't it? Not so much for you, perhaps. You're younger."

"Not so very much. But at least I've nobody dependent on me. And I wasn't brought up to look on an income as something that was just there, as a matter-of-fact. I always knew I'd have to work for my own living."

"Everybody's supposed to be brought up to that nowadays—girls and boys alike. I wonder what my kids'll make of it all."

"Living in a house like Arling, and going to expensive schools, and knowing well enough that they have more or less everything they want, regardless of the fact that it's never quite paid for?" she said, ironically.

"I've always wondered whether it was better to scrounge and save every penny and never let them have a taste of the fun one had oneself, or to let the future go hang—which it'll probably do, anyway—and at least give them a good time to look back on. Anyway, it's Claudia that sets the tune. After all, she pays the piper."

After that, a long uphill slope and the noise of the aged engine kept them silent.

Arling stood in a small park, consisting of rough grass-land and clumps of beeches. A shabby wooden gate, badly in need of paint, led into the winding drive, and a little farther on was another gate, and then a gravelled square in front of the house.

It was a pleasant little house, about a hundred and fifty years old, with no especial features. The French windows of the ground floor faced a long straggling garden where a small stream ran along by the bottom of the tennis-lawn, overhung by a giant pair of weeping-willows.

Inside, it was roomy, shabby, and sparsely furnished. Of the ground-floor rooms, only three were in use—the library, that ran almost half the length of the house and faced south, a smaller room on the other side of the hall, traditionally called the smoking-room, and a square, cold dining-room at the back of the smoking-room.

The hall was also square, stone-tiled, and with a stone staircase leading to the floor above. Nine or ten bedrooms were inadequately served by two bathrooms.

It was a source of satisfaction to the Winsloes, and also to their guests, that Claudia's parents had put both electric light and central heating into the house before the war. The intermediate owners of Arling, beyond repairing the roof and installing a separate boiler for the hot-water system, had done nothing. They had, however, after twelve years, decided to go and live in the Isle of Wight, and this timely resolution had led to the reinstatement of the late Captain Peel's daughter in the home of her childhood.

"I'm not coming in," said Copper, at the open door. "I've got a job in the workshop."

He spent a good many hours in his workshop, an outbuilding behind the stables. Sometimes he repaired small pieces of furniture or turned something on a lathe, but on the whole the visible results of the time he expended there were strangely inadequate.

Sal nodded without speaking, and went into the house.

Her ears were at once assailed by a loud and hilarious outburst of community-singing in German. The wireless was, as usual, turned on full blast in the library, and the door into the hall—also as usual—stood wide open.

She paused for a moment in front of the round gilt mirror on the wall, took off her hat and ran a pocket comb through her short, satin-black hair, and then went into the room.

Sylvia was at the tea table,—auburn-haired, blue-eyed, and innocently pretty; Maurice, small, compact, and sandy, eleven years old, crouched upon the floor near the open window, surrounded by snapshots, a pot of paste, an open album, and innumerable sheets of blotting-paper; and Taffy sprawled gracelessly over an armchair, petting an old and moth-eaten black cat.

The children's grandmother, Mrs. Peel, sat in a sofa corner with *The Times*. At intervals she read aloud an extract from the news, to which nobody paid any attention. Her slim but undefinably elderly figure was clad in thin tweed, her grey hair, piled high upon the top of her head, curled tightly into a neat little fringe on her forehead, and she wore steel-rimmed spectacles.

Standing next to Sylvia, with an awkward air of not knowing what to do next, was a man nearing forty; large and clumsily built, with an ugly, intelligent face and the habitual frown of the extremely near-sighted. This was Andrew Quarrendon.

Sal greeted them all adequately—Quarrendon obviously had no recollection of her whatever, although they had met several times—and sat down by the open window.

"Mother and Frances will be here in a minute. They're only in the garden," said Sylvia. "I've made the tea. We won't wait."

"Sal, do you know His Lordship was thirteen last week?" asked Taffy, petting the cat.

"There was a cat in the *Daily Mail* who lived to be twenty-two," said Maurice, abruptly.

"Oh, dear!" said Mrs. Peel.

This ejaculation was, with Mrs. Peel, almost an automatic reaction.

"*Schön sind die Mädeln mit siebzehn, achtzehn Jahr,*" burst hysterically from the revellers of Leipzic.

"*Must* we have the wireless quite so loud?" said Mrs. Peel plaintively.

"Must we have it at all?" Sal enquired.

"I forgot you didn't like it," Maurice remarked leniently, and went to turn it off.

It was a fine wireless set, of the newest type and very expensive.

"See when the dance music's coming on, though," Taffy besought frantically. "Don't let's miss that, whatever we do. You wouldn't mind the dance music, would you, Sal?"

"I expect I shall be upstairs, or in the garden."

Taffy grinned her understanding of the implication. She was a tall, lanky child of sixteen, of the same loose-limbed build as her father. She had none of Sylvia's golden prettiness, but her small, apricot-tinted face, with wide-apart blue-green eyes set in long, light, curling lashes, was arresting in its air of defiant intelligence. Her straight, sandy hair was cut in a Garbo-like bob that reached nearly to her shoulders. It suited her.

"Here they are," said Sylvia.

Her mother and Frances Ladislaw came in by the long window.

2

(1)

The personality of Claudia Winsloe was of a kind that made it almost impossible for her to enter into any group of people without effecting an immediate alteration in the atmosphere.

In her own home, this was markedly so.

The subtle inner currents running from one person to another seemed somehow accelerated and intensified by her presence, and there was a marked tendency, on the part of her children especially, to refer every manifestation of personality to the bar of Claudia's judgment. This was done simply and without disguise by Sylvia and Maurice, and even to a certain extent by Mrs. Peel. In Taffy, it took an oddly inverted form, causing her to disagree sharply with her mother on every point, although usually by implication rather than directly.

Sal Oliver had formed part of the Winsloe family circle so frequently that her observation of it, though always acute and interested, had become almost a subconscious process. Today her chief preoccupation lay in watching for Frances Ladislaw's reaction to it. She had an idea that behind her obvious inability to conduct everyday life on any but rather muddled and ineffective lines, might lie a quite simple and uncomplicated honesty of outlook that would make her judgments neither muddled nor ineffective. The Winsloes included her happily in their conversation. All of them were naturally good talkers, and Frances was, as naturally, a good listener.

With Andrew Quarrendon they had more difficulty. He did, indeed, appear to listen, but it was with a curious and disconcerting air of intensity, and he turned his large head from one speaker to another as though anxiously awaiting the introduction of some profound thought, brilliantly expounded.

Claudia did her best for him, begging for suggestions for a literary competition. She set one regularly for a weekly paper.

"Make them do a parody!" cried Maurice. "Like the time you said A Railway-timetable as Dr. Johnson would have written it."

"Too difficult," objected Sylvia, at the same time that Taffy ejaculated, "Too easy."

Everybody, excepting Professor Quarrendon, offered suggestions, or rejected the suggestions of other people. Even Mrs. Ladislaw asked, "Why not a piece of poetry?"

"People usually think that sounds too difficult, I believe," said Claudia.

"A cross-word puzzle, then. You do make them up, don't you?"

"Oh yes."

"For two papers," cried Maurice, proudly.

"Claudia!" said Mrs. Ladislaw, with admiration. "It's terribly clever of you."

"It only needs a very good dictionary and a certain amount of general knowledge. One gets into the knack, and after that it's easy."

Quite true, thought Sal, but in some extraordinary way it sounded as though it wasn't really true, but just an expression of modesty.

"Some of Mother's are marvellous," put in Sylvia. "She tries them on us sometimes, before she sends them up."

"A custom in Sparta. Motto of a famous Corsican," muttered Frances Ladislaw, with wide eyes.

"That would be Napoleon," said Mrs. Peel, unerringly.

"Oh yes, I suppose it would. But I didn't really mean anything. I was just thinking about cross-word puzzles, and clues. I can't ever *imagine* being able to make them up."

"Claudia works too hard," said Mrs. Peel, mournfully.

Still, the professor, gazing through his thick lenses at everybody in turn, said nothing and seemed to listen for something.

Sal Oliver could see that Claudia was growing anxious about him. She had brought him to Arling—pleased and dazzled, no doubt, as so many people were, by her brilliant efficiency, her charm and good looks—and now it was obvious that family life and family conversation were proving too much for him. Sal knew already that he was unmarried and lived by himself.

She turned to him.

"Do you do cross-word puzzles?" she enquired.

Quarrendon shook his head.

"I'm afraid not."

"Neither do I," Taffy remarked, in a detached tone. "I wish I did, but I can't see the fascination of them."

Claudia smiled at her daughter.

"That's all nonsense, really. You ought to be very good at them."

Taffy smiled back, though shaking her head, as if to show that she did not relinquish her point. Quarrendon, turning his eyes on Taffy, this time allowed his gaze to dwell there for a moment, reflectively.

The air had vibrated with a faint hint of hostility during the brief interchange of words between Claudia and her younger daughter. Perhaps it was that, Sal thought, which had arrested his attention. She wondered whether he was slightly in love with Claudia. A good many people were.

The conversation went on—inconsequent, cheerful, and allusive.

"Claudia," Mrs. Ladislaw was saying, "you write as well, don't you?"

"Sometimes."

"You must tell me where to find your things. I've been away so long, I don't know anything. Six years!"

"Oh dear! These children must have changed a great deal," their grandmother suggested.

(Taffy and Maurice scowled, and even the gentle Sylvia looked indignant.)

"Yes, they have, of course. But Claudia hasn't. She doesn't look a day older."

"She looks thin," said Mrs. Peel. "Yes, darling, you do. You work too hard."

"Hard work never hurt anybody yet," said Claudia, abruptly. "Besides, there isn't any alternative."

For a moment her face looked older and hard.

There was a smothered shriek from Taffy. Hastily, although with kindness, she shoved His Lordship off her knee and rushed to the wireless.

"There's something I frightfully don't want to miss," she explained, with an apologetic look at Sal. "I'll put it on quite softly."

She flung herself onto the floor and began to manipulate knobs.

"You hadn't got a wireless, when I saw you in London years ago," said Mrs. Ladislaw. "I suppose everybody has one now."

"Nearly every cottage in the village has one," Sylvia replied.

"That," said Mrs. Peel, regretfully, "is perfect nonsense."

Nobody paid the slightest attention to the remark. Of course, thought Sal, it was exactly the kind of thing that one would expect her to say. Women like Mrs. Peel had been talking and thinking—in so far as they could be said to think—in that way for years. The difference now was that nobody ever troubled to argue with them or contradict them.

"*If I love again,*" proclaimed a thin voice from the ether.

Everybody went on talking.

Even Taffy, without altering her position on the floor, joined in.

Then Copper slouched into the room.

Almost at once he turned to his younger daughter. "Switch off that row," he directed.

Taffy, looking sulky, obeyed.

"Tea, dear? Maurice, let Father have that chair."

Maurice obeyed.

"Don't give me that strong tea!" exclaimed Copper. "For God's sake, how long has it been standing? Can't we have some fresh?"

"Of course," said Claudia, equably. "Please ring, somebody."

The whole atmosphere of the room had altered.

Taffy had gone quickly out through the window, carrying the cat with her.

Maurice, in a lowered voice, was muttering to Sylvia about his snapshots.

Presently he let a number of them slip to the floor. But he uttered no exclamation. Helped by Sylvia, he began to pick them up, crawling cautiously about amongst the chair-legs behind his father's back.

"Have you seen the evening paper, Copper? Sal brought one down. I saw it in the hall and put it in the smoking-room."

Claudia, evidently enough, was endeavouring to distract her husband's attention from the youthful clumsiness of their son. For a little while 'she succeeded, by dint of manufacturing remarks about the contents of the evening paper. But Maurice's perambulations, unskilfully conducted, brought him into contact with the leg of his father's chair.

"What the— What a clumsy little owl you are, Maurice! Here—hop it."

"Just let him get his photographs, Copper."

"He can get them later. I want my tea."

Maurice looked at his mother. She smiled reassuringly at him, but signed to him to go out.

Sylvia followed him, by the window.

"Poor little things!" exclaimed Mrs. Peel.

Copper Winsloe scowled.

"Here's some fresh tea," said Claudia. "Look, you've got green sandwiches at your elbow."

She might have been dealing, kindly and wisely, with a spoilt child—and indeed it was as a spoilt child, and a disagreeable one, that Copper showed in his wife's drawing-room. He was not the same person as the man who had met Sal at the station and talked with her on the way to Arling. Sal had seen this metamorphosis of Copper Winsloe before, many times. It never failed to rouse her to mingled regret and exasperation.

The conversation, now, was a completely artificial affair, carefully kept by Claudia on lines adapted to the ill-humour of her husband.

Claudia's own unruffled calm remained admirable. Equally effective was the dramatic suddenness with which the light had left her face and the eagerness fled from her voice and manner.

Words, even tears, could not have served better to underline the boorishness of Copper Winsloe's behaviour.

It was all quite clear to everybody, thought Sal, bitterly, including Copper himself.

Quarrendon, she saw, was observing them both. In the gentle grey eyes of Frances Ladislaw was to be seen a puzzled and deeply-disturbed expression.

(2)

"Have you brought down anything that I ought to see to at once, from the office?" Claudia enquired of her partner.

"Nothing much. Mrs. Ingatestone has fixed up one or two things. I've brought down notes. And there are some cheques for you to sign."

"I'll do those at once," said Claudia, getting up.

"You needn't. And it won't make any difference. No one will get them before Tuesday."

"I'd rather have them now."

Claudia's desire to get things done at once was an obsession. Every night before going up to bed she pulled the day's leaf off the tiny calendar that hung on her desk, so that the next day's date should confront her in the morning.

"Can't you give the office a rest?" Copper enquired.

Claudia shook her head.

"I daren't," she said, simply. "If once I let things begin to pile up ——"

She threw a look at Quarrendon.

"*You* know what it is?"

"Oh yes," he agreed. "I know. But I'm afraid in my case things are allowed to pile up. They're doing it now."

It was the longest speech that Sal had heard from him, and she was struck by the charm of his voice, so much more distinguished and agreeable than was his appearance.

He had risen as he spoke, and moved to the window,

where he stood looking out at the August garden. Sylvia went by.

"Do you play tennis?" she called out.

"Very badly, and I've no racquet."

"Never mind, we'll lend you one. Come along."

He obediently went.

Sylvia came and stood by the window. Her uncovered hair stood out in a bronze halo round her head, and she wore a faded mauve cotton frock that showed the outline of her tall, lithe young figure. She looked incredibly young and slight, lovely with that soft, ephemeral bloom that passes with the last vestige of childhood.

Sal wondered how much the professor noticed, of that enchanting prettiness.

"Frances, will you play, too?" Sylvia enquired of her godmother.

"I should like to come and look on, if I may. I won't play now."

"You will tomorrow," said Sylvia contentedly.

They went off to the court.

"Get me those cheques, Sal, if you please," said Claudia, not in the tone of one who was concerned with what anybody pleased.

"For God's sake, Claudia, let up! It can't make any difference if they're signed tonight," groaned her husband.

"They're upstairs in my case. It'll do if I bring them down at dinner-time," said Sal.

"Darling, do give yourself a rest," urged Mrs. Peel. "You've been at the writing-table all day long."

That's done it, thought Sal.

It had.

Claudia went straight to the door.

"I'll bring down your case, Sal," she said.

Copper Winsloe ejaculated, "O my God!" in a disgusted voice, and left the room.

Mrs. Peel sighed, fidgeted, went to the window, and then came back again to the deserted tea table.

"What do you think of the children, poor little things?" she asked, unhappily.

"They look extraordinarily well and cheerful," said Sal, replying thus on principle, although the words happened also to be the expression of her true opinion.

"Yes, I think they do," their grandmother agreed, without, however, brightening very much.

"Sylvia grows prettier every time I see her," said Sal, encouragingly.

"Oh yes, poor little Sylvia, she's very sweet. She reminds me of a miniature I have at home, of my mother. It's *most* curious," said Mrs. Peel, "but there's a very strong likeness. I don't know why Claudia pretends not to see it."

It was the unalterable conviction of Mrs. Peel that anybody who disagreed with her was only pretending.

Sal, who thought she knew very well why Claudia did not admit the alleged resemblance, made no reply.

"You know," said Mrs. Peel, abruptly, "she works too hard. It's too much for her. I'm very worried about Claudia."

"The holidays make a break."

"She seems to me to work just as hard, only she doesn't go up to London every day. Look at all she does! Her own housekeeping, and her writing, and the

work she gets from the office, going on all the time.
And the children."

"They're growing up, now. In any case, there's no
need for her to wear herself out for the children. She
ought to make *them* consider *her*."

"Of course. It's what I've said all along," wailed Mrs.
Peel.

She hadn't said it all along—and if she had, it wouldn't
have checked Claudia's impulse towards self-immolation
on the altar of her ideal of maternity.

"Has Sylvia heard any more about her job?" Sal
asked, in order to change the conversation.

"Oh, poor little thing! I can't bear to think of it.
But they say that girls all do, nowadays, and I'm afraid
it's more or less necessary. But she'll marry, of course."

Claudia returned, and gave Sal her case.

"Here you are," said Sal, handing her the cheques
in a little sheaf. "If you'll give them back to me when
they're signed, I'll send the lot off to Ingatestone. She'll
be back at the office on Tuesday morning."

"I shall be there myself on Tuesday," Claudia said,
going to the writing-table. "I'm going up with Sylvia,
about a possible job."

"We were just talking of that."

"Darling," said Mrs. Peel, anxiously, "do you really
know what kind of people poor little Sylvia would be
thrown with in this publisher's office? You can't tell
very much in one interview, can you?"

"One interview?" said Claudia, raising her eyebrows.
"But it won't be *my* interview, Mother. It'll be Sylvia's. It's her affair, not mine. She's going to see them
by herself, and to tell me about it afterwards, I hope."

"I thought you said you were going up to London to see about it."

"Oh no. I'm going up because Sylvia asked me to, and because I've got to be at the office. *She's* going up to see about her job. You know I've always made my children make their own decisions."

Sal Oliver, for her part, knew that this attitude on the part of her daughter was one that always drove Mrs. Peel into a frenzy of fretfulness. It implied a not very obscure reproach to her own entirely dissimilar methods of bringing up her daughters, and it also made clear Claudia's complete indifference to her mother's views.

Claudia sat at her desk and signed cheques clearly and rapidly.

Mrs. Peel rustled—an accomplishment lost to any generation younger than her own—ejaculated, and uttered vexed and discursive sounds and phrases.

Sal Oliver picked up the newspaper.

Twenty minutes later Claudia also went out into the garden. A rather curious set of tennis was in progress. Sylvia and Maurice, screaming with laughter, were on one side of the net. On the other, Taffy partnered Quarrendon. Beside her rapid movements and odd, lanky grace he rather resembled a very slowly-moving battleship. When he did hit a ball, it was with a terrific and ill-directed force that invariably sent it out of the court.

"Are you enjoying yourself?" Claudia called out, gaily.

"Very much, thank you. I'm not sure about my partner, though."

Claudia sat down beside Frances Ladislaw.

Maurice was serving. His small, intent face was set.

When he served a double fault, a not-quite-inaudible stream of maledictions came from behind his clenched teeth.

"How earnest little boys always are!" said Frances.

"I wish he wouldn't swear," Claudia admitted. "Is Quarrendon really all right, do you think?"

"Oh yes. He's enjoying it. The girls are marvellous with him. Oh, well *played*!" cried Frances, indulgently rather than truthfully, as Quarrendon, grasping his racquet with both hands, scooped the ball over the net.

"Well played!" shrieked Taffy and Sylvia.

Claudia laughed.

"Come and sit in the old place by the stream. Do you remember how we used to take books there, ages ago, when you used to come and stay in the old days?"

"Indeed I do. It's lovely to find you here again, Claudia."

They strolled along, happily discursive.

"Do you remember the frightful clothes we used to wear—high collars and tight waists?"

"And hair tied up in two black bows?"

"Do you remember Anna putting up her hair, over a huge pad, for the first time? It was when I stayed with you, and you gave a dance."

"And I was so cross because I wanted to wear a black frock, and Mother said it wasn't good style for a young girl!"

They laughed.

"Let's sit here. It's like old times," said Frances, happily, though not accurately. "Tell me about Anna. It's years since I've seen her, and I scarcely know her husband."

"They spend a lot of time in America. They're in London now, though. He—Adolf—is getting richer every day."

"That's a good thing, isn't it?" said Frances, rather timidly. She had an intimate enough acquaintance with the inconveniences of poverty to respect wealth, although she neither envied nor aspired to it for herself.

"A very good thing."

There was a pause, and Claudia turned her gaze on her friend. Her expression was mournful.

"I needn't ever worry about Anna any more. D'you remember how I used to wonder what would become of her, and what she was going to do with her life?"

Frances remembered very well. She could remember also the frantic unhappiness and anxiety of the elder sister throughout the series of violent and disastrous love-affairs that had so thickly bestrewn the path of Anna's youth.

"You don't worry about her any more, now?" she hazarded.

Claudia hesitated, drew a long breath. Then she spoke:

"I couldn't say this to anybody but you, Frances, but you're part of the past, Anna's and mine. Frances—I've lost Anna."

Her friend could only echo in dismay, "Lost her!"

"There's nothing real between us any more. You know what she and I were to one another, all through our childhood and girlhood. Anna was the person I loved best in the world. She is still, in some ways. But she's changed terribly in the last few years."

"Changed? But how?"

"She's grown away from me altogether. I think it began when she married. You see, I didn't like Adolf. I've
got to face the fact that I tried to bring pressure to
bear on Anna. I tried to direct her life for her. That's
what she resents. She's never forgotten it, and I think—
I think she's never forgiven it, either."

Claudia's voice trembled.

"I've got to face it," she repeated, with careful candour. "I've domineered over Anna all her life, more or
less, and she resents it—and always will."

"But, Claudia—not *now*. Surely not now, when it's
all over and she's got her own life and you've got
yours."

"No one knows how deeply those things sink in,"
Claudia said, sombrely. "Anna's resentment of my bully-
ing was probably subconscious for years and years. It
was only after she married and got quite free from me
that she really understood what I'd been doing to her."

"But, Claudia ——!"

"Yes, it's quite true. I've got to face it," Claudia repeated.

Frances, deeply troubled and bewildered, could only
look at her in mute sympathy.

"You've got Arling," she ventured again. "I was so
glad when you wrote and told me."

"Yes. I wanted, almost more than anything, to see the
children growing up where Anna and I grew up. They
couldn't have their early childhood here, as we had,
though Maurice was still quite little, when we came, but
I think they love it."

"How could they help it? And it's all so wonderfully

unchanged. Almost as if there'd never been the war or anything."

"That's what I felt. It's a little bit like putting the clock back. Though, of course, it can't be that, really. We haven't got any of the land, you know. I could only buy the house and the park, and one field—the one between us and the farm—and it's difficult enough to keep it all up, as it is."

"It must be, with things as they are now. Does—does Copper like it?"

"As well as he'd like anywhere, I suppose."

Claudia was silent for a moment, and then she used a phrase that she had used before, that afternoon.

"I couldn't say this to anybody but you. It's almost impossible to make Copper happy, nowadays. He's got nothing to do (that isn't his fault; any number of men of his age are in the same boat) and he sees me earning all the money, such as it is; and the place is mine, really, of course, though I try never to let him feel it. I don't see how he can help minding. Only, it takes the form of making him ungracious—unkind, even. I'm sure that somewhere, somehow, I've made some dreadful mistake in our relationship."

"I don't think you ought to blame yourself," said Frances, startled. "Why should it be your fault? You work so hard—you're such a wonderful mother to the children. Everything depends on you."

"I know," said Claudia, sadly. "It's quite true. The whole thing depends on me. O Frances! what would become of them all if anything were to happen to me?"

"They're growing up, though," ventured her friend.

"It won't be so much responsibility—for you, I mean—later on."

"I know. And I've told them, from the very beginning, that they'll have to work—to look after themselves. That's why I'm spending all the money I can afford—and more—on giving them the very best education."

"It's all one can do for them, nowadays."

"Yes, and to teach them to think for themselves. I've tried so hard to do that. I don't want to make the mistakes with them that poor Mother, with the best intentions, made with us."

"How very little your mother has changed."

"Physically, you mean? Yes, she alters wonderfully little. Mentally, of course, she's been static for years. You'll find that she disapproves utterly of the way I bring up the children."

"But isn't that the prerogative of grandparents?" Mrs. Ladislaw asked, smiling a little. She didn't want to think that Mrs. Peel, too, was adding her quota to the burdens borne by her friend.

Claudia did not respond to the lighter tone. There was something even a little portentous in her unsmiling reply:

"I don't want my children to take their values from her, in any way. I want them free from sentimentality, from her kind of sloppy, easy thinking. Mother, like all that generation, would like them to see everything *couleur de rose*. I don't want that. I want them to face facts, as I do."

"They will—of course they will. How could they help it? Claudia, do you know, I somehow never thought you'd be such a wonderful mother."

Claudia smiled then, a quick flashing of eyes and mouth.

"But we don't know that I am!" she cried, gaily. "The proof of the pudding is in the eating. Sylvia is only nineteen, and the other two aren't grown up. Taffy might turn out—oh, anything."

"But not sloppy or sentimental."

"No, not that, certainly. She's got a funny, hard streak in her. I don't really feel I understand her as I do the other two."

"You don't?" said Frances, bewildered by this strange candour. Never before had she heard a mother openly admitting that she did not understand one of her children.

"I don't think I do," Claudia repeated, calmly.

"She's not at all like you, is she?"

"She's not like Copper, or any of his family, either," Claudia answered, quickly. "Of course, I've got to face the possibility that she feels—antagonistic—towards me. A great many girls do feel like that, about their mothers, although very often they don't know it."

"But if so, it will pass," was all that Frances could say.

"Perhaps, and perhaps not. Most likely *not*, I should say," Claudia returned, judicially. "The thing that matters is that Taffy should develop along her own lines. Whether I'm to be the person she turns out or not, is really quite immaterial."

"I don't think I could ever feel like that, if I had a child. It's very wonderful of you."

"No," said Claudia. "It's just logic, and common sense, and, I suppose, my incurable passion for seeing things straight."

Something in Frances Ladislaw's mind, at that moment, rang a faint, immensely distant, note of warning. Just below the level of conscious thought was a latent fear, not quite sprung into life. She became aware—perhaps not more than half aware—that this frankness, this detachment of Claudia's awoke in herself something that was vaguely and quite indefinably apprehensive.

"You're cold—you shivered," cried Claudia. "Let's come indoors."

They rose and walked slowly towards the house.

Presently Frances said:

"Tell me something about Miss Oliver. I think she's so attractive."

"She's attractive, and she's very clever and capable, and we work together very well, and she doesn't," said Claudia, deliberately, "like me one little bit."

"But, Claudia—! Why doesn't she like you? Why should she be your partner if she doesn't like you? Why do you say such things?" cried Mrs. Ladislaw, breathlessly.

"Say such things?" echoed her hostess. "What things? It doesn't matter, if Sal Oliver has no personal feeling for me, so long as we make a decent job of working together at the office."

"I can't bear it—you're so brave—so good, and I can't bear you to be unhappy—lonely. Anna—and your mother —and Copper—and—and so much to worry you."

"But it doesn't matter," repeated Claudia, quickening her pace a little. "I'm quite used to it all, and there's nothing to be done about any of it. I've just got to accept the fact that it *is* so."

But Frances Ladislaw, breathless and unhappy and

bewildered, could by no means execute the necessary mental *volte-face* that Claudia appeared to expect of her.

Pity and sympathy had welled up within her, and it disconcerted her deeply to find that, all of a sudden, they seemed to be rejected by the very friend whose words had called them forth.

3

They had finished playing tennis.

It was Taffy's turn to put away the balls and let down the net. Sylvia walked slowly towards the house with Andrew Quarrendon.

"I'm afraid I was frightfully bad," he said, apologetically. "I never play games."

"It was great fun," said Sylvia, placidly.

Quarrendon brightened.

"It was, wasn't it? You know, that's a thing one misses very much as one gets older. Nobody ever expects one to have fun—just plain, pointless fun. It's all so serious."

"It's because you're a don, I expect."

"I expect so," he agreed.

"We'll play games after dinner. Shall we? Paper games, I mean. I'm sure you can play those."

"Yes, I can," he admitted. "I'd like that very much. Do you know a great many?"

"A good many, I think. Mother's very good at them, and so's Sal Oliver. I don't know about Frances."

"Which is Frances?"

"Mrs. Ladislaw. The one who was here when you arrived. She was at school with Mother, and her greatest friend. She's my godmother. We haven't seen her for years. Look out!"

Sylvia caught Quarrendon by the arm as he entangled himself with the ropes of the old swing that hung in a corner of the garden.

"Thank you," he said, meekly. "I'm very bad at seeing things, I'm afraid."

"Because of your sight, or because of not being interested?"

"My sight is perfectly all right so long as I'm wearing my glasses. And I always am."

"Yes, I see," said Sylvia.

She liked the dryness of his implications, and the glint of humour that had come into his large, solemn face.

"But you're interested in people," she suggested.

"Oh yes. Always."

"Even when the people aren't interesting in themselves?"

"They nearly always are."

Sylvia felt faintly relieved. In her heart was always the childish fear that she was, herself, utterly uninteresting. At school, Taffy had always been the clever one, the leader, and at home, of course, one's brilliant, hardworking mother was the only personality that really counted. As for being pretty, Sylvia considered that there were many days on which she was anything but pretty. Definitely repellent, she thought.

"Did you know that I'm trying to get a job in a publishing house? Freeman and Forest. I'm going up to see them on Tuesday."

"Are you hoping to get it?" Quarrendon asked, in his odd, intent way.

It somehow caused her to reply rather carefully.

"Theoretically, of course I am. I'd like to do something to help Mother. You know, she earns everything for all of us? At least, she's got a tiny income my grandfather left her, but it isn't much. And I know I ought to work. But I'm afraid, really, I'd have liked to live at home and do nothing. The kind of life girls were expected to lead when Mother was young would have suited me beautifully."

"Arranging the flowers?"

"Yes, and doing things in the village, and gardening, and sometimes going to London for a few parties and theatres and things, and having people to stay."

"The leisured life, in fact?"

"Yes," said Sylvia. "I don't think I've ever told anyone that before. I'm definitely ashamed of it."

Quarrendon smiled.

His ugliness became negligible when he did so.

"Don't be ashamed of it. So long as you're honest with yourself, and know what you really want and why you want it, there's never anything to be ashamed of."

"Is honesty the most important thing?"

"Yes," said Quarrendon.

"I'm not always honest. I say things, quite often, to make myself sound nicer and more interesting than I really am."

"So do most people. Besides, you're confusing honesty with truthfulness. You *know* when you're pretending, don't you? You don't pretend to yourself. So it doesn't matter so very much."

They had reached the house. The old black cat crawled from under the syringa bush near the library window and again Sylvia saved her companion from a disastrous false step.

"Don't walk on His Lordship. He's nearly blind and he gets under everybody's feet."

"In that case he has more excuse than I have for not noticing where he's going," said Quarrendon.

He bent and stroked the cat. The aged creature rubbed its head against him, purring.

"I'm glad you like cats," said Sylvia, pleased. "We've got a dog, too—an Airedale called Betsy—but she's in the workshop with Father. You'll see her at dinner time."

"Do you change for dinner?" said Quarrendon.

"Yes. But don't, if you don't want to. It won't matter."

He put down the cat gently.

"I don't want to in the least, and I shall do so. And you know you'd all be slightly ashamed of me if I didn't. You see how I try to live up to my own theories about honesty."

They both burst out laughing.

(2)

How nice he is, thought Sylvia, running up to her room. Quarrendon had been much more easy to talk to than any of the young men whom she knew. Sylvia was always rather frightened of young men, ever since one, whom she hadn't liked at all, had tried, without a word of warning, to kiss her at a dance when she was seventeen. No one had ever heard about that episode. Sylvia was deeply ashamed of it. Not because the young

man had wanted to kiss her, but because she hadn't liked
it. Her contemporaries, she knew well, took such things
in their stride. It was Experience, they said—and Experience was more important than anything else. Sometimes they carried Experience very much farther than
being kissed. So they said.

Sylvia had gabbled with other girls herself, about sex
appeal and the dangers of repression, or—alternatively—
about the importance of work and the relative unim-
portance of sex.

She felt inwardly sure that she herself had no sex
appeal at all. Looks had nothing to do with it—everybody was agreed about that. Sylvia's own mother, who
was no longer young, still attracted men.

It was funny that one never talked to one's mother
about this terribly important question of sex. She had
been very modern and splendid about it all—told one
every possible thing at the earliest possible age, was prepared to discuss anything freely, and had always encouraged her children to read everything they wanted to
read.

Perhaps it was because she was so much cleverer than
one was oneself, and of course so much more attractive.
It seemed almost impossible that she should understand
the awful diffidence that overwhelmed Sylvia whenever
she thought about the young man at the dance.

Their brief and graceless dialogue was hideously clear
in her memory.

"What on earth's the matter? D'you think I'm tight
or something?"

"I'm frightfully sorry. I don't like that sort of thing."

"My God! are you one of *them*? You don't look it."

"No, no," said Sylvia, distressed. "I—I just don't think that being kissed is any fun."

"I suppose you're temperamentally frigid," said the young man, gazing distastefully at her through horn-rimmed spectacles. He was a Bloomsbury Group young man.

"I suppose I am," said Sylvia, nearly in tears.

The strange idea came to her now that she would like to relate this happening, of which she had never spoken to a soul, to Andrew Quarrendon. She felt that he would be impersonal, although interested, and that he might even make her mind less about it.

She was still thinking of Quarrendon as she changed her mauve cotton frock for an evening one of dark-blue chiffon. It was an old one, bought in the sales more than a year ago, but Sylvia had always liked it.

She was brushing up her shining aureole of wavy hair when Taffy came in.

She, too, had changed, and was wearing a rather ugly apple-green frock with a round neck and short, puffed sleeves.

"Syl, what are we going to do with them all, tonight? Has Mother said?"

"Play paper games."

"Oh, that'll be all right. I thought it would be so awful if we just sat round and talked."

"But that's rather fun, sometimes."

"Not with Grandmother there. And I'm not sure about Frances. Is it all right for us to call her Frances?"

"Yes. She said we were to. Don't you like her? I do."

"Oh, I quite like her. Only I'm not sure if she'd do for paper games—anyhow, not the more subtle ones. I

feel she'd have qualms about being perfectly, perfectly
kind when it came to personalities."

"It mayn't be a bad thing for some one to have a few
qualms," said Sylvia. "You haven't, and Mother hasn't,
and I don't think Quarrendon would have many."

"Neither do I. I like him."

"So do I."

"Do you suppose he's in love with Mother?"

Sylvia felt slightly startled.

"Somehow I never thought of that. Of course, most
of her men are, aren't they?"

"In a way, yes. A sort of intellectual way. It doesn't
mean much. Could I have one of your handkerchiefs,
Syl? I haven't one left."

"Yes. Take one. Do I look all right?"

"You look rather nice. I like you with masses of lipstick on. I hope Daddy'll be late. We can have the wireless on till he comes."

(3)

Maurice had already turned on the wireless. His
evening toilet had been shorn of everything that he
could possibly omit without attracting attention to the
omission. He had rushed downstairs early in order to
obtain possession of the newspaper. Only two came regularly to the house, and of these his father had one in
the workshop.

The other, Maurice knew, would contain a full report
of the summing-up in a revolting and notorious murder
case. He was extremely anxious to read it.

"During the last generation or two," roared a voice—

for Maurice had wholly neglected the recommendations of the little book of instructions that lay on the radio, regarding peaceful tuning—"during the last generation or two there has developed a school of composers and executive artists of great individuality ——"

The voice roared on, and Maurice, impervious to its eloquence, devoured in compressed form the life story of a young cinematograph-operator who had first shot, and then partially burned, an elderly prostitute by whom he had been kept. He had just reached the jury's verdict of "Guilty" when the door opened.

Maurice, drawing a deep breath as he relaxed, stood up politely.

It was Sal Oliver.

"Are you listening to that?" she enquired, obliged to raise her voice in order to be heard.

"Oh no," said Maurice, in surprise.

He abruptly silenced the informant.

"Why do you have it on when you don't even listen?" Sal asked, with friendly curiosity.

Maurice considered. He was a little boy who seldom spoke at random.

"I think the noise helps me to think," he said, at last. "Some people at school have the gramophone on when they're supposed to be studying. They say it's a help."

"In my day it used to be just the other way round. It was supposed to be much more difficult to concentrate when there was a noise going on."

"That's what Grandmother always says. But Mother doesn't. She can always concentrate, however much noise is going on. She doesn't mind being interrupted, whether she's writing or anything. She says it's only a matter of making up your mind to attend to what you're doing."

"I see," said Sal.

"I made up my mind when I was quite young," Maurice said, gravely, "to try and be like her. As far as I *could*, I mean," he added, rather apologetically, feeling that such an aspiration might well sound slightly presumptuous.

His admiration for his mother was enormous, and he saw no reason to suppose that he would ever be hard-working and brilliant, as she was. He knew himself, on the contrary, to be very slow.

But at least he could learn to concentrate, and the people at school always said that was half the battle. Then he might get a scholarship, and it wouldn't be so frightfully expensive for Mother and she wouldn't have to work so hard all the time.

As he thought of it all his small freckled face grew graver and graver and he unconsciously breathed a deep sigh.

Sal Oliver, looking at him, suddenly asked for a cigarette. "And please light it and *start* it for me, Maurice," she said, in a quick, conspiratorial whisper.

Very occasionally Sal would invite him to a couple of illicit puffs.

Maurice flew joyfully to the cigarette-box.

(4)

Taffy had put on the apple-green frock from motives that were obscure to herself.

It was a very old frock indeed, descended to her from

Sylvia—and Sylvia had worn it while she was still at school. It had shrunk badly in its last cleaning, and was now much too short. The sleeves were too tight.

And apple-green wasn't Taffy's colour.

Her mother had said so, and had given her a very pretty frock at Christmas, pale primrose, with tiny orange flowers embroidered all over it. Not a real evening dress, but just right. Taffy ought to have worn it tonight. She had, in fact, meant to wear it, and at the last minute had pulled out the ancient apple-green instead.

She had wondered if Sylvia would say anything, but Sylvia had apparently been thinking of her own appearance, rather than of Taffy's.

On her way downstairs, Taffy rapidly evolved the running commentary that so often accompanied her through her days.

"A tall girl of nearly seventeen was hastening down the stairs. There was a far-away look in her eyes, and it was evident that no thoughts of self troubled her. Yet the hastily-donned shabby frock, faded to a soft pastel shade, served only to show off her slender grace and the deep, dark colour of her eyes. They were eyes of almost emerald green, a colour seldom seen in an English face—gipsy eyes ——"

"Is that you, Sylvia?"

It was her mother's voice.

"It's Taffy, Mother."

"Come in a minute, darling, and help me."

Taffy went into her mother's bedroom. It was a large room, with two windows facing south. Between them stood a sort of combined writing-and-dressing-table.

It was now being used as a writing-table. Papers strewed it, and half a dozen envelopes, already addressed, lay on the floor.

"If you'd stamp those for me while I finish—I shan't be a minute—and it would save time. There are the stamps—under the looking-glass."

Her mother spoke without raising her head, still writing rapidly.

"They won't go tonight."

"I know they won't. But it gets them done."

"But they won't go tomorrow, either. At least, they'll go, but they won't arrive till Monday."

"I know. Be quick, please, darling. I'm going to be late for dinner."

Oh no, you're not, Taffy silently apostrophized her parent as she picked up the stamps and began to stick them on.

Mother wouldn't be late. She'd get her letters finished, and herself dressed with quite incredible speed, and come downstairs at the last possible minute, looking beautifully finished, and with that air of poise that maturity gave to some people—the brilliant, vital ones, like Mother.

"There! That's done, thank Heaven. Why have you put on that frock, Taffy dear, instead of the yellow one?"

How like her! Apparently she'd never once raised her eyes, and yet she knew all the time what one had on and exactly what one looked like. Did she perhaps do it to show how clever she was? Taffy was so disgusted with herself for these thoughts—that another part of herself insisted were unjust and unkind—that her anger sounded in her voice as she answered.

"Isn't it all right?"

"The yellow one would really be better, wouldn't it? This one seems to have shrunk, or else you've grown a great deal."

That was meant to sound as though it was quite a new idea that the green had shrunk. To gloss over the fact that Mother had pointed it out before, and one had deliberately ignored it.

"Honestly, Taffy, I think you'd look nicer in the other."

"There isn't time to change now."

"Yes, there is. Five minutes."

"Have I got to?"

There was a second's pause. Then her mother said, in the carefully neutral tone that she sometimes employed towards her children.

"No, of course not. It's your decision, not mine. Do exactly what you like. I think, myself, the green is a mistake; it's obviously too small for you, and it's not your colour. But it's for you to decide, naturally."

"Then I think I'll keep it on," said Taffy, defiantly.

"Very well. Put the letters in the box as you go down, please, darling."

Her mother sounded calm, almost absent-minded, as though she had already dismissed the whole topic of Taffy's frock from her mind.

Nevertheless, Taffy knew that something was still vibrating in the atmosphere between them, born of that tiny scene.

Only she didn't know what it was.

(5)

Moved by a belated impulse of hospitality, Copper Winsloe emerged from the workshop, his dog Betsy at his heels, with the idea of finding a drink for Quarrendon.

The chap, although extraordinary to look at, seemed to be not a bad sort. He talked less than did most of Claudia's friends, and, although probably clever—"a brain," Copper mentally termed him—had so far shown no offensive signs of it.

Quarrendon was nowhere to be seen. He must have gone upstairs to dress. Copper wondered doubtfully whether the chap proposed to get into evening clothes. Still—Oxford.

He ought to be all right.

Betsy, who was young and light-hearted, made a frivolous attempt to pounce at Taffy's cat, stalking morosely across the hall.

Copper indulgently called Betsy to order.

He was much kinder and more lenient towards animals than towards human beings.

Betsy adored him.

Everyone was upstairs.

Copper, first disposing of a drink on his own account and then of one on behalf of the absent Quarrendon, went up to his dressing-room.

As he took the loose change from his trousers pocket and placed it on the table, he reflected in a detached way that this—three shillings and eightpence—was literally all the money he had in the world.

He had never had any savings. His war gratuity had been spent long ago, and his share of the money his parents had left, divided between himself and two sisters, both of whom had married poor men, had gone, bit by bit, to his creditors.

With bitterness Copper remembered that before the war he had been quite well off and had enjoyed life on a tea-plantation in Ceylon. The climate had never troubled him, and he had had sport, and cheap polo, and the kind of society that he enjoyed. His idiotic war marriage had stopped all that. One couldn't take a girl like Claudia to live in the Far East. She'd have been miserable, out of her element altogether. After the war was over, she had said that of course she'd go if Copper really wanted it. Probably she'd meant it, too. But there seemed to be a doubt about her health, Mrs. Peel making a fuss and insisting on getting an opinion from some old woman of a doctor. And of course the doctor, probably seeing what was required of him, had said that Claudia wasn't any too strong. So they had stayed in England.

Claudia not strong!

Copper's mouth twisted into a smile at the thought. As he had told Sal Oliver, he scarcely knew how he and Claudia had reached the stage at which they now found themselves, and that didn't apply only to the continual financial pressure against which Claudia struggled gamely and to which Copper himself had long since surrendered without resistance.

In the early years after the war he had tried hard to get a job, and had failed again and again.

Then Claudia's father died and she had inherited some money. They had lived on it—and much beyond it—for years. Claudia had decided to start a business that had gradually succeeded and developed into London Universal Services. Then she had bought Arling. It would, she said, be better for the children to live in the country.

It would give Copper something to do.

It would prove cheaper in the long run.

Copper believed in none of these reasons. Claudia wanted to live in her old home, that was all.

He didn't even understand why. It wasn't like her, surely, to be sentimental.

Arling was well enough, but the purchase mortgage remained unpaid, bills were always coming in, and to-morrow's money was never quite enough to meet yester-day's demands.

Copper savagely kicked off his boots. The thought of his financial position always made him sick with impotent fury. He closed his mind to it as far as possible.

But the subconscious knowledge was always there, driving him to irritability with his children—his expensive children—just as his resentment at his own inefficiency made him seek to assert himself with Claudia, grumbling and contradicting like a sulky schoolboy.

He didn't quarrel with her, because Claudia wouldn't quarrel.

She hadn't time, probably.

It was the rush life, for Claudia.

Copper, who never had anything to do that he felt to be worth doing, could only evade the horror of conscious thought by drinking rather too much and taking his dog for long, aimless walks.

There was nothing to look forward to any more, and when the next war came it would settle him. Copper

put his three shillings and eightpence into the pocket
of his evening trousers.

If they played bridge, he might win some money
from Claudia's guests.

Otherwise, there would be nothing more to come
until Claudia, on the 1st of the month, placed five
pounds on his table in the workshop.

It amused him to realize that she should feel herself
to be sparing his pride because she did not hand him
the money outright, as he had seen her hand pocket
money to the children.

(6)

In her room, Mrs. Peel rose fretfully from the bed
on which she had been lying.

She was fretful because nobody considered her important any more, and because her grandchildren were
being brought up all wrong, and her daughter Anna
hadn't written to her for over a week, and her daughter Claudia had too much to do. A vague idea possessed
Mrs. Peel that a general rearrangement of all the lives
connected with her own was required, and that it was
she who was best fitted to undertake it, if only she
knew where to begin and if only they weren't all so
obstinate.

With the thoroughness of her generation, she took
off five or six undergarments, put on several others
instead, curled her fringe with hot curling-irons, and
carefully selected a turquoise brooch, a little turquoise
heart on a gold chain, and a gold curb-chain bracelet to
wear with her black chiffon evening dress. This was cut

with a small V-shaped opening, and it showed a skin whiter than that of either of her granddaughters, for she had been brought up to protect her complexion as carefully as her virtue. Looking at herself in the mirror, she wondered whether Frances Ladislaw, whom she had not seen for years, had found her much changed. A nice creature, Frances—far nicer than Sal Oliver, whom one had never liked.

What Claudia could see in that woman!

At intervals Mrs. Peel had made this enquiry of Claudia, and Claudia had always replied that Sal, who knew everybody, brought a number of clients to the office, and had put capital into the business, besides. She *wasn't* a great personal friend—Claudia hadn't time for friendships with women, anyway—but she was a useful and efficient partner.

"You *cannot* say she's really a lady," was the invariable reply of Mrs. Peel.

It annoyed her that Sal should be spending the week-end at Arling. The presence of Quarrendon, although one would not say that he was really a gentleman, she found more endurable. A man—any man—was always an asset to any party. But there ought to have been a young man, for Sylvia.

"Poor little thing," murmured Mrs. Peel as she shook three drops of eau de Cologne—Johanna Maria Farina—onto a clean handkerchief.

She went downstairs, rustling a good deal. A vague, habitual regret crossed her mind for the long-ago days when she had been the mistress of Arling and everything had been done properly.

Scarcely anything was done properly now at Arling. Claudia hadn't the money, and hadn't the time to spare. Heaven knew, and so did Mrs. Peel, that Claudia did wonders. If anything were to happen to Claudia, thought Mrs. Peel, not for the first time, where would they all be?

4

---

(1)

Exactly as Taffy had surmised, Claudia finished her letters—they were nearly all business letters—and dressed
herself with speed and skill.

Her black draperies, closely defining her slim figure
and leaving her slender arms bare, were very plainly
cut and had cost a good deal of money. Claudia realized perfectly that at forty-three one had to spend
money if one was to appear well dressed. And she cared
a good deal about appearing well dressed. That was
partly the result of upbringing and partly the desire to
attract, which was strong in her.

She dressed, powdered her face, put away her things,
moving lightly and quickly. She was pleased at the
thought of the large party that would sit down to dinner. Copper, after a few drinks, would be in a good
temper instead of a morose one, and she herself, Claudia
well knew, was always stimulated by an audience. The
presence of Quarrendon, too, excited her faintly but
agreeably.

He had been attracted by her, when they first met
in her office. The second time he came Claudia, only
half by accident, had been on the point of going out.

It was nearly one o'clock and they had lunched together.

She had talked to him about her work, and asked about his own. It was Claudia's boast that, unlike nearly all women, she could conduct a conversation that was free from personalities.

That was why men always liked her.

She felt sure that she had no illusions about her powers of attracting men. She never deluded herself that, because she was still good-looking in a distinguished and out-of-date classical style, people still admired her for her looks. How could they, when the world was so full of soft, unlined, pink-and-white faces, heads of bright, unfaded hair, and shining eyes? Claudia never wasted her money on ridiculous and ineffectual attempts to rejuvenate her appearance. She was content with—or at least resigned to—the knowledge that she looked exactly what she was—a highly intelligent, vital, efficient woman of forty-three.

An occasional pang of self-pity might from time to time overtake her when she realized that she was tired, that she was working to the limit of her capacity and beyond it, and that her married life was not a happy one. Claudia told herself that she knew these passing weaknesses for what they were and was not deceived by them. Her clear-sightedness, she felt sure, was beyond question. It was her great asset, enabling her to make allowances for Copper, for her children when they required it, and for her mother when Mrs. Peel's mournful and unending commentary became unendurable.

In her own office, however, Claudia omitted—deliberately and of set purpose—to make allowances. The fury of intensity with which she attacked her own work, and accomplished it, set the standard there.

She always felt that nobody else put work, as she did, before every personal consideration, and although she seldom put the fact into words, she knew that everybody else in the office felt it, too.

Claudia carefully drew her lipstick across the well-cut lines of her mouth. It was not at all a bright lipstick—only just enough to relieve the clear pallor of her skin. Not like Sylvia's bold, pretty scarlet curves.

Claudia's thoughts switched quickly over to the subject of her children.

She adored them.

Her relationship with Sylvia was a marvellous one. That was because she'd always, as a mother, been so very careful not to dominate her children. She'd let them make their own decisions, choose their own friends, live their own lives. She herself had just worked for them—was working for them still.

They knew it, and their love and admiration and trust was her reward.

Though Taffy . . . Taffy was going through a difficult phase. Claudia frowned at herself in the glass, then smiled. Sylvia, her eldest, and Maurice, her son, meant more to her than did Taffy. It was better to face the fact courageously.

She loved Taffy, because Taffy was her own child, but fundamentally they were not really in sympathy. Of Claudia's three children she felt that Taffy was the only one to whom she had failed to impart her own passion for absolutely straight thinking.

Taffy, Claudia could plainly see, dramatized herself
continually. It was a difficult tendency to correct, and
Claudia owned to herself frankly that it was a characteristic she found peculiarly irritating. One of the few
things about which it was very, very difficult to be entirely just, detached, and understanding.

"I suppose," she thought, "that's because my own
bent is exactly the other way. I've been honest with myself all my life."

She often made this assertion.

Her little clock struck eight and Claudia lightly
pushed into place the dark waves of hair over her brow,
and went downstairs.

Quarrendon was just ahead of her.

His evening clothes bore a strange, mangled appearance, almost as though they had been slept in the night
before. No doubt he had done his own packing, and
done it very badly.

As they reached the foot of the stairs, he turned and
spoke to her.

"I like your children."

"I'm so glad," she answered, cordially. "They are nice,
aren't they? Don't you think Sylvia's pretty?"

"Oh yes. But I meant I liked them as people. Why
do you call the second one Taffy?"

"She was christened Theodora. I don't quite know
how it came to be Taffy. She's a queer child, in some
ways. Easily the cleverest of them. In fact, the other
two are not clever at all."

Claudia was always careful to display the modern
spirit of utter detachment, in discussing her children.

"She's the only one who's like you, isn't she?" said Quarrendon, thoughtfully.

It surprised her that he should think so. He hadn't, surely, just meant that it was because of her "cleverness" that Taffy resembled her mother? And yet, Claudia thought, she and Taffy had nothing else in common.

But, after all, Quarrendon, psychologist though he might be, hadn't been in the house twenty-four hours yet.

It would be interesting to discuss the children with him later. She could trust herself not to bore him on the subject, as mothers in general were only too apt to bore their listeners, for the simple reason that they were unable to bring a completely impersonal judgment to bear upon the subject, as she had trained herself to do.

In the library, the customary background of sound was missing. Either Copper or Sal Oliver had ruthlessly switched off the wireless.

Claudia was vaguely sorry. She had felt that Quarrendon would see them all in a more characteristic light if the children were enjoying the privilege of their generation—incessant noise—with herself so curiously unmoved by it. Frances Ladislaw had already said how wonderful that was. Dear Frances!

She was talking to Sal Oliver now, her clear, pleasant eyes full of interest and something not unlike admiration, as they rested on Sal's smart black-and-white effect and extremely sophisticated make-up.

Claudia went up to them.

"Are you rested, Frances darling? I'd have come to

fetch you downstairs, but I was writing madly up to
the last minute."

Sal moved away.

Copper was shaking up cocktails.

They were always a help in making people talk. Not
that anybody was being particularly silent. Mrs. Peel
was moaning slightly—perhaps in admiration?—over
Maurice and his snapshots, and Sylvia was talking to
Quarrendon.

"You're not listening to me," cried Mrs. Ladislaw,
unexpectedly.

"Yes, I am! Oh, I'm so sorry. Didn't I seem to be?"

Frances laughed.

"No, but it wasn't at all important. Besides, I know
you've got a lot to think about."

"So much that I sometimes feel as if I should go mad.
Not till the children are grown up, though. I must see
the job through."

"Claudia, oughtn't you to have a housekeeper, or a
secretary or some one, to help you?" asked her friend,
earnestly.

"I couldn't afford either," declared Claudia. "Besides,
I don't think Copper would ever stand having a stranger
in the house permanently."

"He would if it was going to save you from working
so hard."

"Oh no"—Claudia shook her head—"he wouldn't. You
don't understand."

Frances looked perplexed and sorry.

"I'm all right," said Claudia, gaily. "In another ten
years even Maurice will be grown up, and then I can
let everything go."

"You do so very much," murmured Frances Ladislaw. "I can't think how you can go on."

"I can't, either, sometimes. But one does."

"Won't Copper— Isn't there any chance of his getting a job?"

Claudia's expression altered. Her whole face became overshadowed.

"I don't know. It doesn't seem very likely. I suppose he might."

She carefully refrained from adding, as she might have done, that Copper didn't seem to be trying very hard to get a job. It was so self-evident that Frances, like everybody else, must have seen it for herself.

(2)

"Dinner's ready," said Taffy at the door.

To the infinite distress of Mrs. Peel, Claudia's young village parlour-maid was assisted in some of her duties by the daughters of the house.

They went into the dining-room.

"Sit anywhere," said Claudia, again disturbing the mind of Mrs. Peel.

But it sounded worse than it was.

Mrs. Peel sat down, firmly and correctly, at Copper Winsloe's right hand, and Claudia had already smiled at Quarrendon and lightly sketched a movement that invited him to the place beside her. It didn't matter so much about the others.

And the dinner itself, though far from elaborate, was well cooked and served.

"You've still got Mrs. Price. How fortunate," said Mrs. Peel to her son-in-law, referring to the cook.

"She's quite good, isn't she? I don't suppose she'll stay; they never do," Copper observed, callously.

"I can't bear to think of poor little Claudia having servant troubles *as well* as everything else. She's got so much on her shoulders already."

Copper muttered an ungracious something or other —what it was she couldn't hear—and turned to his other neighbour, Frances Ladislaw.

Mrs. Peel, in dignified isolation—for she had nothing to say to Sal Oliver, on the other side of her—drank cold water.

(3)

The conversation was fairly general.

Claudia, an excellent and animated talker, dominated it for the most part.

Quarrendon, although saying little himself, turned his large head towards her almost every time she spoke, and his face crinkled into laughter frequently, for she could be very amusing.

Taffy sat on his other side. She kept up a low-voiced chatter to Maurice; but Maurice answered at random, and often not at all, for he was listening to his mother and the other grown-up people.

Presently Taffy spoke to Andrew Quarrendon.

"Which would you rather, play paper games after dinner or go and see a movie?"

"I'd rather do almost anything than go and see a movie."

"I thought you'd say that. Well, it's a pity. You miss quite a lot. Maurice and I are terrific fans. Not Sylvia so much."

"Tell me something about the fascination of the films," suggested Quarrendon. "You see, I really know very little about the subject."

"But you've been?"

"Oh yes. Several times."

"Whom did you see?"

"I haven't the slightest idea."

"Haven't you *really*? Do you know what the pictures were, then—what they were called, I mean?"

"One of them was a very bad version of Wells' *Invisible Man*. Another was an inaccurate presentation— and a vulgar one at that—of part of the life of King Henry the Eighth."

"Didn't you think my Charles was marvellous?"

"Who is your Charles?" said Quarrendon, a glint behind his thick lenses betraying his lack of ingenuousness.

Taffy laughed.

"I'd crawl anywhere, any day, on all fours, in any weather, to see my Charles act in any film," she remarked, earnestly.

"I always like an understatement," said Quarrendon, mildly. "It gives such an effect of austerity. Tell me some more."

"Have you *honestly* never seen Garbo—or Norma Shearer—or Gary Cooper?"

Claudia, at the foot of the table, turned round.

"It's a great blow to my pride," she said, with mock solemnity, "that my family is completely film-struck.

Film stars, to this generation, are what musical-comedy
stars were to ours, I suppose."

"Oh dear!" said Mrs. Peel. "Lewis Waller."

She added nothing more.

It seemed enough. Her attitude towards Lewis Waller
and his erstwhile unparalleled vogue was clearly indicated, and it was not difficult to gather that, further than
Lewis Waller and the Matinée idol, her mind had failed
altogether to register the march of dramatic popularity.
Claudia began to speak to Quarrendon about modern
plays.

Taffy relapsed into complete silence.

(4)

After dinner—and after Sylvia had dealt with the
wireless until a reasonably-subdued accompaniment of
orchestral music from London had been provided for the
conversation—they played games.

"I shall be very bad at this kind of thing," Frances
Ladislaw confided to Sal Oliver. "I suppose they're all
terribly good at it?"

"I'm afraid they are, rather. But it won't matter in
the least. I'm bad, too."

Claudia had produced pencils and slips of paper.

"Shall we begin with Twenty Things?" she suggested.
"That's easy."

"I know that one," Frances murmured, joyfully. "You
each suggest a heading in turn—an animal or a battle or
a famous man, and they all have to begin with the same
letter. Isn't that it?"

"That's it," said Sal. "Afterwards, everyone reads out his or her list, and duplicates have to be crossed out."

"Are we ready?" asked Claudia. "Let's try and think of original things, not just battles or admirals or famous people. We've had those so often."

A thoroughly disapproving "Oh dear" came quietly, but angrily, from her mother.

"Maurice, you're the youngest. You start."

Maurice was ready.

"A chemical."

"Very well. Taffy?"

"A quotation from Shakespeare. *A* and *The* don't count."

"I'll say a botanical term," Claudia observed.

"Frances, what's yours?"

Mrs. Ladislaw, with some courage, declared for a battle. Sal supported her in the spirit, by saying: "A character in history. Any nationality."

Claudia smiled, and wrote busily.

Copper, as regardless as Frances of previous instructions, gave them an English town. Sylvia took them to a higher level with A Character out of Thackeray. The standard fell again with Mrs. Peel's prettily-worded suggestion of a Sweet-scented Flower and was brought up once more by Quarrendon's more original, if less charming, request for a Famous Murderer.

It was a reasonably successful game, although Claudia and her children obviously enjoyed it better than did their visitors, with the possible exception of Quarrendon.

Mrs. Peel, however, definitely disliked it. She challenged other people's inspirations, defended indefensible ideas and errors of her own, and maintained, in the face of all opposition, that Thermopylæ was the name of a well-known Greek writer.

When Taffy offered to fetch the encyclopædia Mrs. Peel rose and said that she should go to bed. She had, she declared, been fighting against a bad headache all the evening.

Maurice politely opened the door for her, and she went.

Sal said quietly to Frances Ladislaw: "It's a curious thing, but whenever any family plays paper games, it almost always ends in somebody's either being sent to bed, if young, or going there of their own accord, if old."

Nevertheless, they went on playing paper games. Claudia was very amusing and brilliant, and the children frightfully intelligent.

Presently Taffy suggested a game that they hadn't, she said, played for ages.

"You make out a list of qualities, good and bad, and mark people as you think they deserve, with ten as the maximum. One's got to be honest. Nobody knows who puts what, and then each total is added up and one sees where everybody stands."

"What fun," said Copper, satirically. "This is getting a bit too intellectual for me. Come on, Betsy."

He walked out unceremoniously.

"Wait a minute," said Claudia. "Does anybody want the Second News? It's on now."

Her ear was apparently trained to distinguish the time-signal through the noise of any number of people talking and laughing at once.

"I do," said Sal.

She was obliged to move close to the radio in order
to get it, even after Sylvia had adjusted the wave length.
It never seemed to occur to the Winsloes that other
people might not possess the remarkable faculty of their
mother and themselves for attending to several things
at once.

The suave and cultivated tones of the B. B. C. gave
them various pieces of information.

Maurice, looking regretful, rose, said good-night, and
went to bed.

"Cricket: At the close of play today ——"

"All right," said Sal. "Shall I turn it off?"

"We can get something from Paris," Sylvia suggested. "Dance music or something. I'll put it on very
softly."

Presently a muted rhythm crept over the air. An atten-
tive ear could distinguish the accompanying words:
"Last Week we said Good-bye."

"Now!" cried Taffy. "What qualities are we going
to give marks for?"

"Is this really a good game?" Quarrendon inquired
of his hostess.

Claudia laughed.

"It all depends. I shouldn't play it with my mother,
for instance. *My* children enjoy it, but then I've always
allowed them—encouraged them—to criticize other people quite freely, themselves included."

"And yourself?"

"Oh yes. The last thing I want is to be on a parental
pedestal, like the Victorian parents. I want my relationship with my children to be as honest as possible."

He nodded without speaking.

"Have we got to put down what we really think?" Frances Ladislaw enquired.

Taffy assured her that the whole value of the game depended upon complete candour.

"After all," she added, "nobody knows what marks you give. Who are we taking?"

"All the present company," Sylvia suggested.

"O.K. Mother, Sal, Frances, Professor Quarrendon, Syl, Taffy. Now what qualities?"

"Not too many, or it'll be bedtime before we've finished. Supposing we each suggest one?"

"Good looks," said Sal.

"Brains," murmured Frances, wistfully.

Claudia said, "Personality."

"Let's have some bad ones!" cried Taffy. "I'll say 'Morality.' "

Quarrendon laughed.

"That's Copper's old joke," said Claudia, smiling, as she wrote it down.

Sylvia gave them "Common sense."

"Sincerity," said Quarrendon. "I mean honesty of outlook. Call it honesty, for short."

"We haven't had that one before," Claudia observed. She looked pleased.

"The highest marks you can give for anything is ten, and the lowest nought. Everybody to put down what he or she really thinks."

"We don't really all know each other anything like well enough for this," Sal remarked.

"First impressions are valuable," Taffy retorted.

She and Sal were always on excellent terms.

"I suppose," said Frances, with simplicity, "that when

the game is finished we shall all know each other much
better."

"We shall probably none of us be on speaking terms,"
said Sal, grimly.

They wrote, pondered, frowned, glanced sideways at
each other, and wrote again.

When the papers had been gathered together and
mixed in a heap, Claudia drew each one out and read it
aloud. The totals were put down, and the final aggre-
gate announced at the end.

"Sylvia comes off much the best!" cried Taffy, dis-
gustedly. "She gets highest number of marks for looks
and common sense. Can you beat it!"

"I got rather a lot for morality," said Sylvia, de-
jectedly.

"So did I," said Mrs. Ladislaw, sadly.

"Sal got quantities of marks for brains and personality,
and about one for morality."

"I should very much like to talk to the person who
brought my average down by only giving me two marks
for honesty," cried Claudia, gaily. "I consider that if I
have one quality in the world ——"

"Mother! I gave you *ten* for honesty," cried Sylvia.
"No one knows better than your children how terribly
honest you are. Almost ruthless, some people might say."

They all laughed, including Claudia.

Then she grew more serious.

"I think, as a matter of fact, that what Professor
Quarrendon calls honesty of outlook isn't quite the same
as what Sylvia so prettily calls ruthlessness." She turned
to Quarrendon. "Is it?"

"I meant," he said, in rather apologetic accents, "the—

the contrary of self-deception. Knowing one's own true motives and—and so on," he concluded lamely.

"I see," Claudia nodded. "It's important, of course. It's partly a question of being sufficiently intelligent, isn't it? Analysing one's motives, I mean."

The door opened and Copper came in again.

"Good God! Hasn't Taffy gone to bed yet?" he apostrophized his family. "Do you know what time it is?"

The enquiry, not unnaturally, broke up the party.

(5)

Claudia, tidying up the drawing-room before going upstairs, glanced once more at the strip of paper that bore her name at the head.

She scrutinized carefully the objectionable figure 2 under the heading "Honesty."

It rankled queerly in her mind.

She *was* extraordinarily candid, both with herself and with other people. Nobody, surely, who was cowardly about facing facts would so freely permit her children to dissect her in her own presence? Sal, who didn't really like her, might have put that 2—but she knew Sal's small, clear figures, and the ladylike slope of Frances Ladislaw. This was an unfamiliar 2—sprawling, and curly. Was it Andrew Quarrendon's?

She took the question up to bed with her.

5

Saturday was a cloudless day, very hot and steamy after rain the previous evening, and the two girls were anxious to go to the sea and bathe.

"We could all go this afternoon," said Claudia. "This morning I must work. An enormous pile of stuff has turned up from the office, to be typed."

"What is it?" asked Sal. "Cambridge?"

"Yes."

Claudia sighed and turned to Andrew Quarrendon.

"A Cambridge don keeps us busy with some very intricate stuff, all Greek and Hebrew quotations, that's rather beyond the average typing bureau. We advertise a special department for dealing with that kind of thing."

"Why isn't the special department doing it, then?"

"It is. At least it's going to. I *am* the special department. We've nobody else to whom we could trust it. Anyway, the office is shut till Tuesday. This must have been delivered by special messenger last night, and Ingatestone sent it straight on."

"Why didn't the fool of a woman keep it till after the week-end?" growled Copper.

"Because it's wanted by return of post. It always is. And we've never let down the job yet," said Claudia, very decidedly.

"Is there much?"

"Not so very much. Not more than I can manage in the morning. Frances dear, you'll look after yourself in the garden or anything you like, won't you?"

Frances said that she would.

"It's always the same thing," said Copper, when his wife had left the room. "She can't let well alone. Fancy telling Ingatestone to send things on! I'll take any bet it could have waited till Tuesday."

The Airedale, Betsy, came up to him and laid her head against his knee, anxious to restore him to good humour. Claudia hastened in again, caught up some notes from her desk, and went out quickly.

"What would you like to do this morning, Frances?" enquired Sylvia.

"I think it would be very nice to sit on the cliffs with a book. Please don't bother about me, because I shall be quite happy."

"The only sensible way of spending a holiday, in weather like this," muttered Copper, stroking his dog.

"Oh dear! If only Claudia would do the same. I can't bear to see her working herself to death, as she does."

At this well-worn plaint of his mother-in-law's Copper Winsloe went out, followed by the prancing Betsy in hopes of a walk.

Mrs. Peel, in a pale frenzy of anxiety, turned her eyes rapidly from Frances Ladislaw to Sal, Sylvia, and Andrew Quarrendon, as though defying any of them to leave the room before she had said her say.

"She simply can't go like this. She'll have a break-down, sooner or later. Mark my words. Claudia is living on her nerves. She's at it morning, noon, and night. Dashing up to her wretched office practically every day of the week; and the driving, alone, is a most fearful strain—the traffic nowadays—the car not always reliable —and when it's the train she has to get to the station after all—and back at the end of the day ——"

At this point Mrs. Peel broke off, as the only way of extricating herself from a difficult sentence, and began again. Quick as she was, her granddaughter was quicker. Sylvia fled through the window.

The others, more considerate or less agile, were obliged to remain where they were.

"When it isn't one thing it's another, except when it's all of them at once, which it only too often is. This house, and the children, and, after all, there's always endless correspondence over schools and dentists and clothes and things—*and* her office work as well. Claudia," cried Mrs. Peel, frantically, "is doing three full-time jobs at once. If not more. Of course I know she says it's absolutely necessary. But what's going to happen when she's killed herself with overwork?"

Nobody attempted to reply.

"Well, I know it's of no use to say a word," said Mrs. Peel, with some inconsistency. "She'll go on and on until she's destroyed herself, and then Heaven knows what'll happen to them all. They depend on Claudia for every single thing, from their daily bread down-wards. It's she who keeps the whole thing going."

Taffy, to everybody's relief, appeared at the window.

"Is it settled about the bathing?" she demanded.

"After lunch. We'll go to the sea somewhere. Your mother can't get away this morning. She's got some work to do."

"Wouldn't it be better if we went without her?" Frances suggested, timidly. "Then she wouldn't have to hurry. I mean, perhaps she could come down afterwards."

"How far from the sea are you?" asked Quarrendon. "I could come back for her later, in my car."

"That'd be marvellous," declared Taffy, promptly. "It's only seven and a half miles. You could fetch her and the tea."

"Taffy—" said Mrs. Peel.

"She's quite right," Quarrendon remarked. "It's a very sensible suggestion. I don't bathe, but I should like to go down to the sea as early as possible. I can take some of you in my car, and lunch—if we're lunching there— and then come back for Mrs. Winsloe and the tea."

"Yes, yes. The weather may have changed by this afternoon," said Taffy, gazing up at a cloudless blue sky through a faintly quivering heat haze. "How soon shall we start?"

"I'm ready when you are."

"Well, some one had better tell Claudia," Sal Oliver suggested, mildly.

"Oh dear! It seems a great pity to interrupt her," objected Mrs. Peel.

"She doesn't mind being interrupted," simultaneously said Taffy, Sylvia, and Maurice, who had suddenly appeared out of space.

It was evident that Claudia had thoroughly impregnated her children, at least, with a full appreciation of

her remarkable powers of adjusting herself and her work
to the exigencies of family life.

(2)

Sylvia and Andrew Quarrendon sat on a chalk-white
cliff, in glaring sun, and faced a scattering of scarlet
poppies flaunting boldly against the dazzling blue of
sea and sky.

Far below them, on the shore, Maurice and Taffy
alternately splashed about in the waves or sprawled on
the sands. It was a remote little bay, and there were
incredibly few people about. Their father, who had
rather surprisingly elected to come with them, threw
sticks into the water for Betsy and made occasional
efforts at ducks-and-drakes.

Sylvia was in a white bathing-suit that displayed her
pretty sunburnt legs and arms.

She lay flat on her front, her small face supported by
her hands, and told Quarrendon the story of her life.

She had the most extraordinary feeling that he really
knew a great deal about her already, and wanted to hear
more. And she wanted to tell him all sorts of things—
things that she hadn't ever told anybody else.

"I never did anything special at school. I quite liked
it. I never made any special friend. I used to think I'd
like to, frightfully, but they were a bit down on friendships, at school. I suppose they have to be, because of
wells of loneliness and all that sort of thing. Not that
I should think I've got the slightest Lesbian tendency,
myself. Should you?"

"No," said Quarrendon.

"But I know I'm sentimental. Terribly sentimental. In my heart, I think being fond of people is more important than anything else, though I wouldn't dare say so to anybody. In fact, I've often pretended that I thought it frightfully sloppy to care about that kind of thing when I've been talking with the other girls, you know. Being insincere, in fact. Just what you said one ought never to be."

"Well, never mind," said Quarrendon, consolingly. "One has one's lapses. The great thing is that you know about it. You don't cheat yourself."

"I dare say I do, sometimes. But I'm going to try not to. Well"—she drew a long breath—"when the others used to go on about games, and careers, and what they were going to do (mind you, quite a lot of them meant to marry and have children, except a few who disapproved of marriage on principle) I always knew that *really* I wanted, more than anything else, to care very much about somebody and have him care about me."

"To fall in love, in fact."

Sylvia nodded. "I suppose so. Is that sloppiness?"

"No," said Quarrendon again. He stopped, as if to think carefully, and then said again: "No. It's just nature, isn't it?"

"I'm glad you think it's all right," said Sylvia, gravely.

"Quite all right. May I ask you something?"

"Oh yes. Anything you like."

She was surprised that he shouldn't know that.

"Did you ever think of any special kind of love? I mean—it wasn't that you very much wanted children, for instance?"

"No," said Sylvia. "I'd like to have children, quite, but not at all specially. No, it wasn't that."

"I think I understand."

She had never doubted it.

"I take it," said Quarrendon, "that you never have been in love?"

"No, never. And you see—this is really the point— I sometimes wonder if I ever shall be." She hesitated. "Some one—a man—once told me that I was *completely* frigid," said Sylvia, in a low, ashamed voice.

She looked at Quarrendon.

His face had not altered. He was still gazing out, through the thick lenses of his spectacles, in the direction of the poppies.

"It's nice of you not to laugh, or—or despise me or anything," she said, humbly.

"Why should I? In the first place, I'm honoured by your confidence, and in the second, what you've just told me is quite serious. Not because it's true—which of course it isn't—but because you evidently believe it to be true."

"I thought it might be. You see, he kissed me, at a dance, and I simply hated it. He was quite nice, really; I'd liked him till then."

"But you weren't in love with him."

"Oh good Heavens, no! And he wasn't, with me."

"Then, if I may say so, he was a cad, as well as being a conceited fool, to kiss you. What right had he to expect you to tolerate it, let alone like it?"

"Girls do," suggested Sylvia. "At least, they always say they do. It's supposed to be a sort of compliment."

This time Quarrendon did turn round and look full at her.

She had the curious feeling that he could communicate his thought to her without speaking it aloud.

"Do you mean that they just pretend to themselves they like it, because they think they're being modern, or grown up, or something?"

"But some really do."

"Some, yes. But not people like you."

"Nothing to do with my being frigid?"

"Nothing. That was just the young man pretending. It was naturally more soothing to his vanity to see you as frigid, than himself as unattractive."

They both laughed.

"How easy it is to talk to you!" cried Sylvia.

"Is it? You don't mind my being so very much older than you are?"

"Oh *no*! Why should I?"

"I don't know. But it's thought to make a difference. As regards sharing the same point of view, I suppose. I don't quite see why it should, though."

"Neither do I. Do you think it does—in our case?"

He shook his head.

"No. I've had more experience than you, because I've lived longer, that's all. I think that fundamentally we probably see things the same way. That's why *I* like talking to *you*, too."

Sylvia lifted radiant eyes to his.

"It's marvellous, for me."

"Then we're friends, Sylvia?"

"Oh yes, Andrew."

He lightly placed his hand over hers for a moment.

(3)

Quarrendon had for years been the victim of his own susceptibility.

Very few women attracted him, but with the ones that did he usually fell very deeply in love. These affairs interfered with his work, perturbed him profoundly, and always went on long after they should have come to an end—either because he lacked the courage to make a break or because the woman refused to admit that their passion could last for anything less than eternity. He had long ago resolved never to marry. This was partly because he distrusted entirely his own capacity for making any woman happy, and partly because, in the last analysis, freedom to do his own work in his own way was the thing that he most wanted.

His life at Oxford suited him exactly. He wanted to live amongst books, to talk with men whose interests were the same as his own, to write, and to make love to a woman when the desire to do so became overmastering.

The major emotional crisis of his life had been over more than ten years ago. Never, he supposed, would he love again as he had loved the young, unhappy wife of one of his best friends.

The affair had ended, curiously, with the death of his friend. The lovers—they had been lovers in the full sense of the word—had been confronted with the discovery that they had no longer any wish to spend the rest of their lives together in a joint domesticity.

How he blessed her still, for the candour and the

generosity with which she had followed him all the way, in their painful and searching struggle to attain to the disappointing, humiliating truth!

Since then he had cared deeply—though far less deeply—for two women, both of them unmarried, although neither was in her early youth.

The first of them, frankly out for a passionate affair and nothing more, had been a reckless and joyous companion throughout a long summer holiday in Bavaria.

She still wrote to him, and they met occasionally, without emotion, excepting friendly pleasure, on either side.

The other, a passionate, intelligent creature of violent moods, had speedily exhausted both Quarrendon and herself. They had parted, only to come together again and part again.

The final severance had been three years ago.

Quarrendon had not deluded himself, then or at any time, that he was finished with emotional vicissitudes. He knew only too well that sooner or later the fatal spark would be struck again. He was not even sure that he would wholly regret it.

Sheer chance had led him into Claudia Winsloe's office. He had found her intelligence and vitality stimulating, and had been faintly flattered besides that she should take the trouble to make herself attractive to him—for Quarrendon was under no illusions as to his looks, his absence of social adroitness, and his middle-age.

As he had told Sylvia, people always interested him. Claudia interested him, very definitely. He felt that he would like to see her away from her office surroundings.

She still interested him—but it was Sylvia, twenty-one years his junior, with whom he had now fallen in love. Quarrendon realized it with something like dismay, but it was dismay that was rapidly becoming submerged in sweetness.

Her youth, her vulnerability, her transparent candour, all moved him profoundly. Her loveliness, although it gave him an exquisite pleasure, was perhaps the least factor in the growing attractions of which he was so acutely aware.

When he found that Sylvia was drawn towards him, as he towards her, Quarrendon knew that he must fight a losing battle.

(4)

At Arling, Claudia was at her desk, a wild confusion of papers all round her, her fingers flying expertly over the keys of her typewriter.

It was hot, and every now and then she pushed her dark hair off her forehead. But never for one moment did she relax.

The parlour-maid appeared at the door and made a trivial announcement concerning the cook's requirements.

"I'll come," said Claudia.

She took up her keys and went.

As soon as she had reëstablished herself at her machine, the telephone bell rang.

The telephone was in a singularly inconvenient position in the hall.

Claudia listened to a full exposition from the laundry concerning a bath towel, once lost and now found.

As she hurried back to her work, Mrs. Peel rustled through the hall.

"Darling, you're doing too much. I can see it. You've no idea how over-strained you look, and it's *most* unbecoming," said Mrs. Peel, impressively. "I wish you'd have a look at these patterns and tell me what you think. It's for the new cretonne covers in my flat."

They took the patterns to the window. Claudia looked at them carefully and without hurry. It was Mrs. Peel who broke into their discussion a good many times in order to say that Claudia was too busy to attend to it now, and that she had better get back to her desk, and why, oh, why, wasn't she out in the fresh air, giving herself a good rest?

"It's all right, mother," said Claudia, fourteen times.

At last she was at work again, acutely aware of backache, eye-strain and nervous exasperation. She was aware, also, although much less consciously, of having lived up to her own ideal of a woman achieving, by sheer force of will, the next-to-impossible.

She heard the car drive up to the door, and as she worked she smiled.

It would be lovely for the children, by the sea.

Maurice came in and stood beside her, a worried, wistful expression on his small face.

"Are you just off, darling?"

"As soon as the sandwiches are ready. Sylvia's doing them. Have you got a *lot* to do, Mother?"

"Not so terribly much," said Claudia, cheerfully. "I

shall be through by one o'clock, and this afternoon I'll come down and bathe."

"You won't be too tired?"

"Oh no," said Claudia, lightly. "You know I'm hardly ever tired."

Maurice's anxious look seemed to deepen, rather than relax, at this optimistic pronouncement.

"I wish you didn't have to work so very hard. It seems such a shame."

"But you know, Maurice, nearly everybody has to work. I don't mind it a bit, because it's for all of you. If I can earn money, it all helps to educate you and Taffy and Sylvia, and then when you're older you'll work for yourselves."

"And for you," said Maurice.

She kissed his little plain, freckled face.

"Thank you, darling."

The horn of the car was sounded vigorously from without.

"I suppose the girls are ready at last," Maurice observed, morosely. "I hope all your typing will get done quickly, and not be too difficult."

He walked away, very deliberate, still unsmiling.

It was Claudia who smiled, tenderly and proudly.

Ten minutes later the telephone bell rang again.

She went to the door.

"All right, dear!" called Mrs. Peel's voice, shrilly and nervously. "I'll see what it is. Hallo! hallo! *hallo!*" There was a pause, fraught with agitation, for Mrs. Peel was neither calm nor collected when telephoning.

"Clau-dia!"

"All right, mother."

"No, don't come, darling. . . . No, it's all right. I was only speaking to my— I'm afraid I can't hear you. I think there's something wrong with the telephone."

"I'll take it, mother."

"It's all right, dear. You go back to your writing. I think it's some one who wants— Would you please tell me who's speaking? I can't quite hear. Harvey, or Jarvey?"

"Jarvey, the butcher," said Claudia. "Give it to me."

"The line is *very* bad today," said Mrs. Peel, severely. "It might equally well have been Harvey."

With an air of resentment she handed the receiver to Claudia.

"You know, darling, it isn't *right* that you should have to do this kind of thing on the top of all your other jobs. You're doing too much, and sooner or later you'll suffer for it. You may not think so now, but the day will come."

These sentiments penetrated to Claudia's hearing, rather than to her understanding, as she agreed with the butcher that it would be wiser to have a small leg than a large sirloin, in view of the weather.

Then she replaced the receiver.

"Copper ought to do far more than he does to help you," said Mrs. Peel.

Claudia shrugged her shoulders.

Sal Oliver's voice, cool and unexpected, sounded from the stairs, addressing Claudia:

"You're not what I should call an easy person to help. There's that to be said for Copper. Meanwhile, I'll read out that manuscript while you type it. You'll do it much quicker like that."

"I thought you'd gone out."

"No. I haven't gone out and I'm not going out."

"I can manage perfectly well by myself," said Claudia, rather coldly. "Honestly, Sal, I'd rather."

"I think you'd far better do it together," announced Mrs. Peel. "You're only working yourself to death, darling. How is it going to help anybody when you go to bed with a *complete* nervous break-down?"

From this unanswerable question Claudia fled back to the library.

The first hint of impatience betrayed itself in her tone as she curtly bade Sal: "Go on. I'm ready."

Sal Oliver, unmoved, began to dictate.

They worked without interruption until the manuscript was finished.

Claudia ran the last sheet off the machine, slammed down the carriage, and feverishly began to gather together typescript, carbon copies, and sheets of carbon paper.

"I'll sort those," said Sal.

"They've got to be clipped together."

"So I supposed," said Sal dryly.

She took a handful of paper-clips out of the pen-tray and began to put the sheets together.

Claudia flung herself back in her chair and passed both hands across her eyes.

"Thank Heaven that's done. We'll send them off from the post-office on our way down to the sea."

"You know," said Sal, "you really are a perfect fool."

She spoke in chilly and detached tones and Claudia made no pretence of not understanding the meaning underlying the words.

"I've never let a job down yet and I never propose to."

"You'll have to, one of these days. You're not super-human any more than anybody else is."

"I've never supposed I was superhuman," said Claudia, gently. "I'm simply a person—one of the few persons of my acquaintance—who knows the meaning of the word work."

"Fiddle!" said Sal, deftly adjusting the final paper-clip. "Most people know the meaning of the word work quite as well as you do. Why shouldn't they? But they don't get the same kick out of making martyrs of themselves and calling it work."

Claudia remained unmoved.

"I suppose," she said, meditatively, "that you really *do* believe I enjoy working as I do, instead of, for instance, being with my children in the few short weeks in the year that I've got them at home."

"There's no earthly reason why you shouldn't knock off work altogether in August. I've always told you we could manage perfectly well."

"I'm afraid I don't agree. Excepting yourself, there's no competent executive person in the office. In any case, I'd rather work all the time than leave off and then begin again. One only gets unstrung."

"The alternative, as of course you know, being to go on until everything snaps at once."

"Those things are very largely a matter of will power," said Claudia, superbly. "I haven't any intention of letting everything snap at once."

"Haven't you? Well, you've got an almighty crash coming, one of these days. However, it's your show, not mine. I'm a fool to gratify your egotism by talking like this."

"Sal," said Claudia, in her most carefully impersonal tones, "I'd honestly like to get this straight. I've the greatest respect for your intelligence, and yet it seems to me so odd that you should—speaking, of course, from my point of view—have got me so utterly wrong."

The detached candour of this appeal was without any visible effect upon Sal.

"I don't think I've got you wrong at all," she answered. "After all, I've worked with you for five years, and been down here off and on. I've seen you in relation to your work and in relation to your family. But I admit that it doesn't give me, in any way, the right to criticize you unasked."

"Not unasked at all," said Claudia, cheerfully. "I'm interested in what you think, and I'd like to go into it sometime. If I'm deluding myself, I'd very much better know it. I'm quite prepared to consider the whole question absolutely dispassionately. In spite of having been given only a miserable two out of ten for honesty, in the game last night," she added, smiling.

There was a pause as she took out a large envelope from a drawer and carefully began writing the Cambridge address.

Still writing, and without raising her eyes, she added, in a tone of casual enquiry:

"It was you, I take it, who gave me that two, wasn't it?"

"No," said Sal. "But I can tell you exactly who did."

"Can you?"

"It was Andrew Quarrendon."

"How do you know?"

"By a process of elimination," said Sal, dryly.

(5)

When Quarrendon came back, at three o'clock, to fetch his hostess and the picnic tea, Sylvia sat beside the driving-seat.

Claudia had just finished packing the tea-basket. It was the cook's afternoon out.

"I'm just ready," she cried, flying through the hall with the two heavy baskets. "Here, I'll put these in, and then go and get my hat on. I shan't be a minute."

"There isn't any hurry," Sal suggested.

She stood, hatless, by the car.

Claudia was already halfway up the stairs.

When she came down again Mrs. Peel was hovering restlessly between the library and the open front door. She was unable to decide whether she was, or was not, coming with them.

"Is it very hot by the sea?" she enquired, suspiciously.

"It was lovely on the cliffs," Sylvia said. "I suppose it was rather hot."

"We were sitting in the sun," Quarrendon reminded her. His face had burnt to a lively scarlet.

"Have you bathed?"

"I'm afraid I don't," Quarrendon replied, and at the same moment Sylvia answered, "Not yet."

"Not yet!" repeated Claudia, in surprise. "What have you all been doing?"

"The others have been swimming. We just sat on the cliffs and talked."

"I really ought to write to Anna," Mrs. Peel suddenly decided.

"No, do come. We shall all be out. You can't stay all by yourself, Grandmother."

"There won't be room in the car, I'm afraid."

"Heaps," said Sylvia, vaguely.

Mrs. Peel yielded. She explained, in a short and involved speech, that it would be necessary for her to go upstairs first and fetch a hat and a pair of gloves.

By the time she had said this, had gone, and had come back again, wearing a large shady hat and a pair of wash-leather gloves, and carrying a black watered-silk handbag, a parasol, an air-cushion, and a light dust-cloak, Claudia had reorganized the seating arrangements of the car.

"It will be more comfortable for Grandmama if you come in the back, Sylvia, and let her sit in front. We can fit in somehow, and put the baskets on the floor."

This arrangement, so excellent in itself, caused Mrs. Peel to protest.

She unselfishly urged everybody to move, to let her sit in the middle, to let her sit in the corner, to let her take the baskets on her knee, and to leave her behind altogether.

At last she was persuaded into the car.

Claudia took the seat next to Quarrendon.

"Have you liked your morning?" she said. "It was nice of you to go with the children."

"I liked it. Is your work done?"

"Yes, for the moment."

"Why don't you employ a secretary?"

"I can't afford one. Besides, we haven't got room, in

the holidays when the children are at home. And I don't think Copper would like it. He'd hate a stranger always in the house. Most men would, I suppose."

"You work very hard."

"I rather like it," declared Claudia, too brightly. "I've got any amount of energy, you know. Besides"—she broke off for a moment, and then spoke gravely and quietly. "I expect you've guessed that the children have got nobody to provide for them, except me. They're all dependent on what I can earn, practically. I've got a tiny private income, but it's a very small one."

"Your husband can't get any sort of job?"

"He hasn't had one for a long time," said Claudia, evasively. "I'd give anything if he could find something to do, but it's nearly impossible, isn't it, for a man of his age, who's not been specially trained for anything?"

"I don't know," said Quarrendon, apparently taking the question literally.

"I'm afraid it is," Claudia sighed.

She was surprised, and a little disappointed, when he said nothing more.

6

Tea on the sands was a greater success than tea in the library at Arling had been on the previous day. Copper woke, after sleeping in the shade most of the afternoon, in a mood of amiability, and sitting next to Frances Ladislaw, talked with her about South Africa.

The others were cheerful. Even Mrs. Peel, established on her air-cushion beneath her parasol, seemed to think well of her surroundings and accepted jam sandwiches and tea from Claudia's thermos. The conversation drifted.

Sometimes the children joined in, and sometimes they conducted a side-current of their own—a rapid, unintelligible, allusive spate of words that no one but themselves could follow. When they spoke to their seniors, it sounded quite differently. They were then audible and moderately distinct, and made use of coördinated words and phrases. And yet, Frances decided, they were perfectly at ease with their mother and with Sal Oliver. With their father they were less so, and with their grandmother less still.

Quarrendon, who was sitting next to Claudia, spoke very little.

When, presently, Sal Oliver spoke, energetically and with emphasis, of economic conditions amongst the unemployed, the remark met with instant failure.

"In this country," said Mrs. Peel, "nobody need ever go short of food. To say anything else is Absolute Nonsense."

The conversation quickly reverted to subjects more immediately personal.

Frances, saying little herself, sat and listened. She watched her splendid and gifted friend, Claudia, and a sense of growing dismay invaded her.

Claudia was *not* happy, she was not wholly natural, in some queer way she seemed not even quite real. There was a febrile, excited quality about her gay, animated manner, and whenever one of her children addressed her she listened with full attention and answered with a carefully displayed detachment, as though anxious to impress on them her non-parental candour. It would have seemed more natural, Frances could not help thinking, if she had occasionally been absent-minded or even impatient.

In the old days Claudia had been often impatient. The younger, more sweet-tempered Anna had suffered under Claudia's tense, violent, and domineering ways. Even Frances, a frequent visitor at Arling, had not always been spared.

Yet Frances felt that she had liked, and understood, the tyrannical, self-willed youthful Claudia better than she did the mature Claudia, so self-restrained and so unreal.

Frances was grieved, as she dwelt upon her own

criticism, but it did not cause her to bemoan her own disloyalty.

She was fond of Claudia; she would always be fond of Claudia. Nothing of that was impaired because she could not see Claudia as she had, in the years of their separation, seen her. And she reminded herself that there was much, probably, of which she knew nothing, to explain the new Claudia.

Copper, for instance, was—disappointing?

Frances searched anxiously in her mind for the right word by which to describe Copper Winsloe.

One couldn't, she felt, just dismiss him as disagreeable, although he *was* disagreeable, often. Today, though, he'd been more like the Copper that she remembered— nonchalantly agreeable, quite ready to please and be pleased.

"Well, I shall go for a stroll, I think," said the object of her thoughts. "Betsy!"

"Where are you going, Daddy?" asked Maurice.

(*"Darling* Betsy!" said Taffy, extravagantly, as the Airedale capered gaily amongst the brightly-coloured horn mugs and plates of the depleted picnic.)

"I'm going up the cliff."

"Can I come with you?"

"If you like."

"You must be back in about half an hour, Maurice, if you want to bathe again," said Claudia.

"Oh." Maurice paused.

"I don't know how much of a walk you want, Copper. Are you going to go far?" asked his wife.

"Oh, I don't know," said Copper, curtly. "I can't go timing myself to the minute."

He strode off without turning to see whether or not his small son was following.

"Maurice," said Claudia, quickly, "will you help to collect the mugs and things? Then it'll be all done and we needn't hurry over the bathe."

"Don't you ever bathe?" Taffy enquired of Andrew Quarrendon.

He shook his head.

They began to pack up. Claudia worked with deft efficiency and extraordinary speed, leaving very little for other people to do.

The two girls and Maurice ran down to the edge of the water again. The tide was going out. Presently they could only be seen as black dots on a silvery expanse, against the light of the setting sun.

Claudia had invited Andrew Quarrendon to come for a stroll along the cliffs. He moved off, his step shambling and uneasy, his head bent as though he found it necessary always to look at the ground as he walked.

"What a curious-looking creature Professor Quarrendon is!" said Mrs. Peel, in tones of distaste.

Then she announced her intention of going onto the sands, and trailed slowly away down the cliff path.

Sal and Frances followed, Sal in search of a bathing-tent, and Frances to watch Claudia's three children.

It seemed to her a long time since she had been in contact with youth, and she was innocently pleased and surprised because Sylvia and Taffy and Maurice seemed so willing to talk to her and showed no signs of the contempt for her middle-age that various arraignments of the modern young in literature had led her to expect.

On the contrary, she found them polite and kind and very friendly.

Quite soon, as she strolled up and down the wet sands, Taffy came and joined her.

Taffy was wearing a little backless white bathing-suit, laced up at the sides, barely covering her slim breasts, and leaving her back exposed to the waist.

Frances thought that she had seldom seen anything lovelier than those long lines, that smooth, unblemished young body. At first, dazzled by Sylvia's rose-and-gold prettiness, she had thought Taffy's small, freckled face and straight sandy bob insignificant-looking. Now, she wondered how she could ever have thought so.

The girl's eyes would have redeemed any face from insignificance. They were so green, so deeply set between two rows of curving lashes, above all, so ardently expressive.

"Are you going for a walk? May I come with you?"

"I'd love you to—but you mustn't bother about me. Don't you want to swim again?"

"No," said Taffy.

She pulled off her white rubber helmet and shook her hair loose.

"No; the tide's too far out. Sal and Sylvia will have to walk simply miles before they even get out of their depths. I'd like to come with you, if I may."

"It's nice of you," said Frances, sincerely. "Do you remember last time I stayed with you, Taffy? It was when you were living in Hampstead, and I used to take you and the little dog—Jock, he was—for walks on the Heath."

"Of course I remember. Jock died, poor darling. I often think how he'd have liked the country."

"I suppose he would."

"His Lordship was pleased when we took him to Arling," said Taffy, thoughtfully. "At first I was terrified he might run away and go back to Hampstead. You know how they always say cats go miles and miles to find their old homes. But he never did anything of the kind. Just settled down and was perfectly happy."

"He'd probably be happy anywhere with you, wouldn't he?" Frances suggested, kindly. "I'm sure people are most unjust when they say that cats don't get fond of people."

"Of course they do! His Lordship never goes to anybody else when he can come to me. When I'm away at school he never takes any notice of anybody. Not even mother."

Frances felt rather touched at Taffy's earnestness on the subject of her cat. It made her seem so childlike.

"Do you like your school?" she ventured to ask.

"Not frightfully," said Taffy. "I'm not in the least unhappy there, but just slightly bored. I get sick of the chat about games, and mistresses, and school things generally. I shall be glad when I leave."

"What are you going to do when you leave?"

"As a matter of fact," said Taffy, suddenly immensely grown up and not at all the same person that she had been three minutes earlier—"as a matter of fact, I should be rather glad to talk to you about that, if you don't mind. I'd already thought you might possibly be able to help me."

"My dear, what can *I* do?"

"You might talk to Mother—that is, if you don't utterly disapprove of what I'm going to say. You know my aunt Anna—Mrs. Zienszi—don't you?"

"Yes."

"Well, I want to go to America with her. She's got no children of her own, you know, and she's perfectly willing to take me. In fact, she suggested it. She'd send me to college. There's a place called Bryn Mawr that sounds too marvellous. I might get some kind of a scholarship, perhaps, and I'd either spend the hols—vacations I mean—with them, or else get some kind of job out there, like American girls do. Aunt Anna and I have talked it all over. She's frightfully nice, and frightfully generous, and they really are frightfully rich and could afford to have me. And of course, sooner or later, I should be earning."

She looked at Frances, eagerly and rather anxiously.

"What do your parents think?"

"Daddy hasn't said anything—I'm not sure if he even knows about it—and Mother won't take it seriously. But as a matter of fact, I haven't really put it to her in earnest yet. I'm waiting till I've taken my school-leaving certificate. I'm going to talk to my headmistress and get her on my side."

"Will that be difficult?"

"I don't think so. She's got a good deal of sense. Rather an academic outlook, of course, and she's spent too much of her life amongst women and girls; but she's moderately broad-minded and very intelligent. She'll see the point of it."

"The point of it being, really, that you want to get right away on your own?"

"Partly that. Three grown-up women in one house would be a mistake, don't you think? Though I expect Sylvia will marry quite early."

"Perhaps she will. But couldn't you get away, on your own, without going quite so far as America?"

"I could, in a way. There's no question of my having to live at home and do nothing when I leave school, or anything bloody like that. Sorry—but you see, I don't want to live in London, either, and I don't want to go to an English university where everybody rides a bicycle and the food is filthy and it's always cold and people go all earnest about the Great Problems of the Day. I'm quite willing to work, but I want to enjoy myself, too. Aunt Anna could give me a perfectly marvellous time. And girls do have fun in America, don't they? There was a girl from New York at school with me."

"I scarcely know New York," Frances said, "but I agree with you that American girls have much more fun than ours, in a good many ways, especially when their parents have money."

"Naturally," said Taffy. "Well, you see, I know exactly what I want. And—which is probably just as important—what I *don't* want. Amongst other things, I don't want to marry an Englishman."

"I think perhaps you're right about that," Frances murmured.

Taffy shot her a look of mingled gratitude and approval.

"I should hate not to marry at all, and I think experimental marriages are rather silly and anti-social, but at the same time I hate the English domestic ideal. The only men I'm ever likely to meet, if I stay in England

and get a job somewhere, are sort of upper-middle-class young men who either can't afford to marry at all, or else expect one to live in a bungalow somewhere, and have a daily maid and go all deft and home-making, like the ghastly young matrons one sees in advertisements. Unless they expect one to go on in a job and help keep them."

"I thought that was the modern ideal."

"It isn't mine. There's heaps of lovely fun going in the world, and I want to have it, not just spend my youth worrying about expenses and bills and how I can educate my children—if I can afford to have them at all. Look at Mother!"

"Yes, I see," Frances said, thoughtfully.

"I want to work out a *totally* different life-pattern," said Taffy, emphatically. "I think Aunt Anna—and America—are my best chance."

"On the whole, I'm inclined to agree with you. You do thoroughly know what you want, don't you?"

"Absolutely."

"From what I saw of America and Americans, you're much more likely to get it over there. Of course, there are plenty of people there who aren't well off, though their standard of comfort and enjoyment *is* much higher than ours. I expect you've realized, too, that the young matron of the advertisements is a very, very well-known figure in the Middle West? I'm not sure she didn't come from there in the first place."

Taffy laughed appreciatively.

"That's the whole point of Aunt Anna and Uncle Adolf," she explained. "He's got a place in San Francisco, and they rent an apartment when they're in New

York. It wouldn't be Middle West young matrons, or
Middle West young men, with them. Aunt Anna knows
all the amusing people—the rich ones—the kind that I
want to know, in fact."

"You really mean, don't you, the kind that you
eventually hope to marry?"

"Yes, I do," said Taffy. "Naturally, I shouldn't say
this to everybody—it sounds a bit blatant—but you're
being *most* understanding and kind. I definitely intend
to get married eventually, but I won't marry an average
Englishman and lead the kind of life that Mother's led,
and work myself to death for the sake of my husband
and children. Of course, the obvious answer is that one
falls in love with somebody, and then it's all too marvellous and seems worth it over and over again. *But it
isn't really*. Not when the glamour's gone and there are
all the years and years ahead. Falling in love is just
simply nature's frightfully cunning way of keeping the
race going, isn't it? It's no use waiting till one's fallen
into the trap. I'm not going to take any chances; that's
why I've thought it all out beforehand."

Frances was touched, and also slightly awed, by the
girl's outlook, of which she doubted the sincerity not at
all. Looking back involuntarily into her own unsuccess-
ful, muddled history, she felt how very far her generation had been from such ruthless candour, such devastat-
ing clarity of purpose.

"Do you think I'm just hard-boiled and horrible?"
said Taffy. The mixture of wistfulness and of unconscious hopefulness in her tone, as though the thought of
being considered "hard-boiled and horrible" would not

be wholly without its gratification, suddenly made her seem much younger again.

Frances Ladislaw smiled.

"I don't think you in the least horrible, and if to be honest with yourself about your own motives, and your own wishes, is hard-boiled, then it seems to me quite a good thing to be. You're luckier than you know to have been brought up to think for yourself."

"And will you talk to Mother, sometime or other?"

"Yes, I will, if you want me to, but you know I'm only here for a day or two."

"You'll come again, though. You must. Where are you going to live, in England?" asked Taffy, suddenly.

"I don't know. My husband and I had been travelling about for years, before he died, on account of his health, and we had no fixed home. My furniture is stored in London. I want to get a flat, or a tiny house, there."

"Couldn't Mother find you something?"

Maurice came rushing past them, wet and shining, and turned a cart wheel on the sands.

"He's showing off," said Taffy. "I can do that, too, much better."

They rejoined the others.

Sal Oliver, who had already resumed her striped white-and-green washing-frock and miraculously re-stored the shining smoothness of her black hair, strolled beside Mrs. Ladislaw as they took their way back to the car.

A sudden thought struck Frances.

"How are we all going to get back to Arling?" she enquired. "There won't be room."

"Probably Claudia has thought of that and arranged something. She practically never fails on organization."

"I suppose not. Isn't it rather wonderful to combine the literary side and the practical, as she does? People don't, as a rule, do they?"

"No," Sal agreed, "they don't. I always feel that the literary side is natural with Claudia, and the practical acquired. Which on the whole makes it even more to her credit."

"In the old days Anna was the practical one. At least, she was more practical than Claudia. As a matter of fact, neither of them was really brought up that way, as you can probably guess. Mrs. Peel, then, was very much what she is now—only a good deal more cheerful."

"What was the father like?"

"I never really knew," admitted Frances, shaking her head. "One stayed with them, and saw him at meals, and he always made the same joke about having heard us— Claudia and me—talking in her room at night, when we'd been talking all day, and that was all. He was kind. Not very clever, I don't think. Very good-looking. Anna is like him in appearance."

"Anna is clever, though. In a way of her own, not Claudia's way."

"I should like to see her again. She's in London now, isn't she?"

"Yes. They spend about half the year over here. Sometimes they come down here for lunch or tea, and go back the same day. Not often, though."

Frances became silent.

She was thinking of Claudia's devotion to her younger sister, years ago. And now Anna motored down from

time to time with her husband from London, and had
lunch or tea at Arling, and then went away again. She
didn't stay, or even remain for very long.

Frances remembered, too, what Claudia had said on
the previous afternoon—"I've lost Anna."

A pang of pity went through her. Claudia had loved
Anna so much! Why should she feel that she had lost
her?

But through all her compassion and startled regret
Frances kept a very clear recollection of the three prim
Edwardian schoolgirls, with long, beribboned tails of
hair and serge skirts flapping against their ankles, that
she and Claudia and Anna had once been.

And it was Claudia who had led, Claudia who had,
sometimes, bullied, Claudia who had completely dominated the other two, and Claudia who, on the rare
occasions when Anna had tried to assert herself, had always reduced her to submission again by the tempestu-
ous declaration that Claudia wanted nothing—*nothing*—
except what was best for them all.

(2)

Sal Oliver had not over-estimated the talent of her
hostess for organization.

Quarrendon drove the four elder ladies back to Arling
in his car, and Copper, his dog, and his three children
were left to make use of the bus, passing close by, and
taking them to a point only a few minutes' walk away
from the gates.

Only Taffy grumbled as this arrangement was announced by her mother.

"Have we got to walk all that way?" she demanded, in the injured tone of a spoilt child.

"It'll take you ten minutes, my dear. Probably less. I really think you can manage that," said Claudia, laughing a little.

"I hate the bus. I'd have come on my bicycle, if I'd known."

"Well, you can go in the car if you like, and I'll take the bus."

Taffy turned away and Claudia took her place—in the back of the car this time.

"I think the present generation will lose the use of its legs altogether," said Sal, looking over her shoulder from her seat beside Quarrendon. "They can't bear the idea of walking anywhere at all."

"Except 'hikers,' " said Mrs. Peel, plaintively, as one referring to a noxious collection of insects. "Oh dear!"

Claudia was quietly and frankly putting a problem for the consideration of Frances Ladislaw.

"What am I to do with Taffy? You heard her just now. She's a splendid walker, really; she doesn't mind how far she goes; but there's this odd kind of antagonism to any suggestion of mine. I've never been up against it with either of the other two, and it's only a recent development with her."

"Girls get like that. I'm sure, darling, you were *very* difficult often enough, yourself," said Mrs. Peel, plaintively. "I remember lying awake at night, again and again, and wondering what to do with you."

"Well, I don't lie awake at night wondering what to do with Taffy. I'm much too sleepy by the end of the day." Claudia's reply to her mother was offered with cheerful good humour, but as she turned to Frances again she became once more serious.

"I do want to face the facts and not be a typical sentimental, self-deluding mother. My relation with the other two has been so wonderful, always, that I suppose I've got spoilt. Can you see where I go wrong with Taffy? If so, I can't tell you how grateful I'd be if you'd tell me quite frankly."

Mrs. Peel moaned a quiet protest at this strange reversal of the customary order of things, but said nothing clearly.

Frances, on the contrary, felt that perhaps the moment had come, although sooner than she had either expected or desired it, for helping Taffy's cause, if any words of hers could really hope to influence so clear, so judicial a spirit as that of Claudia's.

"Taffy seems to me extremely intelligent and—and definite in her views," she began timidly.

Claudia interrupted her at once.

"Oh yes. She is. I think she's inherited my mentality, although at the moment she's going through a phase of self-consciousness I suppose most schoolgirls do; Sylvia was an exception. But that doesn't worry me; she'll outgrow her little poses and self-dramatizations. It's really her attitude towards me that's troubling me."

"It must be very disappointing ——"

"Oh, it's not on my own account that I mind. At least, I'm nearly sure that it isn't. Not more than is inevitable," said Claudia, with her careful candour. "If one does mind—it's all in the day's work. The real point is the effect on Taffy. We've got to face the fact that I may, with the very best intentions, be the very worst person for her."

"No, no; don't say that. But perhaps ——"

"Frances, haven't you found out yet that I'd *rather* face things quite honestly? It's the only way by which one can ever hope to put them straight, after all."

"I think it's very brave of you."

"No," said Claudia, judicially. "It's my nature. I haven't any temptation to shirk an issue or to let my emotions run away with my judgment. I can see, and accept, the fact that Taffy—like a great many girls—is antagonistic towards me simply, I imagine, *because* I'm her mother. It's nothing reasoned or specific. These things have their roots far below the level of conscious thought. And probably, in some way that I haven't yet understood, I'm to blame—if you can talk about blame in these cases. What I want to do is to get at the fundamental mistake, find out where I've gone wrong, and put it right."

Claudia drew breath, and in the infinitesimal pause Frances had time to reflect that she need not, after all, commit herself just yet to her own opinion, for it was evident that Claudia, lost in her own earnest and dispassionate analysis, had temporarily quite forgotten having asked for advice.

7

(1)

The evening was hotter even than the one before. As soon as dinner was over, everyone drifted to the hall, where the door stood wide open to the breathless, scented night.

"How quiet it is!" Sal said.

Claudia turned to Mrs. Ladislaw.

"It's like the old days, isn't it? One could almost think oneself back, away from the age of hustle."

"No motor-cars, no airplanes, only the horses looking out of their stalls, and the little clinking sounds that used to come from the stables," said Frances, reminiscently.

She started as a sudden violent braying broke into the quiet.

"That's Lew Sydney playing a trumpet solo. Isn't he marvellous?" trustingly enquired Maurice.

"Marvellous indeed," said Sal. "I shall go out, I think."

Claudia laughed a little.

"We're living in the present, all right," she said.

"Don't you want the wireless, Mother?"

"You can have it on if you like, Maurice. I don't mind a bit, though I don't think I shall sit and listen to it."

She stood on the threshold, a slender figure, almost as

youthful-looking as her daughters in the failing light, and looked round as though waiting for some one.

"Where's Andrew Quarrendon?"

"Didn't he stay in the dining-room with Copper?"

"Did he? But he can't want to do that on a night like this. How heavenly it is! But I'm afraid there's going to be a storm."

They stepped outside, and it was hotter without than within.

Voices came from the end of the tennis court, where Sylvia and Mrs. Peel had joined Sal Oliver.

Claudia slipped her hand through her friend's arm.

"They'll ruin their shoes on the grass. It's soaked with dew. Though I dare say my mamma has put on galoshes. But we'll stay on the gravel, shall we?"

"Yes," said Frances, and she gave a little sigh. "One can't really think oneself back, can one? There was a time when we should have ruined our evening slippers in the dew without giving it a second thought."

"I know more about the cost of evening slippers nowadays," returned Claudia, smartly, and Frances felt slightly snubbed.

As they went past the open window of the library the two men came out.

The sounds from the wireless had been abruptly cut off.

"I soon stopped that row," Copper said. "I call it an insult to a night like this."

Sylvia's slim form flitted rapidly towards them and Quarrendon moved forward as if to meet her.

"Wouldn't it be lovely down by the sea now?" said

the girl, breathlessly. "Couldn't we go? It's hot enough to bathe."

"Why not?" said her mother, indulgently. "Couldn't they have the car, Copper?"

"I suppose so. Yes."

"Oh, thank you, Daddy. I'll go and get it."

Sylvia fled, followed by her little brother.

"Why don't you go with them, Copper? I'd be happier, if you would. I know Sylvia's careful, but there is any amount of traffic on the main road at this time of night. People dashing back to London."

"I'm not going," said Copper, positively. "Either the girl can drive the car or she can't. *You* said she was to learn, so that they could go off by themselves without bothering one of us the whole time."

"Yes, I know I did. Very well. Frances, I don't suppose you want to bathe at midnight, do you? Or Sal? Is it too hot for a game of bridge? Grandmamma would love it."

Feeling that she was intended to do so, Frances agreed to play bridge.

"Sal's always ready for a game—and Copper, of course. I suppose I really ought to do some work."

The headlights of the car threw their long beams of light across the garden as Sylvia drove up to the hall door.

She jumped out and came up to them.

"Where's Taffy?" Claudia asked, quickly.

"In the car, and Maurice says can he go, too?"

"Yes, if you're not too late getting back. It's too hot for him to go to sleep, anyway."

"Andrew, are you ready?" said Sylvia, shyly.

Her mother exclaimed in surprise.

"But he doesn't—" She turned to Quarrendon. "You don't really want to go, do you? Please don't think you need because of what I said."

"But I'd like to," said Quarrendon.

"I'm sure you wouldn't! Stay and talk in the garden instead."

Quarrendon hesitated. He seemed not to know what he ought to say.

Claudia took his acquiescence for granted. She turned to her daughter.

"Don't stay too long, darling, or it'll be so late for Maurice."

Sylvia, without answering, stood motionless, looking at Andrew Quarrendon expectantly.

"You're coming, aren't you?" she said to him.

"Yes—yes—I'll come."

"No, no," Claudia protested. "They'll be all right. Don't go unless you really want to."

"You'd like some bridge, I expect," Mrs. Peel suggested, hopefully.

"I'm afraid I don't play bridge," Quarrendon said, hastily. "And if Mrs. Winsloe wants to work ——"

"No, that doesn't matter. It was only conscience, and I can easily disregard it," Claudia said, laughing.

"Oh dear! Of course you ought to relax at this time of night. Nobody but you," wailed Mrs. Peel, "would *think* of doing anything else—and in this heat, too."

"I think," said Quarrendon, gently, "that I must see the bay by moonlight."

He turned and followed Sylvia to the car.

(2)

Claudia, after all, did no work that evening.

The bridge four was made up without her, and the table drawn close to the open window.

She watched them for a minute or two, then lit a cigarette and strolled down to the stream at the bottom of the garden.

Claudia was perturbed.

In a formula that she did not, herself, realize to have become habitual to her, she murmured under her breath: "Now I must look this straight in the face."

To be looked straight in the face was the sudden knowledge that Andrew Quarrendon, her contemporary and possible friend, was attracted by Sylvia.

Claudia had no illusions as to the nature of that attraction. Sylvia was neither intellectual nor an especially stimulating companion, but she was very, very pretty.

It was the first time that Claudia had fully understood that Sylvia was no longer a schoolgirl. Mentally, she had realized and accepted the fact, and had even supposed herself to welcome it. Actually, she had never before watched any man falling in love with her daughter.

"It's natural I should mind, a little tiny bit," she told herself, even smiling a little, just as she would have smiled if she had said the words aloud to somebody else. "No woman can accept, without any pang at all, being definitely relegated to the generation that looks on. . . . No, that's exaggerated. I'm not quite that. I've had friendships—companionships—I've had men in love with me. It's not been their fault that I haven't found myself involved in a love-affair, even at forty-three."

It was true that several men, always of the literary, intellectual type, had attempted to lure Claudia from the Platonic paths in which she, from inclination as well as expediency, preferred to linger. None had ever succeeded.

It had seemed reasonably likely, had she consciously thought about it, that Andrew Quarrendon would follow in the footsteps of these defeated ones. He was Claudia's type of man, he was obviously taken with her intelligence, her vitality and good looks, and he was sufficiently perceptive to realize the emotional barrenness of her carefully-displayed kindness towards her husband. He, like the others, might well have wished to hold long, intimate and analytical conversations with Claudia, ending in a regretful and admiring acceptance of the inevitable—a few kisses and eventually an intellectual friendship, nourished upon correspondence, infrequent meetings, and a shared sentimental recollection.

Quarrendon, however, beginning as almost all Claudia's men friends began, had now broken with tradition. He was falling in love with Sylvia.

Claudia clearly stated the fact to herself. She looked it, in her own phrase, straight in the face. She soon decided that she had fully accepted it. She was not after all, in the least in love with Quarrendon, nor could she ever imagine being so.

Her natural woman's vanity had suffered a slight shock.

That was all.

She smiled to herself again as she reflected on the

slightness of the effort—one frank and courageous admission of the truth—that had enabled her to put all
personal feeling away. It was Sylvia of whom she must
think.

She heard, as if for the first time, the tone in which
Sylvia had said, "Andrew, are you ready?"

Sylvia, poor darling, was attracted, or thought she
was attracted, by Andrew Quarrendon. It was typical
of a very young girl to let her fancy be captured by a
man much older than herself, far cleverer than herself,
and probably wishing to make love to her for no other
reason than that she was young and lovely to look at.

Claudia sighed.

Oh, Heavens! she thought, how I wish it had been a
boy of her own age! That's where she ought to get her
emotional experience, not with a man like Quarrendon.

I can't live my children's lives for them. I shall have
to see her suffer if she takes this at all seriously.

He's going away on Tuesday.

Three days of summer, three nights of moonlight and
sea waves.

Claudia involuntarily shook her head, as if violently
dismissing the possibilities thus conjured up.

(3)

When the car returned it was just eleven o'clock.
(Mrs. Peel, from ten o'clock onwards, had repeatedly
looked at the clock, which was out of order and remained permanently at ten minutes to seven, and said:
"Oh dear!" and "I hope they're all right. With all this
terrible traffic on the roads . . .") The beams from the

headlights could plainly be seen from the library windows.

Claudia half rose from the seat that she had taken and then sat down again.

Sal Oliver glanced sharply at her and she smiled faintly in reply.

"It's much too late for Maurice to be up. I oughtn't to have trusted any of them."

"It's the last time I shall let Sylvia take the car if she can't do as she's told," grumbled Copper, only giving half his attention to the question. "Now I suppose I must go and see that she shuts up the garage properly."

"Oh, Copper, she can do that quite well!"

"How do I know? She doesn't know how to do as she's told."

He left the room, and they heard him speaking peremptorily to Maurice outside.

"Don't waste any more time, now. Cut along to bed. You can't go in and say good-night."

Claudia moved again, uneasily, and said under her breath, "I do wish he wouldn't!"

Maurice could be heard running upstairs.

In another moment Taffy came in.

"His Lordship has gone back to his old parking-place near the garage," she remarked, unconcernedly. "Close to the bed of mint."

"You're frightfully late, Taffy. I don't mind about you two, but Maurice ought to have been in bed ages ago."

"I suppose he ought."

The casualness of her tone held a hint of impertinence. Claudia took no notice.

"Did you bathe?" Frances asked the girl.

Taffy turned to her at once.

"We did. Not the Professor. It was too utterly marvellous. Syl only stayed in a few minutes, but Maurice and I swam out a bit." She glanced at her mother. "His swimming has come on simply marvellously. He's definitely good, for his age."

Her conciliatory intention was evident, and Claudia smiled a recognition of it.

Taffy moved across to the wireless.

"We ought to get Henry Hall and his band. I wish they'd play 'You're just my olde-worlde girl.' It's a marvellous tune."

"It's an extremely inappropriate one," said Sal Oliver, with a laugh.

She began to take up the cards and markers.

Mrs. Peel picked things up, held them aimlessly for a second or two in her beringed hands, and then put them down again in a slightly different position.

Then Copper returned, by himself.

"What have you done with the Professor?" his wife enquired, lightly.

"He's just coming. Is that fellow *all there?*"

"So far as I know. Some people might even go so far as to call him a man of rather high ability," Claudia resumed, mildly satirical.

"That's simply book-learning. I'm talking from the point of view of common sense. He couldn't manage the fastening of those double doors—he might have been a child of two—and I don't think he has the faintest idea of time. I told Sylvia she ought to have been back hours ago, and he asked what time it was, and said he thought it must be 'about ten.' About ten! It's past eleven."

"I'd better go and hurry up Maurice," said Claudia, quietly.

(4)

In the dark garden, Quarrendon held both Sylvia's hands as they stood motionless, a long way away from the open door and the lighted windows.

"Darling Sylvia. I love you."

"And I love you, Andrew. You've made everything in the world quite different."

"But, my sweet, I'm too old for you. And I'm not— Oh my dear, it's no use."

"Does anything matter except us?" said Sylvia, very simply.

"Sylvia, I'm not going to ask you to marry me."

"Oh, Andrew, how silly! What does it matter?"

"I'm being utterly unfair. I shall hate myself for this when I come to my senses, and the best thing would be if you were to hate me. No! I'm dramatizing it all. Listen, Sylvia. I'm terribly in love with you, and I think I could teach you some things and give you some happiness, but you'll suffer in the end. We both shall, but you will most, because you're inexperienced and sensitive and young. Is it going to be worth it, for you?"

"You know it is," she answered, her voice trembling.

"God help me, I knew you'd say that!"

Quarrendon took her very gently into his arms and held her for a moment.

Then he kissed her.

(5)

Claudia waited in vain for Sylvia to come into the library. She did not appear, and her mother was obliged to conclude that she had gone straight to her own room.

Quarrendon came in by the window, blinking through his glasses at the light, and said vaguely that the sea had looked very beautiful. Then he said good-night and went away again.

"What very extraordinary manners he has," Mrs. Peel remarked, coldly. "Why clever people so often think it necessary to behave like wild beasts I shall never understand."

"Hardly *wild* beasts, surely?" Sal Oliver suggested. "More like something timid and clumsy, in a lair."

Mrs. Peel took no notice. She said her own good-nights with extra elaboration, shaking hands with each person in turn, and carrying up to bed with her a glass of cold water from a tray in the hall.

Everybody else went to bed, too.

Claudia went along the passage and tapped at Sylvia's door.

"Come in!"

Sylvia was, unromantically, energetically brushing her teeth.

She completed the operation with great thoroughness, and then smiled brilliantly at her mother.

"I'm terribly sorry about being late," she said at once. "I know I ought to be shot. I meant to come along and tell you I was sorry."

"It isn't good for Maurice to be up so late, and besides
it vexed Daddy."

"Naturally," Sylvia agreed, cordially. "Was he furious?"

"No, of course not. Didn't he say anything to you in
the garage?"

"I wasn't there. I went to hang up the bathing-things
on the line."

"I see."

Claudia paused.

Sylvia powdered her nose lightly before the looking-
glass and jumped into bed.

"Cuckoo! Why do you powder your nose just to get
into bed?"

"I always do. There might be a fire in the night," returned Sylvia, very seriously. "Not that it would wake
me up, most likely. I shall sleep like a log, after that
heavenly bathe."

"Did you enjoy it?"

"Frightfully."

"I wish I'd been there, too," said Claudia, after another pause.

"Did you do any work?"

"No."

"Oh, that's good," said Sylvia. "I wish you didn't
work so fearfully hard, always."

"I like it," returned Claudia, her invariable answer
when any of her children spoke as Sylvia had just
spoken.

"Good-night, darling."

She stooped and kissed Sylvia's soft, fresh cheek.

Sylvia hugged her in return, like a child.

"Good-night, Mother."

"Shall I put out the light as I go out?"

"Yes, please."

With her hand on the switch, Claudia stood for an instant on the threshold.

"By the way, what do you think of Andrew Quarrendon?" she asked, her voice carefully casual.

"He's very nice," said Sylvia, in a cordial, natural, and quite unmeaning tone.

"Good-night, dear."

"Good-night, Mummie."

Claudia turned off the light and gently shut the door. She felt as though something had struck her, hard and unexpectedly.

So that was how one's children deceived one—shut one out of their confidence, told one nothing at all of their real thoughts and feelings.

The idea shocked her profoundly, the more because she had felt completely sure of her relation with Sylvia, always. There had been no need, in thinking or speaking of Sylvia, to make those careful admissions of her own possible deficiencies as a mother that she had always made so readily in the case of Taffy.

Sylvia had been open with her, frank and affectionate and trusting. They had talked things over together. It had been Claudia's secret pride and joy to know that, contrary to every theory and to most experience, there had been no faintest hint of antagonism between her eldest child and herself.

But she must be fair.

There wasn't any antagonism now.

It was just that Sylvia didn't choose to share with her

mother something that, Claudia was perfectly certain, had happened, or was now happening, to her. There had been an inward radiance shining through Sylvia's control, that her mother could not miss.

Claudia went to her own room in a turmoil. She felt suddenly tired almost beyond bearing. She had meant to go to Frances Ladislaw's room and say good-night, but it was too late and she was too tired.

She leant out of the window. It was still oppressively hot. But the garden below lay drenched in moonlight; there was no sign of a coming storm.

It has passed over, thought Claudia, drearily.

There was a tap at the door, and Copper came in, a lean, slouching figure in his tussore pyjamas.

His first words followed her thought.

"The storm's passed over here. I expect they've had it somewhere. We shall have a scorcher again tomorrow."

"I was just thinking the same thing."

She sat down wearily before the looking-glass and began to brush her hair carefully. When she parted it in the middle, there was much more grey to be seen.

"What are you going to do with 'em all tomorrow?"

"Mother will go to church, and I dare say Frances will too. I should imagine the sea will be the best place for most people. I think I shall send the children off for the day. I can take them somewhere in the car directly after breakfast, and fetch them when it gets cooler."

"Better let that fellow go with them."

"Why?" she asked, rather sharply. "If you mean Andrew Quarrendon."

"You don't want him on your hands all day."

"I don't mind," said Claudia. "After all, he came here to talk to me."

"Did he?" said Copper, indifferently. "If you ask me, he's inclined to make himself a bit of a fool over Sylvia."

How like Copper, reflected his wife, accidentally to hit on the truth, clothe it in foolish and inappropriate words, and miss altogether its real significance! There would be nothing at all to be gained by discussing it with Copper, and she felt, besides, a strong disinclination to enter on the subject at all.

In the morning I must find out *why* I don't like the idea of discussing this problem of Sylvia, thought Claudia, conscientiously modern and analytical.

But I think I know. It's almost bound to end in unhappiness for her, poor little thing, and tonight I'm tired out and I haven't the courage to face it all and decide what I'd better do. And it's hurt me, incredibly, that Sylvia should shut me away, out of her confidence.

Claudia threw back her head, with a very characteristic movement.

I'll look the thing straight in the face tomorrow, she told herself.

8

(1)

The next day a telephone message came through quite early in the morning.

Anna Zienszi and her husband suggested that they should drive down from London before lunch, and spend the afternoon at Arling.

Mrs. Peel, who had been moaning in a quiet, restrained manner all the week about Anna's utter neglect and indifference, now exclaimed in concern.

"Motoring from London on a day like this, in the middle of a Bank Holiday week-end! She must be mad. And it isn't considerate, either. This house is full already, as she *must* know, and everything closed till Tuesday. Will your cook ever be able to manage, Claudia?"

"Certainly she will," Claudia declared, promptly. "Anna hasn't been here for ages. I'm delighted she's coming, and she especially wants to see Frances."

"Yes, well," Mrs. Peel said, reluctantly. "But I don't like all this American hustle."

Nobody sought to find out what she meant.

"I scarcely know Anna's husband," said Frances. "I should like to meet him."

"He's *terribly* nice," declared Taffy, emphatically.

She shot a glance at her mother as she spoke, and Frances received the impression that she expected Claudia to disagree with her.

Claudia, however, said nothing.

She looked tired, with dark shadows beneath her eyes. But when Frances, later in the morning, ventured to remark upon this, Claudia replied rather brusquely that she was not tired in the least, she was never tired, and most tiredness was largely a matter of giving way to it.

A hint of the Spartan creed held by her friend had already reached Mrs. Ladislaw. Mildly, but quite decidedly, she repudiated it.

"I don't agree with you. Tiredness is a physical fact, surely."

"That's just what I mean. Most people—most women, especially—are usually more or less tired all the time, after the age of forty, anyway—and perhaps earlier. But if they don't stop and think about it, it needn't make any difference. I make a point of telling the people who work in my office that, and I only wish I could think they'd taken it in."

"Haven't they?"

"Not really. They don't go all out on their work. They put other considerations first—the younger ones especially. Those two girls—Frayle and Collier—they *can* work splendidly, both of them. They've got intelligence and initiative, Frayle especially, but either of them is perfectly capable of saying she feels ill and must go home, when all she really means is that she was up dancing late the night before and feels mildly sleepy."

"Claudia, you must be a kind of female Napoleon, I think."

"Nonsense! I'm not in the least, but when I do a thing I do try and do it thoroughly. If I didn't, well, frankly, where should we all be?"

She glanced round expressively.

"You work terribly hard, I know. I think all you do is wonderful," said Frances, humbly. "When I'm in London, looking for a tiny house, I wonder whether you mightn't be able to make me useful, from time to time. I know you provide escorts for children, or I could do shopping for old ladies, or any odd jobs. You see, I'm quite unattached. I would," said Frances, with a smile, "put the work first, and I don't often get tired. And if I did, I'd promise not to say so."

Claudia smiled also.

"You think me a brute, I expect," she said, good-humouredly. "Honestly, you don't know what it's like to see some one lying down on the job, as Sal calls it, when one *knows* it's just simply that she won't make the effort."

"Like Mrs. Dombey."

"Very like Mrs. Dombey," Claudia agreed. "I'm sure I should have been very angry with Mrs. Dombey—and then, I suppose, she'd have turned the tables on me by dying. That's one thing that none of my office people will ever do, whatever they may pretend to think!"

"Well, I'll undertake not to, either, if you'll find me an occasional job."

"Of course I will. Look here—talk to Sal Oliver about it. She really sees to that side of things. And, Frances, look in at the office one morning and we'll put you on our card index, formally and in order."

"Thank you," said Frances. "Shall I see you, if I come to the office?"

"Unless I've got a rush on. Sometimes I have. It's mostly writing-stuff. We advertize an expert staff of translators, research-workers and so on, but, actually, I *am* the expert staff in person, with occasional help from Sal."

"Couldn't Sylvia and Taffy do something to help you?"

"No," returned Claudia, very crisply and decisively. "Amateur help, for that kind of thing, is of no use whatever. Anyway, I don't want either of them in my office. Taffy's too young, of course, and it isn't in Sylvia's line. I sometimes think"—Claudia hesitated—"I sometimes think I ought to let Sylvia go abroad and get thoroughly at home with, say, French."

"But why? It would be expensive, surely. And I thought she was going to some publishing firm in London."

"I shall let her decide, of course, but I doubt if it's quite her line of country, really. I've thought for some time," said Claudia, "that it might be quite possible to find an opening for her in Paris. She's very clever with her fingers, and our old madame—you remember madame, don't you?—is running a most successful dress-making business. She'd simply love to have Sylvia working there, and it would be a wonderful experience for Sylvia—or for any girl, for that matter. Still, as I say, it's entirely for her to decide."

Frances felt quite surprised.

She had somehow received the impression that Sylvia's initial step into the world of wage-earners had been to all intents and purposes decided upon already, and now depended only on her interview with the firm of publishers.

Evidently she had been mistaken.

(2)

The Zienszis arrived most unobtrusively and silently in a very large and perfect Rolls-Royce, driven by a young, slim, grim-faced chauffeur.

Anna Zienszi's most noticeable quality was poise. Her unfailing taste, combined with enormous expenditure in clothes, was, like the Rolls-Royce, unobtrusive. One observed it consciously only after a little while.

Like her sister, she was tall. Although Claudia was slight, Anna was so slim and apparently boneless that she made Claudia seem almost sturdy. Her naturally fair hair had been artificially platinumed and suited her smooth, painted little face, her shaven eyebrows and carefully-applied scarlet Cupid's bow of a mouth. Nature, supplementing the successful efforts of art, had bestowed upon her very beautiful teeth and exquisitely-shaped hands.

Anna's personal appearance was the cause of continuous conflict in the mind of poor Mrs. Peel. She was unable to resist a feeling of pleasure in possessing a daughter whose appearance attracted attention wherever she went, and she was equally unable to overcome her conviction that Anna's cult of the fashionable was a subtle form of insult to her mother, her Creator, and the canons of good breeding as conceived by Mrs. Peel's generation. Most people, however, greatly admired Anna, who had none of the affectations that her appearance suggested, and was generous, and in many ways simple.

Adolf Zienszi was small, dark, silent, and rather embittered-looking. He was slightly, quite genuinely, bored by most people, whom he found lacking in accuracy either of thought or of words. He was an American Jew and had made his fortune in Wall Street. He was still making money.

The only woman whom he had ever really admired was his wife, and after ten years he was still intensely grateful to her for having married him and for never reproaching him that he had been unable to give her a child.

The Zienszis gave and received greetings, and the whole party sat on rugs beneath the giant willow trees.

Anna was delighted to meet Frances Ladislaw again. She sat next her, and poured forth eager questions and answers.

However much she might have succeeded in altering her appearance, Frances felt that fundamentally the young Anna was still there, unchanged but matured.

I don't get the same feeling with Claudia, she thought, dimly. Why is it she's so competent, so brave and splendid and hard-working, and yet at the same time gives one an impression of—what is it—instability?

Remembering her conversation with Claudia on the evening of her arrival at Arling, she wondered about the relationship between the sisters. They seemed sufficiently at ease together, and there was no doubt of Anna's interest in, and affection for, the children.

"How's His Lordship?" she tactfully enquired of Taffy.

"Feeling the heat, poor old gentleman. It's such a pity he can't go for a nice swim and get cool."

"Are we going to swim this afternoon?" said Anna, delightedly. "I've brought my things."

"Oh, I bet you've got some marvellous new swim-suit!"

"I have, rather," Anna admitted. "I've been dying for an opportunity to show it off."

"We'll take you down to the sea after lunch," Maurice volunteered. "Will you be able to come, Mother?"

"Oh yes. We'll all go."

"If it isn't too hot for you," Adolf Zienszi remarked to his brother-in-law, "I was hoping you might give me a little exercise on the tennis-court this afternoon. This is the kind of weather I can enjoy."

Thin and spare to the point of leanness, and keeping as he did to a rigid diet, it was nevertheless the fear of Adolf's life that he might one day grow stout.

He seized avidly upon every opportunity for taking strenuous exercise.

Copper, with limited enthusiasm, promised him a game.

"I'll play, too," said Sylvia, suddenly. "Let's have a set, unless you and Daddy frightfully want to play singles."

"Not in the least," said Copper. "Who's your fourth? Quarrendon?"

"I'm told that I resemble a cathedral walking when I play tennis," said Quarrendon, with a glance at Taffy, "but I'm willing to provide the spectacle. My play, I ought perhaps to add, is very much what you'd expect from the description."

The conversation continued, pleasantly trivial and discursive.

(3)

Suddenly, as it seemed to Frances, they were in the midst of a psychic disturbance.

It was afternoon. The set of tennis, which had begun late, was still in progress, Mrs. Peel, watching it, had fallen asleep, Taffy and Maurice, their bathe unaccountably deferred by their mother until some unspecified later hour, were entertaining themselves and faintly disturbing others with a variety concert of Hot Numbers from Luxembourg, and their mother and aunt, with Sal Oliver and Frances, sat in the shade and talked.

It was Anna who plunged, with cyclonic abruptness, from detached, aimless chat, into more vital topics.

"Claudia, what about my plan for Taffy? May I have her?"

"Have her?" echoed Claudia, blankly.

"Take her with us, either this year or next, to the States, and send her to Bryn Mawr. She says she's taking school Certificate next term. Of course, there's no immediate hurry, but I'd like to fix things up in good time. Then the college authorities can put her name down for admission next year."

"What a piece of luck for Taffy!" said Sal Oliver, coolly.

The atmosphere seemed suddenly to have become electric. Frances glanced, almost surreptitiously, at Claudia. Was it fancy, or had she become rather paler?

She was intent on measuring two blades of grass one against the other.

At last she looked up, and spoke very quietly.

"You're an angel, Anna dear, to think of it, but, honestly, I don't know what to say. Taffy's only sixteen. I suppose you wouldn't like to transfer the offer to Sylvia?" She laughed as she spoke, so that none could tell whether she was in earnest or not.

"I'm afraid not," Anna said. "Sylvia is a darling, and gets prettier every time I see her (that girl's too wonderful, she's *always* prettier than one expects her to be), but I think Taffy suits Adolf better. Besides, she's wild to come."

"She'd be most unnatural if she wasn't," observed Sal, briskly. "And I quite agree that she's the one that ought to go. It's none of it my business, Claudia, I know, but you know what I think about Taffy."

"Quite well, Sal dear. So well that I don't think we need go into it just now. Anna, may I think it over?"

"Well," said Anna, "I don't believe that means anything at all, unless it's a civil way of refusing. So if you don't mind, why not let's discuss it here and now? Frances is your greatest friend, and one of my oldest ones, and Sal here knows all about all of us and is cleverer than the whole of the rest of us put together. You like facing facts, Claudia, so let's face them."

Claudia gently laid down her two blades of grass.

Then she said, with great sweetness:

"But of course, Anna dear, if you want to. Though I don't know that I quite see what facts there are to face."

"I do," Sal Oliver irrepressibly broke in.

Claudia kept a careful silence.

It was Anna who turned to Sal and said:

"You know what I mean, don't you? Taffy's a splendid child, with any amount of personality, but she's getting self-assertive and aggressive. She knows it too."

"She's very intelligent," said Frances softly.

"Has she talked to you, about what she wants to do?" Claudia asked quickly.

"As a matter of fact, she has."

Claudia laughed, with a slightly impatient sound.

"For Heaven's sake, my dear, don't sound so apologetic about it! Whatever else I may be, I'm not, and never have been, a possessive mother. What does it matter whether Taffy talks to you, or me, or anybody else? All that matters is that she should develop freely and on her own lines."

"Which is just what she probably isn't doing," Anna observed, in a detached tone. "You see, my dear, you've got a terribly strong personality, and, with the best will in the world, you do dominate your surroundings absolutely. You've told me yourself that Taffy's attitude—her sort of defiance towards you—has worried you."

"Yes"—Claudia admitted it thoughtfully—"that's quite true. But it isn't anything so very unusual, after all, in a rather self-willed, rather egotistical, schoolgirl. Especially when her father—to be quite frank—doesn't set her a particularly good example of courtesy or self-control. Besides, you're all talking as if the alternative to Anna's scheme was that I should tie Taffy to my apron strings in the good old-fashioned style. Directly she leaves school she'll go into a job, just exactly as Sylvia is going to do. Unless I can afford to send her to Oxford or she gets a scholarship."

"I wonder what you'd say if it was an indifferent case—somebody not in any way connected with yourself," Anna observed.

"I should say exactly the same. Why, Anna, you know I should! I have *always*," said Claudia, with emphasis, "always refused to allow my own personal feelings to interfere with my judgment."

"Darling, you haven't. I know you think you have. But you haven't. Honestly and truly, you're deceiving yourself completely."

There was absolute silence for a long moment. Frances Ladislaw's hands gripped one another nervously.

Claudia, who had flushed deeply, opened her lips once as if to speak, and then closed them again firmly.

"Fly at me," urged Anna, childishly, "be as angry as you like. I know it's an awful thing to have said. But it's true." She fixed her eyes tearfully on her sister.

"It's this awful picture that you've built up of yourself in your own mind, as a bread-winner, and a wife, and a mother—and it's all artificial and unreal. It never goes below the surface for one minute."

With Anna's outburst, Claudia seemed to recover her self-command—if, indeed, it had ever been in jeopardy.

"You know, Anna, I don't think you're quite a fair judge, where I'm concerned. In fact, I'm sure you're not. I'll tell you why in a minute. But first, I'd like to know if Frances thinks as you do."

She turned her great eyes towards Frances Ladislaw.

"We've known each other all our lives, practically, and nothing is going to alter the fact of our friendship. Please tell me, is there any truth in what Anna's been saying, or is it just that she's utterly biassed, utterly

fixed in some old, unconscious resentment that has its
roots—we may as well face it—in the fact that I bullied
her and domineered over her as a child and as a young
girl?"

Never, it seemed to Frances, had her brilliant friend
been so fluent, so outspoken, and so wholly unconvincing.

"Please answer me," urged Claudia, gently. "You see,
if what Anna says is in *any* way true, I want to face it
quite frankly and honestly, and accept it with my feelings as well as with my mind. That, really, is the only
way to put things right, isn't it? At the moment,
naturally, I can't accept any of it—Anna seems to me
quite incapable of forming an impartial judgment where
I'm concerned, and Sal—and I'm saying this quite without any kind of resentment—Sal doesn't happen to like
me very much."

It almost seemed, thought Frances, rather dazed, as
if Claudia was unable to stop talking.

At last, however, she drew breath.

"Well, Frances dear? Is it true that I dramatize myself
all the time, that I'm not honest as to my own motives?
That's really what Anna has been saying, isn't it? Is
it true?

"It isn't all the truth," Frances answered, "but I believe it's part of the truth. I'm sorry, Claudia. You asked
me to tell you what I thought."

Claudia, unexpectedly, broke into a ringing, oddly
febrile, laugh.

"But why be sorry, my dear? As you say, I asked you.
It's interesting, if it's nothing else. Besides, you may be
absolutely right. Anyhow, all I can do is to look the

whole thing straight in the face, as dispassionately as I can. I do promise you that I'll do that." She got up with a resolute movement. "I don't want to break this off at all. It is, quite honestly, extraordinarily interesting. But if I don't go and see about making the tea we shan't get any. Come when you're ready."

She smiled at them calmly, and walked away.

"Poor darling!" said Anna, frowning a little. "She's angry."

"Very angry indeed," Sal Oliver responded, tranquilly. "But I don't think she knows it."

9

(1)

Sylvia was an admirable tennis-player, Adolf Zienszi good although never brilliant, and Copper played a nervous, erratic, spectacular game. Quarrendon, as he had rightly told them, was very bad indeed. In whatever combination they played, Quarrendon and his partner invariably lost the set. It constituted, he gently pointed out, a discouraging coincidence.

"Let's leave Daddy and Uncle Adolf to have a single," suggested Sylvia.

They crept quietly past Mrs. Peel, whose head had fallen on one side, but whose hands, encased in white wash-leather gloves, were still neatly folded in her lap.

"She's asleep," Sylvia murmured. "Do you know, *now*, I feel I can't bear to waste a single minute in sleep. I want to be awake every minute of the time, just to realize how happy I am. I never knew life could be anything like this. Do you mind, Andrew, if I say all the things that have been said before by novelists and people like that? You see, I never realized before that they could actually be *true*."

She turned her shining eyes towards him, and he thought he had never seen anything so lovely.

"Where are we going, darling?"

"I was going to take you to a lane behind the orchard. No one ever goes there; it isn't a proper lane at all. I'm not sure that even Mother knows about it, although this was her home when she was a child. That's why we came here, of course. We lived in Hampstead before."

"You ought to live in the country. You're so like a flower."

"What a lovely thing to be told! But I shall have to live in London soon—at least except for the week-ends, I suppose. I may be going to get a job almost at once. Andrew, are you ever in London?"

"I'm going to be," said Andrew, promptly. "Quite often."

"Let's talk about what we'll do."

Instead of answering, he took her hand in his and held it lightly. Thus they walked down the slopes of the cherry-orchard, and then Sylvia showed him a steep bank thickly covered in cow parsley.

"We can get over that, and then we're in the lane. I'll go first."

She was up and over the bank with the grace of a wild young animal. Quarrendon blundered after her, regretfully conscious of his weight and his awkwardness.

The lane was a disused bridle-path, deeply sunken between hedges and with the trees meeting overhead in a dense canopy.

"If we go here—" said Sylvia. She guided him to a tiny mound at the foot of a great beech tree, and they sat down on the ground.

It was a long while before either of them spoke. Then Sylvia said:

"What are we going to do about seeing one another again?"

"I can meet you in London. When do you go to see about the job?"

"Tuesday."

"The day I go. I'll drive you up."

"That'll be lovely. Andrew."

"My dear."

"I'd like to ask you something. Don't answer if you don't want to."

"I think I know what it is. Of course I'll answer. We ought to talk it out, if it's what I think it is. Why did I say that I shouldn't ask you to marry me. Is that it?"

She nodded. Her very childlike face expressed no anxiety—only complete trustfulness.

"I'm not the right man to marry anybody, my sweet. I shouldn't make any woman happy for long, and I shouldn't be at all happy myself. I suppose that's really at the bottom of it. I'm too selfish. And I hate the domesticities. The pram in the hall—the weekly budget —the inevitable monotony that must creep into any kind of orderly, shared life—and yet the horrid results when people try to do without it. It's no use, Sylvia, my loveliest one. I can't delude myself into thinking that we should be different, that those things needn't over-take us. They would. Even us."

"Even us?" she echoed, a kind of piteous entreaty in her voice.

"Yes. Am I hurting you by talking like this?"

"A little bit," said Sylvia, her eyes full of tears. "But I want you to go on. We've got to be honest with one another."

"You know, Sylvia, you're rather wonderful. Such a lot of people say they want the truth; but they don't, really. You, I think, do."

"Go on," she repeated.

"There's my work. I'm not only interested in it, but I want complete freedom for it."

"Couldn't you have that with me? I'm not trying to persuade you against your own convictions, only I want to understand."

"I know. You see, I've seen too many of my friends —men with, as it seemed, a career ahead of them. They've married. It's been wonderful at first. And then, bit by bit, one has seen it hampering them at every turn. There's the eternal economic question. A man with others dependent on him can't take risks—experimental work that may or may not succeed—that's not for him any more. He's got to think in quite other terms about his work."

"Sometimes the woman works, too."

"Yes. I think she should, if she wants to. But even that doesn't solve everything. And there's the question of children. Almost every normal man or woman wants to have children, sooner or later."

"I wouldn't want children if you didn't, Andrew," she said, in a low voice.

Deeply moved, he kissed the hand that he was holding.

"You can't realize how every word you say makes me feel more utterly and completely ashamed of myself. No, that's not absolutely true. I have, at least, told you the truth."

"I'm glad you have."

"Darling, darling Sylvia. Will you forgive me? You know I love you. More and more every minute we're together."

After a time she said:

"Then what's going to happen, Andrew? Are we going to become lovers—just for a little while?"

"Would you, Sylvia?"

"Yes. I think so. Not yet, though."

"No. Not till you want to. Not ever, unless you want to my darling."

"There's something else, Andrew. Sooner or later my mother will have to know. I couldn't tell her lies or deceive her. She's always been sweet to us, and terribly uninterfering and modern, and she's always said we were to make up our own minds about everything. She's been like that from the time we were little."

"But, my sweet, could any mother, however modern, understand about this and not try to influence you—at your age especially?"

"I don't know, quite," Sylvia admitted. "But she wouldn't do *more* than try to influence me. I mean, she wouldn't make fearful scenes, or forbid me to see you again, or any of the things that I feel sure poor dear Grandmamma would certainly have done. She'd be rational and kind. She always is."

"You love her very much, don't you?" said Andrew, watching her.

"Yes, I do. I shall hate thinking I've made her unhappy. But she'd rather—and I would, too—that she was made unhappy than that I should try and deceive her."

"What about your father?"

"He doesn't count nearly so much. He'd make much

more fuss, of course, but probably Mother would manage him. She generally does. Anyway, he couldn't stop me, poor darling."

"You'll have to do as you think best about telling them," Andrew said. "Only warn me first, won't you? The least I can do is to give them an opportunity of saying to my face some of the things they'll certainly say behind my back."

"I suppose it means you won't come here any more, once they know," said Sylvia, wistfully.

"Yes. It's bound to mean that, of course. One could hardly expect anything else. But then, I couldn't come here any more, anyway. Not to make love to you, sweetheart, in your parents' own house, without their knowledge. That would be too unfair."

"It's got nothing to do with anyone except you and me!" Sylvia cried, with sudden spirit.

"Then don't tell them," rejoined Quarrendon. "Listen, darling. Whatever you do I shall know is right, and I want you to decide. But if you feel your mother has got to know, it's going to make things much more difficult for all of us. Wouldn't it be possible to wait till you've got your job and are living in London independently? If you like, I won't see you again till then."

"I couldn't bear that," whispered Sylvia, and with a sudden unexpected movement she turned and threw herself into his arms. "I love you so terribly, darling Andrew. I can't ever do without you any more."

Holding her slender weight against his thumping heart, Quarrendon was sorely tempted to echo the words.

(2)

When they came back to the house it was after five o'clock.

A languid tea was drawing to a close. Mrs. Peel, regarding it as a serious meal, had folded and eaten one or two thin slices of bread-and-butter, but most of the others drank tea or lemonade and ate nothing.

Anna Zienszi refused everything, and sat on a garden seat just outside the window, nursing the old black cat. He had crawled on to her lap, and lay there contentedly, occasionally digging a still sharp claw into the thin pale silk of her dress.

Anna was the first person to notice Sylvia's return.

She moved to make room for her.

"Sit down here with me," she urged. "You haven't got the awful English tea habit, have you? It'll ruin your lovely figure in the end."

"Couldn't I drink something?"

"Professor Quarrendon would get you some lemonade. They've got some inside."

She smiled at Quarrendon, and he obediently stepped across the low sill, into the room beyond.

Claudia was sitting at the head of the table. He wondered whether it was the strong sunlight, filtered through half-drawn blinds, that made her face seem unusually pale and full of strange shadows.

She looked at him as he came in, smiled, and suggested tea.

Nothing in either the look or the words held any but the most ordinary significance. Andrew Quarrendon told himself ruefully that probably it was a guilty conscience that caused him to feel as if something faintly sinister, resembling a vague threat, was in the atmosphere about him.

(3)

Claudia was, indeed, extraordinarily tired.

It was a sensation to which she was for the most part unaccustomed, for it was true that she was, as she said, a strong woman and one not at all given to dwelling on her own minor symptoms. She thought that it must be partly the heat that was upsetting her, and the trouble of her increasing anxiety over Sylvia's affair with Quarrendon. The talk under the willow tree she had resolutely determined not to think about until later. She knew that it had hurt her, and would hurt her more when she came to dwell upon the remembrance of it.

What Sal had said didn't matter. Sal was unjust because she was prejudiced. Claudia had always known that.

Frances—poor Frances—could be dismissed, although with a little pang for her failure in loyalty. Sal Oliver, with her easy effect of slick, modern cleverness, had perhaps slightly dazzled simple, old-fashioned Frances. She was not—and never had been—any judge of character.

It was Anna's criticism that hurt and rankled. Anna, who as a little girl had so uncritically admired and adored her elder sister.

Why couldn't that childish relation—so happy, so uncomplicated—have been maintained between them? It was not Claudia who had changed. It was Anna. Resentment, anger, and bewilderment, surged in Claudia. She found continually that in despite of her determination to the contrary her thoughts were circling round and round the same subject. Again and again she resolutely checked them. Her mind turned restlessly hither and thither, nowhere finding solace.

Sylvia and Quarrendon! They hadn't come in; they were somewhere together.

She felt that she had too much to bear, but still she went on mechanically talking and even laughing, and when Quarrendon at last appeared, she smiled at him.

After all, she wasn't angry with him. There was no cause for anger.

Claudia even began to wonder why she had been so deeply troubled by the realization that he and Sylvia were mutually attracted.

Perhaps they would marry.

But, no; Quarrendon was too old. He wasn't the right type of man for little Sylvia. He didn't, she was nearly sure, really want to marry anyone. He was the kind of man to find emotional satisfaction in a close friendship with a clever woman of his own age. . . .

Suddenly she was thinking of Anna again, and of the things Anna had said. Were they very important things, or was it just that the cruelty of them, the utter lack of understanding they betrayed, had hurt so much that one couldn't dismiss them?

Claudia almost involuntarily put her hand up to her aching head.

She moved her chair back from the table. Tea was finished.

"When are we going down to bathe?" Maurice whispered, urgently.

"Now, if you like—and if Daddy will take you, or let Sylvia drive the car."

"P'r'aps Aunt Anna would let us go in the lovely Rolls. The chauffeur's had a long rest," Maurice suggested.

She smiled.

"Go and ask her."

They were all leaving the room now.

Claudia felt too wearied to move.

Suddenly Mrs. Peel, with an air of determination, came and sat down in the chair next to hers. O God! thought Claudia, she's going to be tiresome, poor darling!

It was a true foreboding.

"You look very tired, dear," began Mrs. Peel, automatically. "*And* thin," she added, rather absent-mindedly, for she was thinking of something else.

"Where is poor little Sylvia? Why didn't she come in to tea?"

"She's outside, with Anna. I saw her go past the window. I suppose she didn't want tea. Girls never do seem to want any tea, or breakfast, nowadays."

"I dare say it's better for them to go without," perversely said Claudia, not averse from irritating her mother by the advancement of a theory which she did not, in actual point of fact, really hold at all.

"Nonsense, nonsense! They'll probably all die of consumption before they're forty. They'll have no powers of resistance whatever. Any doctor would tell you the same. I'm worried about poor little Sylvia."

"Why, Mother?"

"I don't like this idea of her going off to work in some horrid London office. You know I don't mean yours, darling, but some ordinary office. I know it's of no use speaking to you, Claudia; you never dream of taking my advice, although I'm your mother and have had far more experience than you have—but *what is* this place you're sending her to?"

Claudia replied, with a mildness that surprised herself:

"It's a perfectly well-known publishing firm, entirely reputable. I've met one of the senior partners. Sal Oliver heard that this job was going, and it was Sylvia's own idea to try for it. She's always known that she'd have to take a job when she left school."

Mrs. Peel groaned faintly in disapproval.

"There must surely be better jobs than grubbing about in a dirty office with a lot of third-rate young men. After all, Sylvia's a lady."

"Mother! What *has* that got to do with it? People don't think in those terms any more."

"The world," said Mrs. Peel, stoutly, "would be a much better place if they did. Look at Germany! Look at America!"

"I'm not thinking of sending Sylvia either to Germany or to America. If she gets this job, she can even go on living at home if she wants to—anyway at the week-ends."

"And what is she going to do when it isn't the week-ends? Sleep in the Park, I suppose," witheringly suggested Mrs. Peel.

"I think the sensible thing would be for her to share a small flat with a friend, as so many girls do nowadays.

Though I suppose we ought really to consider what's least expensive."

"How much is the poor child likely to earn?"

"Very little, to begin with. She won't be worth a great deal. Sylvia's not really in the least clever, except perhaps with her fingers."

"Why don't you let her learn dressmaking or something of that kind, properly?"

Claudia, startled, looked up.

"You mean in London?"

"Paris would be better. And there's dear old madame, who we *know* would look after her and probably be only too delighted to board her; and think how good for her French!"

"What made you think of it?"

"Seeing that very disagreeable Professor, as he calls himself, hanging about her," promptly answered Mrs. Peel. "I don't blame him for admiring her, naturally, but from what he says he's continually popping up to London—I always say these university people haven't anything whatever to do—and what's to prevent him, I should like to know, from seeing her three or four times a week, if she's in London?"

"Nothing, I suppose." Claudia spoke quite abstractedly.

Her mother's suggestion, in the most extraordinary way, chimed in with some scarcely-formed scheme in her own mind.

Mrs. Peel went on arguing earnestly and illogically, making assertions that had no foundation in fact, adducing inaccurate reasons that bore no particular relation to the point at issue, and several times contradicting her own exaggerated statements. Yet Claudia, as never before, found her mother singularly convincing.

The habit of years, no less than her deep-rooted instinct never to relinquish her own ideal of modern parenthood, caused her to make her customary protest.

"Sylvia will have to decide, of course. You know how completely free I've always left them—all of them —to make their own decisions."

Mrs. Peel, perhaps elated by Claudia's unusually considered reception of her advice, looked calmly at her daughter. Her pale, ringed hand patted her grey pompadour approvingly.

"Nonsense, darling! It's all very well to talk like that, but we all know that, however much you let them make their own decisions, as you call it, they none of them *ever* think anything but what you've taught them to think."

(4)

"Of course you may go in the car," said Anna to Maurice. "As many of you as you like. Tell Uncle Adolf I said so and he'll send a message to Kane."

"Can I sit next the chauffeur?"

"Certainly."

Maurice rapturously thanked her and rushed away. Anna and Frances exchanged smiles.

"He's a dear little boy."

"Yes."

"Anna, I'm so unhappy about Claudia. She minded dreadfully, this morning what you said—what *we* said."

"I know she did. But I still think I was right to say

it. (It was I, more than you.) It isn't that the question
of whether Taffy comes with us or not matters so
terribly. I think it would be good for her, and we should
like having her, but after all, sooner or later Taffy's
going to break away, and probably sooner. She's practically seen through her mother already."

"Don't, Anna. Why are you so bitter about Claudia?
Why do you talk like that?"

"Because it makes me so *furious*," declared Anna,
vehemently. "She isn't honest with herself—never for
one minute. She's dramatizing herself, and her relationship with her children, and even her position as the
gallant, hard-working wife of that unlucky wretch of a
husband of hers. But because she's too intelligent to
pose consciously she has to make herself believe in her
own legend."

"Anna, you're not being fair. Claudia does work hard
—she's doing marvels. I suppose she makes mistakes—
who doesn't?—but, after all, she's got the whole weight
of everything on her shoulders—the house and the children and everything. It isn't easy to educate three
children in these days, after all."

"Adolf is paying for Maurice's education, and has
promised to send him to his public school, and Mother
helped with all Sylvia's school bills. I suppose," said
Anna, quietly, "Claudia didn't tell you that."

Frances stared at her in silence.

"That's what I mean," said Anna. "I'm perfectly certain she doesn't deliberately mean to deceive you, or
anybody, when she talks about being the only support
of her children. That's simply a phrase that serves to

convey the picture of herself she's got fixed in her
mind, and that she wants you to see."

"But that would mean that she doesn't ever really
face facts at all."

"Except when she wants to. Claudia's anything but
a fool. Haven't you heard her analyzing herself, admitting all sorts of faults and failings, asking for criticism and accepting it in the most candid, most simple
way in all the world, and then going on just as before,
not altering, or attempting to alter, anything at all?"

Frances smiled in almost involuntary recognition of
the description.

"She was rather like that in the old days. I remember
her at school."

"Of course you do. And God knows I remember her
at home," said Anna, feelingly.

"Oh, Anna! Claudia always adored you."

"I know she did. But think how completely she ruled
me—and always *pour le bon motif*. Don't you remember
how she always had such good, sensible, excellent reasons why you and I should do exactly what she told us
to do? If ever a child had a power complex, that child
was Claudia! I'm sure she deceived herself quite as much
as anybody else, as to her real motives. She *hadn't* any
motives except determination to get her own way and
dominate everybody else. And as she couldn't admit
that motive, she had to invent others. I suppose lots of
people do the same kind of thing when they're young
and undisciplined, but you see Claudia has carried it on
into maturity, and doesn't know it."

10

Taffy experimented, expertly, with the wireless. Sunday evening, she reflected, was nearly always a very bad time. Nothing really amusing to be had. For the moment even Luxembourg failed to provide her with the syncopated rhythm she wanted.

Buzz—crack—CRACK ——

Atmospherics.

". . . *et du Saint Esprit, ainsi soit-il.*"

Small incongruous bursts of unrelated sound sprang into life as Taffy tuned in, in rapid succession, to a variety of stations.

". . . Followed by Schubert's Ave Maria arranged by . . ."

"Will you very kindly address all contributions, which will be gratefully acknowledged, to . . ." .

"Aeth ym laen a'i astudiaeth yn y . . ."

A loud and powerful chorus: "Full salvation! Full salvation! Lo, the fountain opened wide."

Taffy wrathfully switched off the wireless altogether.

Why did one so hate anything that wasn't either very noisy or cheaply sentimental—above all, that hadn't got the queer fascination of rhythm? Taffy genuinely enjoyed listening to classical music, and was possessed of some elementary knowledge of harmony and of musical theory. But it was not music at all that she found so indispensable as a background to existence. Rather was it an expression, often clothed in vulgar words and cheap and derivative tunes, of something within herself that could find no other outlet.

She propped her chin on her hand and thought:

"Abstract speculations frequently occupied the mind of the young girl. A superficial observer, noticing merely her strange, exotic beauty, would have been surprised ——"

The turn of the last sentence was unsatisfactory.

Before Taffy could reconstruct it her grandmother came into the room.

Since it was Sunday evening, Mrs. Peel was not wearing an evening dress. She had changed her black afternoon frock for another one that looked exactly like it and had substituted a black enamel locket on a gold chain for a cameo brooch.

"Oh dear! The evenings are drawing in. Are we the first ones down?"

"Yes," said Taffy.

Did old people always talk like this? Would her mother, for instance, one day cease to be amusing and interesting and forcible, and make trite and foolish observations to which other people could make no reply beyond a bald assent? It seemed difficult to imagine Mother like that.

"Don't get the stares, darling," advised Mrs. Peel.

Taffy, much annoyed, blinked rapidly.

Then Maurice came in, flew to the wireless, was

checked by his grandmother, and retired rather sulkily to the Sunday newspaper.

The room filled.

The Zienszis were staying to supper.

It was a cheerful meal, with a good deal of laughter and talk.

(2)

Everything seemed like a dream, to Sylvia. She was conscious of scarcely anything that went on round her, although she performed the customary actions of the supper table automatically and heard her own voice joining in the conversation.

Afterwards, she and Andrew must go out, by themselves, into the darkening garden.

Her mind refused to admit the knowledge that they had only one more day to spend together at Arling and that after this week-end was over there must come a change in their relations. She scarcely dared look at him because to do so made her heart beat so violently that she was afraid of fainting.

She could hear his voice, from time to time, replying to her mother, sitting next to him.

Almost immediately after supper the Zienszis went away.

The whole party assembled to see them driven away in the magnificent Rolls-Royce.

The heat held all the oppression of a coming storm.

Sylvia's father raised his head.

"There's the first drop of rain," he said.

"Good-bye, Aunt Anna!"

"Good-bye, Maurice. Good-bye, Mother dear. Let me know when you get back to London . . ."

"Good-bye!"

They got into the car; the door was closed and the chauffeur, with almost imperceptible movements, set it in motion.

It glided away.

As it did so, heavy raindrops began to fall.

"I think I heard thunder just now. We shall get a storm," Claudia predicted.

Taffy said, "There won't be any thunder or lightning once it's begun to rain."

"I hope you're wrong, Taffy," Claudia said, mildly. "I think a real thunderstorm would be very refreshing just now."

"I don't," Taffy declared. "Besides, thunder makes me feel sick."

There was a small outcry at Taffy's pretension to this interesting peculiarity of which none of her family had ever seen any signs.

Sylvia joined in with the others, scarcely knowing what it was all about.

Suddenly a loud crack of thunder was heard.

"There!" exclaimed almost everybody.

"I hope His Lordship is indoors," Taffy said, in tones of concern.

"Run and shut the upstairs windows, you girls," Copper directed. "It'll be coming down in torrents in another minute."

Taffy and Sylvia obeyed, and when they came down found everybody established in the library.

In deference to Mrs. Peel, who was known to dislike

the idea of playing games on a Sunday, none was suggested.

Sylvia sat on the window-seat and gazed unseeingly at the rain that was now drenching the garden, giving herself up to the bliss that pervaded her whole being.

Only as the evening wore on did she slowly wake to the consciousness that there seemed little chance of any moment alone with Andrew Quarrendon.

She looked at him.

He was talking to her mother, but as Sylvia's eyes turned to find him he also looked at her, without moving his head. She knew that the thoughts that were in her mind were in his also.

It seemed to Sylvia that nothing in the world was so important as that she and Andrew Quarrendon should see one another alone once more that evening.

(3)

The chances grew less and less.

Copper Winsloe embarked upon a seemingly endless dissertation on the government of India, and although it appeared evident that, whilst half his audience disagreed with him, the other half was not listening to him at all, he talked on with a fluency in inverse ratio to his habitual taciturnity. Maurice went up to bed, and presently Taffy disappeared, without saying good-night.

India, at last, was abandoned and Sylvia glanced at the clock.

It was half past ten.

"I think that I shall go to bed," announced Mrs. Peel. "Claudia, you look tired. No wonder."

"Shall I get your glass of water, Grandmamma?" Sylvia enquired, wondering whether, if she went out of the room, Andrew would have enough *savoir-faire* to follow her.

"Thank you, dear. Just plain cold water. And I do hope there's no *ice* in the jug, as there was at luncheon. Iced water is so unwholesome."

"Unwholesome!" echoed Copper. "What an extraordinary theory. Iced water, in moderation, is a great deal more wholesome than ——"

Sylvia slipped from the room.

She left the door open, and could hear her father's raised voice, and then her grandmother's in plaintive, obstinate contradiction.

Ice was in the jug, and Sylvia carefully avoided letting any slip into the glass as she slowly poured. Then she waited anxiously.

". . . the coats of the stomach," came angrily from her father.

"Without going into that, there can be no doubt whatever that the Americans *all* owe their *incessant* digestive troubles to this iced-water habit," Mrs. Peel retorted.

Quarrendon appeared in the doorway.

She moved quickly towards him.

"Damn the rain," he muttered. "What waste of an evening! I must see you alone, Sylvia—I must."

"I know," she whispered.

"Could you come down again, after they've all gone to bed? Would you?"

"Daddy always stays up so frightfully late. I think he goes to sleep, as a matter of fact, but Betsy's always with him, and she barks at a sound. You'll have to come up to the schoolroom, Andrew."

He nodded eagerly.

"What time? Where is it?"

"You know the passage where your room is? Go straight to the end of it, and there are two steps down. And be very, very careful, Andrew, because Grandmamma's room is just there, and the boards creak so. The schoolroom is the door on your left."

"And you'll be there, my sweet? What time?"

"Half past eleven. O Andrew!"

"My darling."

They stood there, looking into one another's eyes.

"Sylvia!"

Her mother stood in the doorway, smiling, and yet somehow faintly disapproving.

"What *are* you doing? Poor Grandmamma is waiting for her glass of water."

"I'm sorry. I was just coming."

Sylvia took the glass into the library, where the discussion had by no means ceased.

"Any doctor in the whole world, I don't care who he is, will tell you exactly the same thing as I'm telling you now."

"Regardless of the fact, I suppose, that in certain illnesses ice is what they prescribe?"

"If you mean ice at the back of the neck, Copper, or to stop bleeding, it's an entirely different thing. No doctor on earth . . ."

The words "ice," "doctor," "incontrovertible fact," and "absolute nonsense," rang through the room.

In vain did Frances speak about American ice-creams

and Sal talk of skating. These red herrings were of no avail.

Copper became more and more angry and Mrs. Peel more and more hurt and offended.

From iced water they proceeded to other, less impersonal topics. Mrs. Peel, in a ladylike way, reminded her son-in-law of mistakes that he had made at the bridge table, and of errors of judgment as to the investment of money. Copper retaliated with indignant references to the utter inadequacy of the water-supply at Arling as originally installed by the Peels.

In angry distress, Mrs. Peel rose to her feet.

"Say what you please about me, Copper, if you can't control your dislike of me, but at least let the sacred memory of the dead be safe from insult."

"My God! as if I meant ——"

"Mother dear ——"

Claudia went to her afflicted parent and led her gently out of the room.

"Copper, you really are an owl," Sal remarked as the door closed.

"She likes a scene," said Copper, impenitently. "Besides, it's such nonsense. Every sane person knows that ice, in moderation, is *not* unwholesome."

(4)

Although it seemed to Sylvia that the evening would never end, at last she was in her own room and had flung off her clothes and slipped into her flowered cotton pyjamas and heel-less green slippers.

She brushed her auburn hair with her stiff-bristled

brush until it shone like silk and stood out round her head in a halo.

She hoped ardently that Andrew would think she looked pretty and attractive.

Then her breath caught in her throat, with a kind of sob.

As if it mattered—as if it mattered!

One wanted to look pretty and be admired by ordinary people—people who didn't matter.

Andrew was different.

Sylvia knelt down by the bed and hid her face against it. She was not praying consciously, but some fire of inarticulate rapture and gratitude consumed her. Life was wonderful—it was incredible—it *couldn't* be like this always. To be so happy, to love so intensely, was an unendurable ecstasy.

She crouched on the floor, trying to achieve a return to sanity.

Suddenly the clock on the landing outside chimed a single stroke.

It was half past eleven.

Sylvia sprang to her feet and stood listening.

She knew that her father had not yet gone to bed, but he was in the library downstairs.

She opened her door softly.

Round the corner of the landing was the twisted staircase that led to the attics of Taffy and Maurice. On either side of her were closed doors. A thin line of light beneath one of them revealed that Sal Oliver was still awake. The others were in darkness.

Sylvia moved swiftly and noiselessly down the familiar passage, and down the two shallow steps that led to the schoolroom. Groping her way in the darkness, she switched on the reading-lamp at the far end of the room and stood waiting.

Quarrendon's approach, when it came, was far from noiseless.

Sylvia heard his door open cautiously, his foot creak upon the boards, and then his slow, careful approach.

A spasm of laughter seized her, born of sheer nervous excitement.

She stood pressed against the wall, her hands raised to her mouth, stifling her laughter.

The cautious, clumsy step came nearer, stumbled, and then halted altogether.

To Sylvia's horror, she heard the click of a handle slowly turned.

Was Grandmamma coming out of her room, or was Andrew opening the wrong door?

She dared not move.

Then came the sound of a door closing.

An instant later she sprang forward, opened the door, that she had purposely left unlatched, and drew Quarrendon inside the room, closing the door noiselessly behind them.

"What *did* you do?"

"I opened the wrong door," groaned Quarrendon. "I lost my bearings and I couldn't remember if you'd said the one on the right or the left. But the second I'd turned the handle I knew it was wrong. It felt unfamiliar, and I could hear some one asleep—breathing."

"Grandmamma," Sylvia gurgled. "Do you think she heard you?"

"I didn't wait to find out. But I shouldn't imagine so."

"She'll suppose she's had a dream. O, Andrew!"

"O, my Sylvia!"

"I thought the evening would never, never come to an end."

Time was no longer.

(5)

At a quarter past twelve, Copper Winsloe woke from dozing on the library sofa, said, "Come on, Betsy. Time to go to bed," and moved slowly and heavily upstairs, turning out the lights as he went.

On the landing, to his astonishment, a figure advanced to meet him.

It was Mrs. Peel, in a wadded grey silk dressing-gown, with a little piece of lace draped round her head and a book in her hand.

"I don't wish to disturb anybody," said Mrs. Peel, "but I'd fallen asleep, when I suddenly awoke, and as I awoke something flashed into my mind. It really was most curious. Almost as though something had woken me on purpose. This little book, Copper ——"

She held it out to him.

"Page two hundred and fifty-two," said Mrs. Peel. "There is an article, by a medical man, on the injurious effects of drinking iced water. I haven't read it, or even thought of it, for years. But I awoke—suddenly and abruptly—a thing I never do—as though a voice had called me—and remembered this."

A solemn triumph sounded in her tones.

Dazed, Copper took the book.

"What is it?" he asked.

"Dr. Pepper's *Scientific Dieting in the Home*. Old-fashioned now, of course, but thoroughly sound in all essentials, that I *do* know. You mustn't think me obstinate," said Mrs. Peel—not very reasonably, Copper felt—"but I really do wish you'd read what Dr. Pepper says. I think it will convince you."

"Do you?" said Copper. His ill-humour had left him. "Well, p'r'aps it will. Anyhow, I'll have a look. Iced water isn't any great catch in this country, I suppose."

Mrs. Peel met generosity with generosity.

"Americans certainly do *over*do it," she admitted. "Though I must say, in those terrible overheated rooms one can perhaps understand it. Oh dear, I feel it must be very late."

"It is."

"Well, good-night, Copper. I hope . . ."

Mrs. Peel's hope trailed away indeterminately, but it was evidently of a conciliatory nature.

"Yes, that's all right," her son-in-law responded. "Let me see you to your room."

He followed her along the passage.

Suddenly she stopped dead, nearly causing him to walk straight into her, and muttered, sepulchrally.

"*What?*" said Copper.

"There's somebody in the schoolroom. I distinctly heard a man."

"How do you know it was a man?"

"I mean a burglar," Mrs. Peel said.

Copper shook his head. He snapped his finger and thumb and Betsy hurried eagerly up.

"She'd have spotted a burglar long ago," he explained. "But nobody's got any business up there at this hour."

He strode up to the door of the schoolroom and threw it open.

The little reading-lamp on the desk at the far end of the room was turned on, and showed him Sylvia, leaning back in the old, shabby, wicker armchair.

Quarrendon was on his feet, facing the door.

"What the devil—" began Copper.

He swung round very quickly, but not quickly enough. Mrs. Peel was at his elbow.

"I'm sorry," Quarrendon said. "I'm afraid I've disturbed the whole house. I was in search of a book and blundered into the wrong room. I'm extraordinarily stupid at finding my way about."

"I see," said his host, grimly. "Well, your room is the one on the left, at the end of the passage." He jerked his head in an odd, backward gesture, as though inviting Quarrendon to return there without delay.

Sylvia rose, looking frail and childish in her thin pyjama suit.

"I heard a noise—" she began, valiantly.

"Not even a dressing-gown," moaned Mrs. Peel.

Copper eyed his daughter strangely.

"You'd better clear off to bed, hadn't you?" he enquired, with none of his wonted irritability.

Sylvia threw him a surprised, grateful look.

"I'm going at once," she said. "Good-night."

Her smile was half relieved and half mischievous. They heard her flying down the passage.

Mrs. Peel, standing aside, clutched her thick dressing-gown more closely round her.

"I had better leave you," she said, gravely, to her son-in-law. Her eye avoided the figure of Quarrendon, who, however, still wore his proper complement of clothing.

"We'd better all leave each other," Copper said, stifling a yawn. "It'll be morning before we get any sleep, at this rate."

Mrs. Peel, seeming a little bit disappointed that there was to be no scene, after all, bowed in a stately fashion and moved away.

Quarrendon immediately went out, and Copper Winsloe extinguished the light.

(6)

Always an early riser, Claudia was in the rain-washed garden just before eight on the morning after the storm.

The air was indescribably fresh and clear and full of the scents of the country, intensified by the heavy rain.

She stood on the gravelled space outside the front door and looked round, remembering, as she so often did, her own childhood and early youth. It was as a setting for those past selves that she still, invariably, saw Arling.

What a long way she'd travelled since then!

Claudia was thinking of it as Copper came out of the house and joined her.

She turned to him, smiling.

"Isn't it lovely?"

"That rain's done good," he assented, "though it's knocked things about a bit. I say, have you seen your mother yet?"

"No. Is anything the matter?"

"Nothing's the matter, but she's certain to pitch you

a long yarn about having found that ass Quarrendon
fooling about in the schoolroom last night."

"In the schoolroom?"

"With Sylvia," explained her husband. "Silly little
fool, there she was, sitting about in her pyjamas, asking
for trouble. I must say, girls do some funny things
nowadays."

Claudia's frame of mind as she listened was a strangely
complicated one. Intuition and common sense alike told
her that there was no question here of a vulgar attempt
at seduction. Yet she was both astonished and angered
that her husband should so evidently take this same
view. She found such perspicacity, in Copper, discon-
certingly unexpected.

She assumed a gravity almost portentous.

"Copper, I don't understand. What, exactly, do you
mean?"

"Exactly what I said," he returned, impatiently. "I
heard some one in the schoolroom at about half past
twelve last night, and went in, and there was Master
Quarrendon striking an attitude in the middle of the
room, and Sylvia sprawling about in her pyjamas. I
told you I thought he'd fallen for her."

"But it's—it's undignified and cheap and hateful to
have her meeting him like that in the middle of the
night. And a man of his age ——"

"He ought to know better," Copper assented, "but
there's nothing *in* it, I'll take my oath. I mean, people
do these things nowadays, don't they, and it doesn't
mean a hoot. Damned bad form, of course, but then
what can you expect of a chap like Quarrendon?"

"It's unnecessary. It's ugly," said Claudia, with decision. "It's not like Sylvia."

"Girls are all alike, aren't they? I suppose you'd better blow her up, hadn't you?"

"You don't understand. But I'll talk to her—and to him, too."

"Isn't that making too much of it? He can't mean anything serious. I expect the sort of girls he's accustomed to go and sit in men's rooms half the night, jabbering away, and nobody thinks anything of it."

Copper's tolerance, as unexpected as it was unprecedented, exasperated Claudia almost beyond her powers of self-command.

She stood for a moment stockstill, breathing hard. When she did speak she had made her voice unusually gentle and restrained.

"You said something about Mother. How does she come into it?"

"That's just sheer dam' bad luck. She was hanging about upstairs, wanting to show me some rotten little book or other where she'd found some nonsense about iced water. So I escorted her back to her bedroom door and she suddenly said there were robbers in the schoolroom and naturally we looked to see. I hustled her off to bed pretty quick, but, as you may suppose, she was all ready to believe the worst. She's probably looked up the address of a Home for illegitimate kids by this time."

"Don't, Copper."

"It's no good being tragic and highfalutin' about it, Claudia. We're not living in the old days now, and if you stuff up your children with a lot of modern ideas about freedom and living their lives their own way, what can you expect? Especially if you ask chaps like this one to come and stay."

In a curious way, Copper's reversion to his habitual ungraciousness and habit of blaming his wife, however unreasonably, for everything that displeased him, helped Claudia to regain her balance.

"I agree with you," she said, in level tones, "that there's nothing in it except that he's obviously attracted, and Sylvia, I suppose, flattered. What would have been called in our day a violent flirtation. (Not that it could ever have taken that form.) I'm sorry Mother knows about any of it."

"She'll make fearfully heavy weather, I suppose."

"I'll talk to her."

"Well, if Quarrendon has any sense he'll clear off today. Otherwise, things'll be a bit awkward. But you'd better make Sylvia understand that as long as she lives at home she's got to behave herself. I know there's nothing *wrong* about it, but there's no sense in making herself cheap."

"Sylvia will probably come and tell me about it."

"As she knows she's been found out, she probably will."

Claudia turned towards the house.

After all, she thought, Copper knew nothing whatever about his daughter, nor was he capable of understanding the relationship between her and her mother.

Secure, at least, in her own comprehension and sympathy, Claudia went straight to Sylvia's room.

Her daughter was not yet out of bed. She lay covered only by the sheet, her tousled auburn hair giving her a more than usually childlike aspect, her eyes meeting those of Claudia frankly and fully.

"Mother? Oh, has Grandmamma told you?"

"No. Daddy has."

Claudia sat down on the foot of the bed.

"Can you tell me about it, darling? It's just that you wanted a—a mild sort of adventure, isn't it?"

"Not exactly that," said Sylvia, slowly. "I'd like to tell you. Of course, I meant to, anyway. I don't mean about last night, but the whole thing."

"The whole thing," echoed Claudia.

A cold dismay had begun to invade her. She realized that she was feeling slightly sick.

"Shall we talk after breakfast?" she suggested. "The gong is going to ring in a few minutes. I only wanted to be sure you were all right, darling."

"Mummie, you're marvellous," said Sylvia, joyously. "Of course I'm all right."

11

Damn that old woman, thought Quarrendon with angry futility.

He felt that if it hadn't been for Mrs. Peel there need have been none of those private conversations that had now, he saw, become inevitable, and in which it would be almost impossible for any of the participants to convey their true meanings one to another.

Copper Winsloe, he realized with a certain surprise, would have understood, without too many explanations, that his rendezvous with Sylvia had not been of the kind that demands parental interference.

But Mrs. Peel . . .

Andrew Quarrendon walked up and down the garden paths, his head bent and his hands behind his back.

Breakfast would be very embarrassing, and there was nothing for it but to go in to breakfast and hope that Mrs. Peel would have the good sense to take hers in her room.

She had.

Claudia, who was pale and looked very tired, displayed a sort of febrile animation in conducting the conversation and it seemed to Quarrendon that she was especially careful to address him, frequently and with an air of rather special consideration.

She knows, he thought. She's showing me that she isn't angry.

Sylvia came in late. At the single look that she gave him—half ashamed, half mischievous, and wholly radiant —he forgot everything else.

Sal Oliver asked whether the storm had done much harm to the garden, and when breakfast was over she went out with Copper.

Taffy and Maurice earnestly debated the items in the Bank Holiday program of the *Radio Times*. Frances— the only person willing to listen to them—was assured that she would enjoy hearing an item from Normandy. It was, Maurice said, the best that could be had early in the morning. Frances amiably followed him to the library.

Quarrendon stood uncertainly in the hall.

Sylvia was close beside him.

"It's all right," she murmured. "It's really only Grand-mamma. Mother will understand. You know I was going to tell her, anyway."

"I know. Sylvia, my sweet, I'm so ashamed. I've made things difficult for you."

"It's all right," she repeated. "I think I'll get it over quickly and I'll come out to you in the garden. Will you wait near the stream?"

"I love you," he whispered.

"So do I."

"Sylvia, will you fetch me if I can do anything to make things easier?"

"Yes. But it'll be all right."

He wandered wretchedly into the garden.

(2)

It was not Sylvia who came to find him, half an hour later, but her mother.

Claudia advanced with her light, quick step, moving so swiftly and youthfully that it caused him a second of strange surprise when he saw the lines graven on either side of her mouth and the slight discoloration beneath her eyes.

"Will you come in?" she said, directly. "I think you could help us. Sylvia and me, I mean."

Quarrendon, without speaking, fell into step beside her.

"She tells me," Claudia said, "that you and she have fallen in love with one another. I didn't know. I hadn't realized that at all. I thought you were attracted by her because of her looks and her youth. Even after last night, I thought it was just that."

"No," said Quarrendon as Claudia paused, as though expecting him to say something. "No, it isn't just that."

"Can you explain, a little bit?" Claudia asked, gently. "You see, I don't think anything matters, really, so long as we're honest about it. My husband, as you've probably guessed, takes a rather conventional view of these things, and as for my mother—" She laughed a little. "Well, it's particularly unlucky that she should know anything about any of it. I don't mean, you know, that she suspects you of anything worse than what she probably calls 'compromising a young girl'—but that's quite enough to make her ask very seriously what your intentions are."

"A question," said Quarrendon, gravely, "that you, at least, have the right to ask."

"I'm afraid so," she agreed. "However much I believe in letting my children live their own lives and buy their own experience, I've got to remember—we've both got to remember—that Sylvia is very young. You know that."

"Yes," he said.

He followed her up to the schoolroom, where Sylvia was.

She moved across to Quarrendon's side at once.

Something in the gesture caused him to put out his hand and clasp hers strongly.

"Mother's being marvellously understanding and kind," Sylvia said. "Only she doesn't realize, exactly, that the thing that's happened to us, Andrew, is so important. The sort of thing that changes all one's life. She just thinks—don't you, Mummie—that it's something quite passing and—sort of trivial."

"You've known Sylvia three days," said Claudia, looking at Quarrendon.

It was not a reproach, but only a statement of fact.

"Yes," he said. "But she's quite right. The thing that's happened to us *is* important."

"Then," Claudia said, "you want Sylvia to marry you?"

Before he could answer, Sylvia had begun to speak.

"That's just it, Mother. We're not sure we want to get married at all, and, anyway, we don't want to be engaged and have a fuss and everybody knowing. This is something that only concerns Andrew and me and we haven't decided anything yet."

He felt her small, strong fingers pressing his as though to reassure him as she spoke, and the gesture stirred him profoundly.

"Do you feel that, too?" Claudia asked Andrew, in a low voice.

He was torn between his passionate love for the valiant, loyal child beside him and his own unshakable inner certainty that marriage, shackling his freedom and crippling his powers of work, was not and could never be what he wanted.

That Claudia must think him a cad and a coward mattered very little, but that he must hurt Sylvia was unendurable.

The sweat broke out on his forehead.

"Sylvia is perfectly right," he said hoarsely. "This is something that concerns only ourselves. I don't mean that you haven't the right to know—she's living under your roof, she's your child—but any decision should be hers and mine."

Claudia shook her head.

"No," she said, and her voice was now very clear and decided. "Sylvia isn't a woman of eight or nine and twenty. She's almost a child still, without experience and without real understanding of what it is that you're asking. It's this, isn't it? You want to see her continually, to make love to her, to absorb her imagination and her thoughts and her dreams, so that everybody else is excluded from her mind for the time being—and perhaps, later on, to become her lover. (I'm going to put this all into plain words. We're going to get it absolutely

straight.) What you don't want is to make the tie a
permanent one—to marry. And you're quite right.
You're a man of, I suppose, my own age. Sylvia is nineteen. You're in love with her now, but what you really
want is to follow your career, to go on with the life to
which you've grown accustomed, to have the right to
consider your own interests first, to spend your money
as you wish to spend it, to keep your absolute independence. You're quite right. It isn't for you to marry
any girl of Sylvia's age. But what you can't do, Andrew,
is to have it both ways. That's really what you're asking
for, isn't it?"

Her great eyes were boring relentlessly into his.

Everything she had said was true, and yet he had the
strongest conviction that she was speaking falsely. She
wanted to separate Sylvia from him, but it was for reasons other than those that she had given.

"Do you want me," he asked, "to give up seeing her
altogether? To have nothing more to do with her?"

Before Claudia could answer, Sylvia had spoken.

"Mother couldn't possibly want that," she said, con-
fidently. "She isn't cruel and tyrannical. You've always
said, haven't you, Mother? that we were to make our
own decisions and to judge things for ourselves. You
couldn't possibly go back on that now when this is the
most important thing in my whole life. Perhaps it sounds
rather silly to say that when I'm only nineteen, but it's
true. I can't tell you exactly how I know, but I *do* know
that it's true."

Claudia smiled very faintly.

"You've known him three days," she said.

Quarrendon felt a quick contraction of the muscles

of the hand clasped within his own, as if those five words had revealed something to her suddenly.

She said, piteously:

"Mother, don't you understand?"

"Yes," Claudia said. "I see that you love Andrew. I don't know—neither do you, none of us does—whether it's something that will last and that may affect your whole life, or whether it's only a vivid emotional experience, not a deep one. But, my darling, darling child, whichever it is you've got to be hurt and I wish to God I could take it for you. Don't you see that—he doesn't love you enough?"

"That's not true," said Sylvia, simply.

"No," said Andrew, "it's not true."

He turned and looked at Sylvia. He saw that her eyes were brimming with tears, but her soft, childish mouth broke into a quivering, courageous smile as their eyes met.

"I know it isn't true," said Sylvia. "I know you love me, Andrew, just as I love you. I don't want us to get married, or anything like that. I don't think I believe in marriage, anyway. But I'm not going to give you up unless you want me to."

Claudia put up her hand and pushed the hair away from her face with an oppressed, exhausted gesture.

"Darling, you're not old enough, and not sufficiently experienced, to make a decision like that. You don't even realize what it would imply. How do you suppose Daddy would ever tolerate a situation of the kind you're suggesting? Even from a purely practical point of view, it's impossible."

"No," said Sylvia. "If I get a job, and go and live in

London, it's not impossible at all. What I do there is my own affair. I quite see about Daddy. I know he'd never understand—and I couldn't live at home and do what he'd think wrong—but it was all settled, about my going to London, ages ago. If I don't get one job, I shall go on looking till I find another. And then Andrew and I will be able to be together whenever he comes to London."

Claudia turned and looked at Quarrendon.

He answered the look.

"It was I who asked her if she'd do that. I asked her yesterday."

"You can't do it," said Claudia, calmly and directly. "You can't do that to Sylvia. You and I know, if she doesn't, that it means her breaking her heart sooner or later, and though the heartbreaks of nineteen don't last, the things that they do to us last. They take something away—for ever. You can't do that to Sylvia, if you love her at all."

"I do love her," said Quarrendon.

He saw that Sylvia was crying.

She pulled her hand away from his and brushed the tears from her eyes with a childlike gesture that caused them to run in long smears down her face. When she spoke, her voice shook, and every now and then broke into a sob.

"Listen, Mother. I do know what I'm talking about. I know that I love Andrew and that he loves me, and that that will always be worth whatever comes out of it, even if it's what you call breaking my heart. I don't want him to marry me. He's told me why he doesn't want to marry anybody, and he's quite right. I understand. He's told me that I may have to suffer—that both of us may. I don't care. I don't believe that suffering is a dreadful thing we've got to avoid. It's one side of experience, just like happiness is the other, and that's the greatest thing in the world, and Andrew—Andrew will give it to me."

She put her hands over her face, sobbing and crying.

Quarrendon put his arm round her and gently placed her in one of the creaking wicker chairs. He knelt on one knee beside her. He could see nothing through the dimming of his thick lenses, and he took them off and looked up at her.

"Sylvia," he said, "will you marry me?"

She shook her head vehemently.

"No—no. You mustn't marry anybody. You've got to be free."

A pang went through him as he realized afresh the truth implicit in her words.

"We'll make it mean freedom for both of us. And I can't let you go, Sylvia."

Claudia left them.

(3)

She went along the passage, hearing without noting the eternal blare of the radio from below, and went into her own room. She felt wretched and exhausted.

Although it seemed to her that her whole miserable preoccupation was with Sylvia and Sylvia's emotions, yet her mind continually dwelt on the thought of Andrew Quarrendon.

Then she'd been utterly wrong about him?

He was not the academic philanderer that she had expected him to be, he was not particularly attracted by the thought of a close intellectual affinity with herself, as so many men had been. Her sincerity, her direct intelligence, her faculty for real and vital conversations, really meant nothing to him at all. But after all, she hadn't expected him to fall in love with her. She had long ago faced the fact that sexual appeal, in herself, had waned rapidly after the age of thirty. The men who liked her, who mildly fell in love with her—only she preferred to call it friendship—were attracted by quite other things. And it was those other things that kept them bound to her, regardless of the toll claimed and taken by the years.

No, she hadn't expected Quarrendon to fall in love with her.

But she hadn't expected him, somehow, to fall in love with anybody else.

A housemaid came to the door, hesitated.

"It's all right," said Claudia. "I'm going."

Feeling as if there was no refuge for her anywhere, she sought the library. The room was deserted, and the wireless turned off.

As she sank into a chair, Copper appeared at the open window.

"Well?"

Claudia sat upright, as if with a great effort. One could see her striving to dominate the lassitude that bound her.

"Come in, Copper. I've seen them both. He's asked her to marry him, but I don't think he really wants to marry anybody, and she knows it."

"My God! If he doesn't want to marry her, what does

he want? Does he suppose she's the sort he can keep
in a flat in a back street somewhere?"

"Don't. What's the use of talking like that? It doesn't
mean anything at all, in a case like this."

"Supposing, instead of lecturing me," said her husband, disagreeably, "that you tell me what's happened.
Is Sylvia engaged to this blight?"

Claudia shook her head.

"I don't think they've settled anything. I've spoken
to them both, as honestly as I could. It did make a difference—at any rate to him. But the decision now rests
with Sylvia. I feel, more than ever, that I've got to do
what's really the hardest thing of all—leave her to live
her own life without imposing my wishes, or even my
views, on her."

"My God! Claudia, stop theorizing. If you'd brought
that child up properly, I don't suppose she'd be in this
mess at all. And, anyhow, there's no sense in talking as
if it was grand tragedy. She can't be seriously attracted
by the chap; and if she is it won't last, at her age. But
for Heaven's sake don't go putting it into her head that
there's any question of her making a life-and-death
choice. That's all nonsense."

Claudia gave him a look of mingled weariness and
scorn.

"It's no good, Copper. You don't even begin to understand. Never mind. I'll do what I can, about Sylvia;
you needn't think about it any more. I imagine you'll
admit—even you—that I do want what's best for my
children. You'll give me that, won't you?"

"I tell you what," said Copper, with great delibera-
tion. "I can't put things into words like you can, as

you very well know, but there's something wrong about you somewhere, Claudia. You may do all the right things for the children—I suppose you do, God knows you're clever all right—but you do them for the wrong reasons, or something. I don't know what it is. But you just think it over."

So saying, he left her.

Ten minutes later Frances Ladislaw, entering the room, found Claudia there in tears.

She scarcely ever wept, and her tears had evidently exhausted her.

"It's all right," she said, and summoned a smile for the reassurance of her startled friend. "It's all right, Frances dear. One or two things combined to upset me, and I'm tired, perhaps—and then Copper came in."

"Claudia, I'm so sorry."

"It's all right," Claudia repeated, and she stood up, with the old weary gesture of pushing back her hair from an aching forehead.

"He doesn't mean to be unkind," she said, in a low voice. "But they're rather incredible, sometimes, the things Copper says to me. I do everything that I can for the children—I've always done every single thing that I could for them, ever since they were born—but I suppose I make mistakes sometimes. Of course I do. Who doesn't? I try to face them and acknowledge them. But he—he waits until I'm anxious or unhappy, and then—flicks me on the raw."

"No, Claudia, no. Don't feel that. Copper may hurt you sometimes—as you've just said, who is there that doesn't make mistakes?—but it's not on purpose. He couldn't hurt you on purpose."

"Oh yes, he could," returned Claudia, decisively enough. "Never mind. I'm used to it by this time, and I don't let it interfere. One grows a protective shell, I suppose. And it doesn't hurt as things that are true might hurt. Copper talks at random—just relieving his own impatience and dissatisfaction with quite meaningless accusations or reproaches. They don't hurt," repeated Claudia, "as they might hurt if they were true."

12

Mrs. Peel was wandering about, searching, although she scarcely knew it, for somebody to whom she might talk of her grave apprehensions concerning her grand-daughter Sylvia.

Copper, to whom she had addressed a preliminary "Oh dear!" had at once walked away, and Mrs. Peel had decided that he could not have heard her.

Claudia was nowhere to be seen. Sal Oliver, whom Mrs. Peel could not endure, seemed to meet her eye wherever she looked, but Mrs. Peel and Sal Oliver were at least at one in their conviction that a tête-à-tête conversation between them could afford no gratification to either. With equal determination they ignored one another in spite of repeated encounters, until Sal at last accepted an invitation from Maurice to come and develop photographs with him in the cellar.

What affectation, reflected Mrs. Peel, unjustly. She can't *really* want to dabble about in a dark cellar.

Irritated, she sought the library once more. Taffy was sprawling across the sofa, reading a book and eating caramels.

"*Ha, ha, ha, mais les hommes, les hommes sont rigolos!*"

This merry proclamation rang stridently through the room and assaulted the ears of Mrs. Peel three times in rapid succession.

"Really," said Mrs. Peel.

Taffy, looking very glum, rose without speaking and, still reading her book, walked across the room and turned off the wireless.

"Where are the newspapers?" patiently enquired Mrs. Peel.

"It's Bank Holiday. They don't deliver any newspapers today," Taffy reminded her.

Giving her grandmother a glance full of hostility, she walked out at the open window.

Really, the children!

Mrs. Peel sat on the sofa and thought how very odious children became the moment they ceased to be children.

Even her own Claudia and Anna, although perfectly brought up, seemed to her just as tiresome, ungrateful, inconsiderate, and unreasonable as did Taffy and Sylvia, who had not been perfectly brought up at all, but quite the contrary. She gazed sadly about her and felt relieved when Frances Ladislaw looked in at the window.

"Come in, come in," said Mrs. Peel. "I've not been downstairs very long, but I didn't have a good night."

"I'm sorry. Perhaps it was the storm? It feels so fresh and nice outside, now."

"What about a little stroll?" mused Mrs. Peel. "I don't know *where* Claudia is," she added, resentfully.

"I think she's upstairs."

"Writing. Oh dear. Have you noticed how round-shouldered she's growing, with all this stooping over a desk and scribbling? How I wish she'd take advice!"

Frances smiled sympathetically, without, however, endorsing the aspiration.

"Would you care for a walk before lunch, just to the bottom of the drive?"

"Yes, certainly. Is it very wet underfoot?"

"It is a little, but the sun's drying things up."

"I shall not be one moment," said Mrs. Peel.

A quarter of an hour later, wearing pointed black walking-shoes, a large straw hat, and a pair of washing gloves, she joined Frances outside.

"Quite like old times," she sighed.

She had always liked Frances. A quiet, nicely man-nered girl, without the good looks, brains, or personal-ity of Mrs. Peel's own daughters, and yet with sufficient intelligence to enjoy their friendship and the privilege of being a frequent visitor at Arling.

Without any particular intention of doing so, Mrs. Peel found herself telling Frances by degrees all about her anxiety and distress over Sylvia. She had meant to be vague and general, and so indeed she was, but the story of Sylvia and Quarrendon found together in the schoolroom in the middle of the night filtered itself through her lamentations.

(2)

When Frances had disentangled the brief facts from Mrs. Peel's storm of apprehensions, deductions, and analogies with her experiences of one, if not two, pre-vious generations, Frances felt that she understood Claudia's distress earlier in the morning.

Claudia, too, had known of the crisis, and it was on that account that Copper and she had quarrelled.

Frances quickly amended the thought, even in her own mind. Claudia didn't quarrel, ever. She said—Frances had often heard her say it—that quarrelling was uncivilized. But Copper, if he didn't quarrel, was frequently aggressive and disagreeable and would certainly hesitate not at all in blaming Claudia for anything that vexed him, whether justly or unjustly.

That was why Claudia had said that she did all she could for the children. And of course, thought Frances, so she did. Could any woman have worked harder or made more sacrifices? And surely her relationship with them was exceptional in its frankness and freedom?

Except, perhaps, Frances admitted, in the case of Taffy. But it wasn't, now, Taffy who was in question.

Frances instinctively reserved judgment as to the affair of Sylvia and Andrew Quarrendon. The only account of it that she had received was from Mrs. Peel, and not only were the general inferences of Mrs. Peel always peculiar to herself, but she was also strangely unable to distinguish imagination from fact on any question that excited her personal prejudice. Would Quarrendon now leave Arling, not waiting for the natural completion of his visit on Tuesday? And would Claudia carry off the whole situation with her customary high-handed calm? Frances asked herself these and similar questions as she paced slowly along beside Mrs. Peel and made, at suitable intervals, sounds expressive of commiseration, and of modified agreement that she hoped did not amount to actual untruths.

Presently Claudia came towards them from the house.

She still looked pale but there were no traces left of her recent weeping and her voice was cheerful and matter-of-fact.

"Lunch is cold. I hope nobody minds. I was wondering what we could do that would be amusing, this afternoon. I'm afraid the court won't be dry enough for tennis, and the roads, of course, will be quite impossible and the beach, too, so that rules out bathing."

"What about a picnic?" Frances suggested. "We could find somewhere that's dry enough to sit down, with rugs, and it needn't be too far away. Do you ever picnic on the little common, where we used to go? That's right off the beaten track."

"What a good idea!"

"Darling, the servants," Mrs. Peel said. "Won't it be giving them extra work?"

"The children get their own picnics ready," Claudia returned, crisply. "The maids are having the afternoon off. The girls can quite well cut sandwiches and pack up tea. I'll give them a hand."

"You ought to rest. I think you do too much, Claudia."

Claudia, as usual, made no reply, nor did her mother appear to expect one.

(3)

The picnic eventually resolved itself into a party consisting of Sal Oliver, Claudia's three children, and Andrew Quarrendon, who showed no signs of any intention of curtailing his visit.

Copper Winsloe retired to his workshop and Claudia

declared that she had some writing to do. Mrs. Peel was persuaded into ringing up an old friend in the neighbourhood, and allowing herself to be fetched and taken over to play bridge.

"If you don't very much want to go for the picnic, Frances, will you stay and keep me company?" Claudia murmured.

Since she had been told by her mother that Frances was aware of the crisis, it seemed to Claudia that she could find a certain relief in talking to her friend.

After an hour of tense, concentrated work at the writing-table she turned to Frances, placidly glancing through the pages of a novel in the window-seat.

"That's done! Who was it that originally said life was just one dam' thing after another?"

"The mother of a family I expect," Frances suggested.

"Probably. Frances, I'd like your advice. Mother says she told you what happened last night."

"I hope you don't very much mind," Frances apologized.

"I don't a bit mind your knowing. I'm rather glad. I wanted to talk to you, but it seemed a little unfair, perhaps, to tell you. However, I might have guessed poor mother wouldn't ever keep it to herself. I'm staving off, with the utmost difficulty, the long talk that she's certainly determined to have with me sooner or later. But what's the use of long talks, after all, with some one who simply takes a preconceived, conventional view of the whole thing?"

"I think she realizes that meeting a man in the middle of the night isn't quite the wild indiscretion that it would have been in our day."

"Does she?" said Claudia abstractedly.

She came and sat on the broad window-seat beside her friend.

"You see Sylvia, poor darling, has fallen in love. Don't ask me why—these things can't ever be explained. He isn't in the least attractive, that I can see, but I think it may be partly because he's so much older, and a man with a certain reputation. It's flattering. And of course he's made love to her."

"Would it be quite out of the question?" Frances asked.

"You mean for them to marry? I think it would be a very great risk—but, after all, it's Sylvia's own life. One could only advise her and beg her to wait, and then leave her to decide. But, you see, Andrew doesn't really want to marry her at all."

It caused Claudia a faint surprise, after saying this, to observe that Frances looked thoughtful, rather than pained or astonished. She was also surprised by her comment:

"I think I can understand that. He's not a man who'd want to be tied, I suppose, and perhaps he feels that his work would always come first. I can imagine that he'd be honest with himself, about that and everything."

"But, Frances—!" Claudia felt a little impatient. "A man who feels that he doesn't wish, or intend, to marry, is hardly justified in making love to a young, inexperienced girl. Surely you see that?"

"Oh yes, I see that. But after all, most of us do things we're not justified in doing, at one time or another. And it's no use pretending that young girls are anything like as silly and ignorant as we were. They're not.

Your children especially, Claudia, who've always been
taught to think. Sylvia and Professor Quarrendon, I'm
sure, must have realized from the very beginning that it
wasn't necessarily a question of getting married."

Claudia, astonished and a little disconcerted, raised
her eyebrows.

"My dear, I hadn't any idea that your views were as
modern as all that. You feel, then, that I'm not justified
in objecting if Sylvia, aged nineteen, becomes the mistress of this man who must be over forty?"

"No, no; that isn't fair. I never said that."

"I beg your pardon. What exactly did you say, then?"

Claudia was conscious of the bitter edge that had
crept into her voice, and strove to keep it under control, but she knew that she was angry. That Frances, of
all people, should take up this attitude!

"I meant that it didn't seem to me fair to take it for
granted that Sylvia was being deceived, as you or I
might have been deceived at her age. They fell in love
with one another—I don't see how any man could help
falling in love with Sylvia—and then, I suppose—I feel
sure—he told her the truth, and they talked it over
together. Isn't that the way they do things nowadays?"

Claudia's reply was indirect.

"If it had been some one of her own age one could
have understood it so much better. They could, as you
say, have discussed everything frankly from the same
point of view. But Andrew Quarrendon—after all, he's
a very clever man; he's been about a good deal; he must
have known a great many women of his own sort.
Sylvia can't mean anything to him at all, beyond a

pretty face. But she, poor little thing, is taking it all seriously."

Frances continued to look at her friend with eyes that betokened perplexity and doubt, rather than un-qualified sympathy and understanding.

"What are they going to do?" she asked, at last.

"He's asked her to marry him and she's said No. Honestly, she's quite right. He doesn't want to marry at all and she knows it. I see exactly what's going to happen. Quarrendon has made his gesture, trusting to Sylvia's generosity, and she, poor little thing, is going to give him up and go through a very, very bad time. (So am I," Claudia added, in a parenthesis, dashing her hand across her eyes with a smile for the childish ges-ture. "But that doesn't matter.) One thing, I shan't let her go and work in London now. That would be alto-gether more than she could bear, just yet."

"Perhaps she'll want to get away."

"Oh no she won't!" returned Claudia, quickly. "Syl-via has never really cared for the idea of leaving home at all. Don't you remember, how we've always laughed at her for saying that she'd have liked best to stay at home and do nothing except arrange the flowers and take the dogs for walks?"

Frances, with a strange and new obstinacy that Claudia felt became her very ill, pursued her point.

"But I think she might feel quite differently now. Surely you'll let her go if she wants to go?"

"But of course. When have I ever imposed my own wishes on my children? As a matter of fact, I think I can manage to let Sylvia get right away, if she wants to. I think it would be possible to send her to old madame

—you remember madame, of course?—to Paris. I believe in a complete change of environment, at her age—and she'd like using her fingers far better than working in a stuffy office."

"You mean that it would put her quite out of reach of seeing Quarrendon, which of course she'd almost certainly do if she was in London."

Claudia frowned involuntarily.

"I don't know that I'd looked at it particularly from that point of view. I'm not a Victorian mother, to send Sylvia off out of reach of an undesirable admirer. Far from it. I don't want to do anything at all except what's going to help her most. Surely you must see that, Frances?"

"Yes, yes, I know. Of course I know you only want to help her—poor little Sylvia! I'm so sorry about it all."

"I think I'd rather," Claudia said, gently, "that you told me just what's in your mind. I can see there's something, and you know my passion for getting things straight."

Frances hesitated.

Seeing her so deeply disconcerted, Claudia felt her own irritation diminish.

"Please do be absolutely frank with me," she urged. "If you think I'm quite mistaken, or even quite wrong, I'd so much rather you told me so. I'd rather face it. You know I'm quite good at facing facts."

She waited.

At last Frances, raising troubled eyes to Claudia's face, spoke.

"I'm so stupid at putting it all into words," she murmured. "I know how marvellous you are about the children—how devoted to them—and that you've always said they ought to be quite free in every possible way. Only I feel now about this—please, please forgive me, Claudia—that you seem to be doing the right things, only somehow not for the right reasons."

Claudia, confronted by so odd and unexpected an echo of Copper's random accusation of a few hours earlier, could only stare at her in astonishment.

(4)

The picnic party broke up early.

It had not been a success.

"Things aren't nearly so much fun when you're not there," Maurice told his mother.

She kissed him.

"But you mustn't feel that, darling. I can't always be there, you know."

"Were you resting?"

"Well, I had a nice long talk with Frances, sitting in the library," she replied, evasively.

"Shall you have to go back to work tomorrow?"

"Of course, Maurice dear. The office will be open again tomorrow morning. I dare say I shan't have such a tremendous lot to do. I've got through some of it here, this week-end."

"I wish you had proper summer holidays, like us," he said, wistfully.

"Never mind. I like my work, you know."

She dismissed Maurice, smiling, and felt comforted.

He was such a dear little boy, and so touchingly impressed by his mother's position as breadwinner for the family.

From her desk she could see Sylvia, alone, walking across the lawn. Perhaps the others were carrying the picnic things to the kitchen entrance.

On an impulse Claudia went out and joined her daughter.

She was shocked by the pallor of Sylvia's small face. It was drained of all colour.

Almost involuntarily Claudia exclaimed:

"You poor little thing!"

"Mother," said Sylvia, "you think I ought to give him up, don't you? He doesn't *really* want to marry me, does he?"

"What does he say, himself?" Claudia temporized.

"He asked me if I'd marry him. You heard him yourself," said Sylvia, proudly. "And at first I thought perhaps it was all going to come right. But I couldn't help remembering what you'd said this morning—it seems like days and days ago, somehow—about Andrew's really wanting to follow his own career and be free and keep his independence. And I know, in my heart, that it's true."

"Yes," said Claudia, in a low voice, "it's true."

She told herself, even as she spoke, that whatever agony it might be to herself to hurt Sylvia, she owed her the truth, whole and complete.

"He isn't the kind of man to marry any girl and make her or himself happy. I expect he's told you that himself. Hasn't he?"

"Yes."

"If you were much, much older, my darling Sylvia,

you might have the right to decide on breaking the rules and going to live with him, though I don't think, myself, that it would bring real happiness to either of you; but I can't believe he'd ask you to do that, at the very beginning of your life."

"No," said Sylvia. "He knows you're right, about that. He told me so this afternoon. Oh, mother, I can't give him up!"

She was in tears again.

Claudia, the tears standing in her own eyes, looked at her child in silence, sharing to the full in her suffering.

She knew, with penetration sharpened by experience, that Sylvia, though perhaps not yet aware of it herself, had capitulated. Claudia thought, "I've saved her."

13

The week-end was over.

On Monday night Andrew Quarrendon told his
hostess that he wished to make an early start, and hoped
that nobody would see him off. If somebody could
knock on his door at seven o'clock, that would do very
well, he added. Claudia, with equanimity, agreed that
this should be done.

She had given Quarrendon one or two opportunities
for speaking to her alone, but he had taken advantage
of none of them.

After all, thought Claudia, she had said all that it
was necessary to say that morning—and it had produced
its effect.

She herself was to motor up to London on Tuesday
directly after breakfast taking Sal Oliver with her, and
Sylvia.

Mrs. Peel, after saying a good deal about the
traffic and the strain of driving, had determined to go
by train.

Frances was to remain at Arling for a few days before
establishing herself in her club while she looked for a
flat.

"It feels more like the end of the summer holidays

than the beginning," remarked Maurice, hearing these various departures arranged for.

(2)

Long before seven on Tuesday morning Andrew Quarrendon was quietly going downstairs, carrying his own bag.

Sylvia had promised to be there.

She was already unfastening the chain that held the front door.

They went out together silently into the dewy freshness of the summer morning and Sylvia unlocked the door of the garage.

"Sylvia," he said, desperately, "for the last time, will you marry me? I love and adore you."

"I know you love me," said Sylvia on a sob, "and I won't ever marry you. But I—I—I'll always love you, Andrew, all my life."

He took her in his arms and she clung to him.

All that he said in a shaken voice, was:

"There's been nothing but what's true between us."

"I know. And I'm glad, and I'll *always* be glad. And proud, Andrew, because you thought me worth it."

He held her for a long time, kissing her hair, her wet eyes, her trembling mouth.

At last, without saying anything more, he went away.

(3)

"I don't think I'm coming up to London with you," Sylvia said, tonelessly, to her mother, two hours later. "I don't want to see about that job, after all."

Claudia agreed quietly.

"Very well, darling. Stay here and look after Frances and the children."

"But I quite see that I mustn't just do nothing. Besides," said Sylvia, piteously, "I'd like to help you, if I could. Only I don't think I want to work in London. Will you think of something for me, Mother?"

"Yes," Claudia said, "I will, my darling."

As she wrote her letter to Paris, later in the same day, Claudia reflected, with wondering thankfulness, on the complete trust reposed in her by Sylvia.

Copper—Frances—Sal—Anna—all of them were unjust, lacking in perception.

Whatever they might say, Claudia could reassure herself completely.

She had not failed to live up to her own ideals, her own high standard of motherhood.

It was they who had failed to understand her.

PART TWO

October in the Office

*

1

As she sat in the office in Norfolk Street, Claudia Winsloe became a different person.

She was, in her own phraseology, "on the job." She instinctively discarded everything that impinged upon her conception of herself as a breadwinner. Over the door of her private office was a fearful red electric-light globe. When this light was switched on from within the room it served as a signal that she was not to be disturbed.

Even Sal Oliver, whose own tiny room was on the top floor of the building, unprotected from the assaults of interrupters, seldom disregarded it. Nobody else ever did.

From time to time Claudia forgot to turn off the red light and sat within in solitude whilst Miss Collier, agitated, or Mrs. Ingatestone, infuriated, moved up and down the dark stairs, clutching to themselves urgent problems. Miss Frayle, the young, pert Miss Frayle, was neither agitated nor angry. She only muttered obscenities below her breath, and then drifted back to the downstairs office again, indifferent. She and Miss Collier both got through a great deal of work, drank quantities of tea, smoked innumerable cigarettes, and talked, in the intervals of work, about their employer, themselves, how best to reduce (Miss Collier weighed eight stone, and stood five feet seven, and Miss Frayle, five feet eight, turned the scales at seven stone twelve) and about twice a week one of them told the other that she was going to leave, and allowed herself to be persuaded not to.

They were both of them objects of awe and admiration to young Edie, the messenger girl, who was fifteen, fat and obliging, and whose duty it was to make herself useful to everybody in the office.

Mrs. Ingatestone, in a more responsible position than either Miss Collier or Miss Frayle, but held by them to be of inferior social standing in private life, was agreeably condescending to them and to Edie alike, but had terrific outbursts of temper, attributed by herself to nerves and by the imaginative Miss Frayle alternately to drink, drugs, and hereditary insanity. She was a widow with one child—a girl of twelve at school near Dorking. It was in order to educate her daughter that she was obliged to work.

On Monday mornings the atmosphere in the office was always impregnated with the slight strain that is the result of a holiday which has been at once too short and too long.

Miss Frayle and Miss Collier greeted one another with modified enthusiasm.

"Hallo, Collier. Had a good week-end?"

"Lovely. I played badminton all Saturday and must have taken off pounds."

"And ate sweets all Sunday and put them on again," said Miss Frayle, cynically. "I know, because it's what I did myself. Except that I danced as well as played badminton."

She danced almost every Saturday night, nearly always with a different man. Frayle, said the office, knew thousands of men. The question of her virginity was sometimes gloomily discussed between Miss Collier and Mrs. Ingatestone.

"Winsome Winnie arrived yet?" asked Miss Frayle, languidly uncovering her typewriter. By this engaging sobriquet she sometimes referred to her employer.

"Yeah. The red light's on."

"Oh, hell! It can't be. It's too early. What frightful affectation!"

"Well, there it is. Oliver hasn't turned up yet."

"Dirty slacker."

Miss Frayle had a terrific crush on Sal Oliver, and of this the whole office was well aware, but she invariably referred to her in terms that were either slighting or abusive.

"Is there much in, this morning?"

"Edie hasn't brought the letters yet. She's getting them from Ma Ingatestone now."

"When she comes, we may as well tell her to get a kettle going. It'll do for eleven o'clock," said Miss Frayle, glancing at her wrist watch. It was just before ten o'clock.

It was not Edie, however, who brought in that selection of the letters known as "routine work," but Mrs. Ingatestone.

"Good morning, good morning," she chanted, with a hasty breeziness that denoted that she was in a good temper but had no time to waste. "Now look here, I've got to go out to Streatham this morning, to help that Lady Maitland who's moving house. Miss Oliver's dealing with the school for that child—what's his name?—whose parents are going to India. She'll probably go out there this afternoon. You're to go to her first, Miss Frayle, and take down her letters, and then to Mrs. Winsloe."

There were no unadorned surnames in the vocabulary of Mrs. Ingatestone.

"O.K. But Oliver's not come yet."

"Yes she has. She arrived with Mrs. Winsloe and they're in her office together. She's going to ring when she's ready for you. Now, Miss Collier, here's the routine stuff."

"O.K."

"I shan't be back in time to sign before the post, so you'll have to take it to Miss Oliver."

"O.K."

"I must say," observed Mrs. Ingatestone, "you girls don't look much the better for your week-end. As for you, Miss Frayle, you might have been on the tiles the whole of last night, from the look of you."

"So I was. Didn't you hear about it? Collier came and bailed me out of Vine Street police station at two o'clock this morning."

"Vine Street nothing. More like Limehouse Street," said Miss Collier.

A buzzer sounded sharply.

Miss Frayle muttered, "How well I know that fairy touch," and snatched up pad and pencil. As she ran up the stairs she passed Sal Oliver.

"Good morning, Miss Frayle."

"Good morning, Miss Oliver."

"I hope you had a nice week-end."

"Marvellous, thanks."

Doris Frayle lifted her eyes for one moment, observed accurately and in detail everything that Sal Oliver was wearing, and went on to the room of her employer.

She knocked at the door, but received no answer. That was part of Mrs. Winsloe's impenetrability. At the third knock she was told to come in. A wilderness of papers lay strewn about the table.

"Good morning, Mrs. Winsloe."

"Good morning. Take this down, please. To the Manager of the Westminster Bank: Sir ——"

"She's off," thought Miss Frayle. "And she's in one hell of a mood, blast her."

(2)

An hour later, Miss Frayle was downstairs again with a sheaf of notes.

She began to type, rapidly and accurately—for she was a good worker. A cup of tea stood on the table beside her. From time to time she picked it up and drank out of it, holding it in one hand whilst she continued to type with the other.

Miss Collier sat at the other table, entering figures into a small ledger.

At twelve o'clock they spoke.

"Do you know, I haven't touched a potato for over six months?"

"I haven't touched sweets—well, not to speak of. And I think bread's pretty fatal, too."

They then said nothing more until it was time to go out for lunch.

"Are you coming, Frayle?"

"I'm meeting my aunt."

"O.K. Where's she taking you?"

"I'm taking her, worse luck. I suppose you couldn't possibly cash me a cheque? I haven't got time to get to the bank."

"How much?"

"Well—a pound. I must get some stockings."

"Oh, I haven't got a *pound*," said Miss Collier, in rather shocked accents. "You can have three bob, and pay me back on Friday."

"Is that really O.K.?"

"Yeah. Young Edie may have something."

"I won't ask her, poor kid. She gets so frightfully little, and her mother takes most of it off her. I'll see if my hairdresser'll lend me fifteen bob. He does sometimes."

Miss Frayle combed her blonde, waved hair, applied a stick of highly-expensive lipstick, and tipped a tiny little black hat well forward on her head. Miss Collier did more or less exactly the same things, with less hair, a cheaper lipstick, and a scarlet hat, and they left the office.

Doris Frayle took her aunt—a bewildered provincial spinster—to a small restaurant in the Strand, listened to her uninteresting chat about relations very nicely and politely, gave her a better lunch than she could afford, and put her carefully into the right bus for Kensington High Street.

Margery Collier ate sardines on toast at a Lyons Corner House and rushed to a lending library in order to change her mother's book for her, and to a tobacconist for her father's birthday present, and on her way back to the office spent eightpence on some pallid-looking roses because the woman who was selling them whined piteously and had with her a small child in a push-cart.

(3)

Young Edie sat in the office whilst her seniors were at lunch. To this arrangement she had no objection whatever. Her mother always gave her cake or sandwiches to take with her and she sometimes heated things out of little tins in an old saucepan over the gas-ring.

Moreover, Edie was writing a novel, and this interval in the day's work was her best time for getting on with it.

Today, however, an epidemic of telephone calls assailed the office. Edie wrote down the various messages, and placed them on Miss Frayle's desk.

Suddenly the buzzer sounded.

Edie, who had supposed herself to be alone in the building, flew upstairs. Either it was *Her* wanting God knows what, but certainly something that Edie wouldn't be able to do properly, or else it was A Murderer.

Edie's thoughts frequently dwelt upon murderers, and in any emergency murder was always her first fear.

On this occasion the lesser alternative alone confronted her.

She sat at her desk, smoking a cigarette.

"I haven't time to go out to lunch today. Do you think you could fetch me something?"

She was actually smiling, and looking at Edie—almost for the first time in their association—as though she really saw her.

"Yes, Mrs. Winsloe. Only, I'm on the telephone. Miss Collier and Miss Frayle have gone to lunch."

"You can have the calls put through in here. Get me two or three sandwiches—anything will do—and could you make me a cup of tea?"

"Oh yes, Mrs. Winsloe."

Edie, with incredible speed, put on the kettle, arranged the best cup and saucer on a little tray, hitherto sacred to Mrs. Ingatestone's use, and dashed out into the Strand.

She was upstairs again in less than fifteen minutes.

"Down there, please. *Not* on the papers."

Edie obeyed, gasped, and retreated as quickly as she could to the door.

"Thank you very much indeed. I'm so much obliged to you."

"Don't mention it, Mrs. Winsloe."

Raising her eyes, Edie again received a look of full recognition and a smile.

Dazzled, she went downstairs. Instead of writing her novel, she sat eating caramels and thinking about Her.

(4)

Sal Oliver returned to the office at four o'clock. She had personally inspected the school destined for the little boy whose parents were going to India, had found herself satisfied with it, and had had a long conversation by telephone with the little boy's father. She was to see him at five o'clock. There would just be time to sign her letters and clear up.

"If you please, Miss Oliver, would you go in to Mrs. Winsloe?"

Sal nodded at the messenger girl.

She went in to Claudia.

"Look here, a frightful rush job has just come in. That American woman wants us to provide an escort for her child to Paris—get her clothes, see about passport and everything, and get her there by Thursday. Not flying; it seems she's nervous."

"Ingatestone must do it. We can manage without her for a couple of days, easily."

"Ingatestone telephoned half an hour ago to say she's gone to Dorking and will be away at least two days."

"Gone to Dorking! Why has she gone to Dorking?"

"Because," said Claudia, in a low, furious voice, "she thinks, or pretends she thinks, that her wretched child is ill. It's an absolute excuse, of course. And even if it isn't, the school authorities can look after her, surely. There's no question of her being in danger, or anything like it."

"What's it supposed to be?"

"I don't know. Tonsillitis. Ingatestone got a message

at Streatham, apparently, and she must have rushed through the job there and gone tearing off to Dorking. They're all alike—putting personal considerations before their job."

"She's never let us down before."

Claudia struck the table with her fist.

"It's perfectly maddening! This American job may be worth any amount of work to us. I'd go myself, but I've got that article to write, and the big cross-word before tomorrow. I simply can't."

"Of course you can't. I'll do it, Claudia. I can manage it perfectly."

"Who'll take your work?"

"Frayle and Collier can do anything that absolutely won't wait."

"One of them will have to deputize for Ingatestone. God knows how long she means to be away."

"Not longer than she can help, I imagine."

"As long as I live," said Claudia, "I shall never understand the mentality of people who take on a job of work, and then put every sort of personal consideration ahead of it."

"I suppose if one of your children were ill—" began Sal, and then stopped. What was the use of arguing the point?

"I can only tell you," said Claudia, arrogantly, "that in six years of running this show I've never found it necessary to let my private affairs interfere with my work."

"Well, you've been dam' lucky, that's all," returned Sal, unmoved. "Now look here. I've got an idea. Get Mrs. Ladislaw here for a week. There are any amount of things she can do, and I'll be responsible for showing her the work."

"I don't like amateur work."

"It's only for a week, or less. Till Ingatestone turns up."

"It's a bad principle," Claudia enunciated, slowly, "to try and combine friendship with work. It never answers."

"There isn't much friendship about you, in this office," said Sal, dryly.

They looked at one another for a moment in silence. Then Claudia, with one of the unexpected flashes of humour that enabled Sal Oliver to tolerate her autocracy, burst out laughing.

"I suppose you're right. Very well. Tell them to get me Frances on the telephone. I'll speak to her myself."

"Right."

Sal went out.

Why, she thought, didn't Claudia want Frances Ladislaw in the office? She had only agreed to send for her because the pressure of work really was great, and this American job important.

Most likely, Sal thought, Claudia felt that it would be difficult to reconcile her office personality with that aspect of herself that she had presumably always shown to her friend hitherto.

(5)

Frances Ladislaw arrived on the following morning, pale with agitation and excitement, and, since Claudia's

red light was burning, was taken straight up to Sal
Oliver's office by Edie.

As they went upstairs, Miss Frayle cautiously opened
her door without a sound, and applied an eye to the
aperture. With equal noiselessness she closed the door
again and turned to Miss Collier.

"It's the one who came in one day last August. Quite
nice shoes and stockings and utterly meaningless hat.
Looks as if she might be a lady."

"Really a lady?" demanded Collier, sceptically.

"Yeah. A relic from Winsome Winnie's palmy days,
I should say."

"Oh, she is. They were at school together."

"God! Collier, how do you always get to know
everything? What are we going to do with our Polish
friend, now we've got her?"

"Polish?"

"Yeah. She's called Mrs. Ladislaw, and that's a Polish
name. I know it is because I saw a film once—Cossacks
and dogs and all like that—and the chap was called
Ladislaw. I thought it was rather sweet."

"I say, Frayle, I *honestly* think I'm putting on a stone
a day, if not more. *I* don't know what to do."

"Try handing me the duster for this bloody machine.
I won't half give young Edie hell for leaving it like
this!"

Miss Collier threw the duster at her colleague's head.
Miss Frayle caught it neatly with one hand, waved it
above her head, twirled round once or twice on the
tips of her toes, said, very gravely: "Nymph dancing
naked in the woodlands," and began to dust the cover
of her machine.

"A nice fool you'd look if your precious Oliver had come in then!" observed Miss Collier, dispassionately. "Has anybody heard what's happened about Ingatestone?"

"The old bitch isn't coming, Edie says. There was a telephone message or something. Her child's got to see a specialist."

"My God! how awful! Is she really bad?"

"Not frightfully, but Ma Ingatestone's got the wind up. I'm sorry for the old hag."

"So'm I—and won't she get hell from Winnie! 'Putting personal considerations before the work! I can only tell you that in six years of running this job I've never found it necessary to let my personal affairs interfere with my job,'" mimicked Miss Collier, with appalling fidelity.

"I tell you what, Collier, let's send the kid an aspidistra in a pot or a pennyworth of tomatoes, or something. Wouldn't it be a gesture?"

"Yeah. Let's. We'll pop round to a shop at lunch time. Poor little wretch—it's a shame. And Ma Ingatestone works like a black, I'll say that for her."

"After all, it isn't her fault if she looks like an overworked tart and weighs eighteen stone," tolerantly observed Miss Frayle.

She looked at herself in the glass.

"Would you say I looked *utterly* repellent in this frock, or only just repellent?"

"Anyway, you don't put on about six pounds every other minute, like I do. I ask you, Frayle, *have* you noticed my seat lately?"

Miss Collier twisted herself into various attitudes, in

an endeavour to obtain a view that nature had never meant her to obtain.

"I think you're going batty, Collier. Truly I do."

Young Edie came in.

"Please, Miss Frayle, will you go up to Miss Oliver?"

"O.K."

Frayle skimmed out of the room and up the stairs. She moved with an almost incredible effect of speed and lightness. As she went out she blew a kiss with the tips of her fingers to her colleagues, murmuring: "Exit ballet queen, featuring as Cupid the Winged Messenger."

Edie giggled.

"I don't know whatever keeps Miss Frayle off the stage," she gurgled, ecstatically.

"Unless it's the manager's foot," Collier agreed. "Now, you hop off and get the kettle going. I'd sell my soul for a cup of tea."

"I can get you one in a minute, Miss Collier, if the telephone doesn't ring and I'm not sent for."

"*You* won't be sent for. Don't flatter yourself. Get a move on."

"O.K., Miss Collier."

Edie grinned and went out.

(6)

Miss Frayle, outside Sal Oliver's door, assumed an air of preternatural discretion and went in.

"Good morning, Miss Oliver."

"Good morning. Mrs. Ladislaw, this is Miss Frayle, who deals with most of our correspondence, and has charge of all the personal files. I think the best plan would be for her to go through them with you and give you some idea about anything that's got to be dealt with this week."

Mrs. Ladislaw shook hands, smiled rather nicely, and murmured that that would be very kind of Miss Frayle.

"Mrs. Ladislaw is going to help us till Mrs. Ingatestone can come back. Is there any news of the little girl this morning?"

"She's to see a specialist. I don't think she's really much worse, but she's always been delicate, and I think they're afraid of glands or something."

"Poor Mrs. Ingatestone!" said Sal. "I suppose she's frightfully worried."

"Frantic, I should think. She's crazy about the little creature. When I see what these mothers go through, it's me for Marie Stopes every time. I hope that woman gets a monument when she dies."

"I'll put you on the job, if we're asked to compose the inscription," promised Sal. "In the meantime, can you find a table for Mrs. Ladislaw in your room? I think we'd better leave Mrs. Ingatestone's undisturbed as long as possible, don't you?"

"I should think we better *had*," expressively murmured Miss Frayle.

"I'll ring down as soon as Claudia is disengaged," Sal assured Mrs. Ladislaw. "And—unless she's already booked you?—do come and lunch with me somewhere, at about one o'clock, and tell me what you think of our beer-garden."

Frances murmured acceptance and gratitude and followed her guide downstairs.

(7)

Frances had been downstairs for more than an hour before a message came summoning her to the presence of Claudia.

She had had a good many files shown to her and their contents briefly and clearly explained by Miss Frayle, whose sophisticated mannerisms disappeared magically when she was at work, and reappeared instantly whenever she was not; she had been given a cup of tea, with two biscuits in the saucer, by young Edie, and she had exchanged several amiable observations with Miss Collier.

Frances inwardly felt afraid of the two girls. They looked so young, so competent and assured, and their successful permanent waves, lipstick and nail varnish all combined to give each of them an air of poise that she secretly envied.

They were very kind to her.

"Please ask me anything you want to know. You will, won't you?" said Miss Frayle.

"I'll type anything you want done, Mrs. Ladislaw. Just say the word," said Miss Collier.

At intervals one or other of them looked up and asked, "O.K.?"

And Frances always smiled and said, "Yes, thank you."

She heard them talking to one another—brief, ejaculatory phrases in the intervals of work—and she guessed that her presence was making them self-conscious. Well, theirs, if they only realized it, was having much the same effect upon her.

She liked them, though, both of them.

Then young Edie came and primly said that Mrs. Winsloe would see Mrs. Ladislaw now, and would she please come up?

Frances got up, and Edie held the door open for her. "Won't you show me the way?" said Frances. Edie, politely murmuring, "Pardon me," preceded her to the stairs, omitting to shut the door behind her.

Frances heard the unguarded voice of Miss Collier: "Twee, isn't she? I hope W. W. doesn't reduce her to a nervous wreck within twenty-four hours."

"My God! Collier, what a hope! If Ingatestone doesn't turn up by tomorrow, we're all for it."

Mrs. Ladislaw sedately followed the messenger up the stairs and to Claudia's office.

Her mind, already sufficiently agitated by the number of new impressions confronting her, refused resolutely to take in, at any rate for the moment, the full implications of the light-hearted dialogue she had just heard.

2

Mrs. Ingatestone's child was declared not to be seriously ill but she must, said the doctor, leave school at once and spend at least six weeks in the country, drinking milk and living as much as possible out-of-doors. At the end of six weeks he would see her again.

Mrs. Ingatestone, whose home was a two-roomed flat with a bath-kitchenette in Bloomsbury, at once said that this should be done.

"Splendid," said the doctor, much encouraged. "Injections would be advisable as well."

"Certainly," said Mrs. Ingatestone.

She could not imagine how any of it was going to be done, but done it should be.

She had very few relations, and had quarrelled with most of them, and none of them lived in the country. Nor would it be in the least possible for her to take Diana away anywhere herself. If country lodgings, milk, doctor's fees, and travelling expenses were to be paid for at all, it could only be achieved by continuing her work.

Since nothing in the world except Diana was of the slightest importance to Mrs. Ingatestone, she would have had no hesitation in throwing up her job, at whatever

218

inconvenience to her employers, if to do so would have benefited Diana.

But on the contrary, it would have cut off their sole income, and would have made even smaller the already small chance of getting another post later on.

Mrs. Ingatestone, like most workingwomen, found it easier to earn than to save. There was a small amount in the Post Office Savings Bank, and she paid regular premiums to a life assurance company. Everything else went on Diana's school bills, the upkeep of the tiny flat, and such minor self-indulgences as cheap cigarettes, sweets for Diana, visits to the cinema, and a yearly holiday by the sea.

For all these extravagances, except the last one, Mrs. Ingatestone now blamed herself bitterly.

Not, however, for long. She was preëminently a person of action.

She rang up the office.

"Mrs. Ingatestone speaking. Is that you Edie? . . . Put me through to Miss Oliver, like a good girl. . . . What? . . . Thank you very much, Edie; she's better, but I'm a bit worried; the doctor doesn't think her any too strong, poor kiddie. . . . It does seem a shame, doesn't it? How are things going at the office? . . . Well, I know, dear, but it couldn't be helped, not in the circumstances. As to when I'll be back I couldn't say at all. See if you can get me through to Miss Oliver."

There was a pause. Mrs. Ingatestone could plainly hear the buzzing and whining noises that indicated young Edie's efforts to obtain a reply from the telephone on Sal Oliver's table.

"I'm ever so sorry, Mrs. Ingatestone, I think she must be out. I can't get any reply."

"Damnation!" said Mrs. Ingatestone, clearly and forcibly. And she added—to herself, for she knew how to keep subordinates such as young Edie in their places—"I suppose it'll have to be Her Ladyship. Just exactly what I didn't want."

"Miss Frayle would like to speak to you, Mrs. Ingatestone," piped Edie's attenuated voice.

"O.K."

More buzzing. Then the familiar drawl of Frayle's young, light voice.

"Oh, hallo! It's me. I say, how's Diana?"

Mrs. Ingatestone, irresistibly compelled to it by Frayle's tone of deep concern, poured forth a concise history of her child's illness, partial recovery, the advice of the doctor, and the absolute necessity of following it.

"Yeah," said Miss Frayle at intervals. "Yeah. . . . I see. Of course. . . . *Every* time. . . . She'll be all right, Mrs. Ingatestone. I knew a child *exactly* like her, only miles worse, and they sent her to Weston for three months and she put on stones, and she's been as strong as a horse ever since. It's utterly sickening for you, of course, and frightfully upsetting, but she'll be O.K. directly you get her into the real country. You mark my words."

Never, in the course of their office association, would either of them have expected for one moment that Mrs. Ingatestone should think any words of Miss Frayle worth marking—unless of a sufficiently blasphemous or indecent nature to be curtly rebuked as "*anything* but ladylike."

Now, however, Mrs. Ingatestone gasped in grateful tones: "Do you really think so?" and Miss Frayle replied, reassuringly, "Yeah, sure I do."

"I've been sorry to let you all down, I must say. How have you been managing?"

"A friend of Mrs. Winsloe's has taken over for a bit, and Collier and I are helping out. It's quite all right. We're as slack as hell, for the moment. I suppose you're not likely to be back just yet?"

"I shall need a couple of days to get things settled, and then I want to get right back to work," Mrs. Ingatestone declared, vigorously. "Get Edie to ask Mrs. Winsloe if I can speak to her for a minute."

"O.K. Oh, Mrs. Ingatestone! Would Diana like any books to read? I could lend her some detective stories and frightfully light novels and things, that we got last year for mother when she was laid up."

"I expect she'd love them. She's a regular bookworm. It's very kind of you indeed, and we'll take every care of the books."

"Oh, that's all right. I'll send them along. 'By-bye. Love to Diana. I'm writing her a letter, to cheer her up."

"That's a nice *girl*," said Mrs. Ingatestone emphatically to herself, as she waited for Edie to put her call through to Mrs. Winsloe's room. And she added, quite mistakenly: "I've always vowed and declared that, for all her disgusting language and immoral ideas, Frayle was a thoroughly good girl at heart."

"Yes?"

Claudia Winsloe's voice, crisp, and decided, came across the wires.

"This is Mrs. Ingatestone speaking. Good-morning, Mrs. Winsloe," said her employee, very correctly.

"Good-morning. I hope the child is better."

"She's better, thank you, Mrs. Winsloe. I hope to be back at work by the end of the week—to-day's Tuesday —say Friday morning—if you could possibly spare me till then."

There was a silence that Mrs. Ingatestone decided was an unfavourable one.

"I'm extremely sorry, but I've got to make one or two arrangements for sending Diana to the country."

"Yes, I see. Well, of course, Mrs. Ingatestone—I can't say it's very convenient to do without you just now; we're as busy as we can be—but I suppose I must give you till Friday."

"I appreciate that very much, Mrs. Winsloe, and I can assure you that I fully intend to make up for lost time once I get back," Mrs. Ingatestone said, in tones of entirely false cordiality.

"Till Friday, then. Oh, by the way. I suppose you couldn't possibly look in here for half an hour sometime this afternoon? I do want to ask you about one or two things, and it would be a great help to Mrs. Ladislaw, who's doing what she can with your work."

"Certainly, Mrs. Winsloe, with pleasure. About three o'clock?"

"Excellent, thank you. Good-bye."

The click of the replaced receiver reached Mrs. Ingatestone's ear before she could utter her own good-bye.

"No time to waste, as usual," she muttered, and smiled rather grimly and not without a certain admiration.

(2)

Claudia and Sal Oliver lunched together that day.

They did this from motives of expediency, rather than from any special inclination for one another's society, since it afforded them an opportunity for discussing minor points concerning the office and the staff.

It had been decided by Claudia, with a strange mixture of candour and autocracy, that Frances Ladislaw, so long as she worked in the office, had better not join them.

The restaurant they chose was a very small and modest one. They ate fish salad and bread-and-butter, and finished with stewed fruit and black coffee. Claudia smoked throughout, nervously and almost incessantly. Sal not at all.

"Ingatestone rang up this morning, didn't she?" Sal enquired.

"I was going to tell you. How did you know, by the way? Edie is supposed to treat all telephone calls that come to me as confidential."

"It's all right; she's been perfectly discreet so far as I know. Mrs. Ingatestone spoke to Frayle. She asked for me first, but I was out. It was Frayle who came and told me about it."

"We'd better find a little more work for that girl to do, if she's got time on her hands. Well, Ingatestone admits that the child's more or less well again, but she wants to make some arrangements or other about her—Heaven knows what—so I've given her till Friday. She's to come in for half an hour this afternoon, to clear up one or two things."

"Yes, I know."

"Frances is really doing a lot to help us, but of course she's a complete amateur and has to be told every single thing. It holds up the work quite a lot."

"But it couldn't be helped," Sal pointed out.

Claudia looked at her in surprise.

"Of course it could have been helped. If Ingatestone put her job first, instead of her private concerns, she needn't have been away at all, for more than a couple of hours to take the child to the doctor. It isn't as if she was very ill. She's not. It's the same old story. Private lives first, and the job second. Women are all alike."

"Except you."

"Very well, except me if you like. I'm not in the least ashamed of saying so. I always have thought that I was the only woman of my acquaintance, almost, to understand the meaning of hard work."

Sal shrugged her shoulders.

"Wait till Maurice gets acute appendicitis, that's all."

"But that's not the point, Sal! The Ingatestone child *hadn't* got acute appendicitis, or anything else that meant a real crisis. I could understand, if it had been that kind of thing. But this was just feminine fuss, and nerves, and disregard of everything except her own personal feelings. Why on earth does she want to be away for the next two days, for instance?"

"What did she tell you?"

"Something vague about getting the child to the country. I told her she could stay away till Friday, and I only hope she understood what I thought of her."

"I've no doubt she did. She's heard your views on the subject of unnecessary absence quite often enough. I imagine that's why she didn't tell you any details. You see, I heard the whole story from Frayle."

Sal stopped, and Claudia said: "Well, go on. I can see you mean to tell it to me."

"Yes, I do. If Ingatestone hadn't been terrified out of her senses at the thought of getting the sack, she'd have told you herself. Well, this child's the only thing she's got in the world. The husband was a bad hat, and drank, and he left her without a penny, having previously pawned most of the furniture."

"I know all that, except about the furniture, which I believe you invented."

"Very well," continued Sal, imperturbably. "The whole of Mrs. Ingatestone's screw goes on this child, naturally. I don't know whether she has any relations to help her or not; anyway, none of them is in a position to take her now, and the doctors have ordered her into the country. The point of all this is that Mrs. Ingatestone, between now and Friday, has got to find a suitable place and make all her arrangements. I suppose she means to take her there, wherever it may be, at the week-end."

Claudia made a sound expressive of concern.

"Yes, I see. Why on earth didn't the idiot tell me? Of course I should have understood."

"How was she to guess that? She's heard you say— the whole office has heard you say—that you've no patience with slackers and people who are always putting their own concerns before their work. Naturally she thought you meant it, and that you'd probably sack her if she asked for more than two days."

Claudia uttered an ejaculation, more expressive of impatience than of contrition.

"The woman must be a perfect fool. What a mercy she's coming this afternoon. Of course I'll tell her she can have a week or ten days—whatever's absolutely necessary—on full pay, while she gets the child settled."

"I knew you'd say that."

"It's the obvious thing to say."

Sal called for her bill.

"Could we possibly offer her anything to help at all, with the expense? After all, she's been with us from the beginning."

"I should think we might," Claudia said. "Anyway, I'll try this afternoon. Poor wretch! It's bad luck. I hope there's nothing really wrong with the little girl."

"I don't think it's terribly serious, from what Frayle said. Ingatestone will probably tell you about it this afternoon."

"Apparently that's exactly what she won't do. Fool! I do think people might realize," said Claudia, half laughing, "that one's bark may be worse than one's bite."

"It'd be a lot easier," Sal returned, "if you didn't say things that you don't really mean, just to live up to your own idea of yourself as an employer."

(3)

"Never again," remarked Mrs. Ingatestone, emotionally—"never again shall it be said in my presence that Mrs. Winsloe is hard. She is *not* hard. No one could have been kinder, or more generous, or more of an *absolute* lady than she's shown herself to me."

"That's good," said Miss Frayle, cheerfully. "I thought Saucy Sal's example would tell, in time. To say nothing of Collier's and mine."

"I'm afraid I'm going to desert you all for a week, but the very first minute I can I shall be back again. How is this Mrs. Ladislaw managing?"

"Oh, she's O.K.," Miss Collier conceded. "I say, does Diana like chocs? I've got some here for her, just to pass the time away."

"That's very kind of you—really it is. I do think you girls have been sweet."

Miss Collier and Miss Frayle looked embarrassed, and the former said, quickly:

"Actually, I shouldn't offer my worst enemy chocs. There's nothing like them for putting on weight. But if you're a kid, it doesn't matter. Aren't they lucky!"

"They aren't the only ones," said Mrs. Ingatestone. "My word, no!"

(4)

In a very few days Frances Ladislaw had begun to feel as if she had been at work in the office of London Universal Services for quite a long while.

She became attached to her—or Mrs. Ingatestone's—card index, and enjoyed entering up particulars on the cards and signalizing a completed transaction by the affixing of a red paper disk.

She liked Miss Frayle, Miss Collier, and young Edie—whose surname she never learnt. Quite soon Frayle and

Collier forgot that Mrs. Ladislaw was a friend of their employer's, and behaved in her presence very much as they would have behaved without her, except that they referred to Mrs. Winsloe only as *Her* or *She*. Miss Oliver they simply called, behind her back, Our Sal, or Sally-in-our-Alley. The violent language used by the slim, baby-faced Doris Frayle ceased to surprise Frances. From time to time she took part, quite earnestly, in passionate discussions about Miss Collier's weight.

As the weather turned colder she fell more and more into the tea-drinking habit.

Much of her work, however, lay outside the office. She packed, washed underclothes, and mended, for agitated and often unreasonable women; she took small children to walk in Kensington Gardens or visit the Zoo—Frances liked the children and hated the Zoo—and she continually visited a small Servants' Registry Office run in close connection with Claudia's organization.

One day, to her surprise, Copper Winsloe walked into the office just as she was preparing to go out to lunch.

"Hallo, Frances! Good-morning."

"Good-morning. It's nice to see you. Shall I see if Claudia's ready?"

"She isn't expecting me. I came up by train, after she'd left," said Copper, coolly. "Had to see a man."

"We'll ring through, and let her know you're here."

Ringing through only revealed that both Mrs. Winsloe and Miss Oliver had left the office a quarter of an hour before.

"*What* a pity!" Frances cried. "I wonder if Edie knows where they were going."

"Never mind. It doesn't matter. They'll be here this afternoon, won't they?"

"Yes. We've got an inter-departmental conference."

"*What?*"

"We meet in Claudia's office for a sort of general discussion about the various jobs and who's doing what. It's supposed to prevent overlapping and to give us all a chance of bringing forward suggestions. I think it's a very good idea. Not that I've attended one yet. They only happen once a month."

"You were just off to lunch, weren't you? Come and have some with me. We'll go to Simpson's."

Her impulse was to protest at the extravagance, but she checked it. Copper scarcely ever made any suggestion, if one came to think of it, and when he did so—at any rate at Arling—it was not usually successful.

"Thank you very much," she said, gently. "I'd love to come. What an exciting place!"

"I used to go there sometimes in the old days before the war," Copper explained.

He took her to Simpson's, expressing disapproval of the way in which London had altered, and they sat down to lunch.

"What cocktail would you like?"

She saw that he wanted her to accept the cocktail, and, although with a foreboding that it would make her feel sleepier than ever between the fatal hours of two-forty-five and three-thirty, she chose a dry Martini.

When the drinks came, Copper said, rather shyly:

"I want you to drink a toast. To a possible job!"

"Oh, I will!" cried Frances, eagerly. "Copper, I'm so glad! Here's the very best of luck."

She drank excitedly, and choked at the taste, which she hated.

They both laughed.

"Do tell me about it, please."

"That's what I came up about. It's not exactly settled yet, but with any luck it will be to-night, before I go home."

"What is it? Does Claudia know yet? Is it a permanent job?"

"Claudia doesn't know. I shall tell her this afternoon. As a matter of fact, it partly depends on her. I say, what are you going to eat?"

They discussed the question. Copper's childlike absorption in the menu, and his anxiety that Frances should have what she liked, rather touched her. At Arling he had been sullen and very often disagreeable, although not to her.

Now, away from Arling and with a new hope in front of him, he had become again the Copper Winsloe that she had known in earlier years. When the waiter had received his order, Copper leant back and drew a long breath, looking at his companion.

"I'll tell you," he began. "Sure you're not bored?"

"O Copper! Go *on*!"

(5)

The job, it appeared, had to do with a new country club, to be started outside a big midland town by an enterprising speculator and his wealthy wife.

"The woman, as usual, being the moving spirit and

having most of the money," Copper threw in, with a grin.

Copper, whose name had been sugggested by an old Ceylon tea-planting friend, had actually received a letter asking him whether he would consider taking up the management of the golf-house and club that were to form an integral part of the scheme.

Frances listened to him with absorption, uttering low ejaculations of excited comprehension from time to time. Copper was not, as a rule, an eloquent speaker, and even to-day he did not achieve more than articulateness.

But his face, indeed his whole personality, were transformed.

"Decent of old Branscombe to remember me, wasn't it?" he kept on repeating.

"It's splendid!" said Frances. "I suppose they wanted a gentleman?"

"That's the idea, I believe."

"But, Copper, tell me some more. Would it be residential? Is it permanent?"

"It's residential, naturally, to start with. They're only suggesting that I should do it for six months, to get the thing thoroughly started, and after that I imagine it's up to me. Old Branscombe didn't seem to think there'd be much difficulty about getting in with them permanently, if the thing's a success."

"Oh, it must be!"

"It's bound to be, isn't it?" he agreed, earnestly. "They've got any amount of money, and apparently the house and grounds and everything are all O.K. The list of members is as long as your arm."

"Is it open already?"

"Opens next week. They want me to go up before that, naturally. Then, if I get the job, I can meet the people—the members, I mean—when they have the opening show. Lord Mayor coming out as large as life, and all the local big-wigs. After that—carry right on."

"It's marvellous! How excited Claudia will be."

"D'you think she will?" he asked, wistfully. "Lord knows it'll be a change to have me earning some money. There's only one snag about it, though. They want me to put a couple of hundred pounds into the show—just as a guarantee of good faith."

"Would that be very difficult to manage?"

"Impossible, so far as I'm concerned. I shall have to have it from Claudia, I suppose. If she can't, or won't, I dare say I could borrow it. It's worth it, to me, to get something to do again."

"Oh yes, yes!"

"You must have another drink," said Copper.

"No, really I won't."

"You *must*," he insisted. "I'm going to. You must drink to the success of the job, now you know what it is."

Her head was already swimming slightly, and a pleasant feeling of irresponsibility invading her.

"I shan't be able to attend to anything this afternoon," she murmured.

"You won't have to if there's this what-you-may-call-it conference. Unless I'm mistaken, the talking will all be done by Claudia."

Copper ordered two more cocktails.

He was happier than Frances had ever seen him since

the early days of their acquaintance. She remembered, pleasantly sentimental, how much she had liked him then, and how disappointed she had felt at the change in him.

"When can you tell Claudia?"

"After this blessed conference, I suppose. Will it take long?"

"I don't know. About an hour, I think the girls in the office said."

"I tell you what, I'll call at about four o'clock and take her out to tea or something. Don't say a word, will you?"

"Of course not."

He raised his glass.

"Well, here's to it!"

"Here's to it," repeated Frances, obediently.

She liked her second cocktail better than she had her first. It seemed less unfamiliar. Moreover, the agreeable sense of irresponsibility was increasing rapidly.

"I never, never," she said, with great earnestness and distinctness—"I never, never was so pleased about anything. I can't tell you, Copper, how sorry I've felt for you heaps of times."

"It's been pretty rotten—and not only for me. I know I've been a brute often," said Copper Winsloe, candidly. "I seem to have got into a bloody awful state when I couldn't do anything but curse. I've felt a different man since Branscombe's letter came."

"When did you get it?"

"Two days ago, but I wasn't going to say anything till I'd actually seen him. I didn't even let Claudia know I was coming up this morning."

"Is it actually all settled? Oh no—there's the two hundred pounds."

"There's the two hundred pounds," he agreed, "and one's got to see the place and the people and get the once-over. But Branscombe thinks it's a certainty, all right, if I can produce the capital. They were quite prepared to take his recommendations. Save them the trouble of advertizing and so on, I suppose."

"Where would you live?"

"In the guest-house, to start with. They've got one, of course, for week-end visitors. I'd have a bedroom and an office there. Later on, I suppose it might be a question of something more permanent.

"Do you mean—living there altogether?"

"Well, I don't know. But you see, Frances, it might be worth it. Supposing—just supposing—we were to sell Arling, mortgage and all, we could kind of start fresh, couldn't we?"

Frances felt dimly that there was a drawback to this scheme and that she ought to put it forward. The idea, however, eluded her.

She took another sip at her cocktail, hoping that it might clear her brain.

Copper was speaking—from rather far away, and without her having heard the beginning of the sentence.

". . . and not only is Arling much too big for us, but it's too expensive. It was a perfectly mad thing ever to buy it. But Claudia wanted it so frightfully."

"She's very fond of Arling."

"It's a nice enough place," he conceded, "but not for people situated as we are. The fact is Sal Oliver once put the whole thing in a nutshell. She's a clever woman, Sal."

"Oh, very, very," said Frances, enthusiastically.

"She said that what Claudia really wanted was to see an extension of her own personality in the children. History-repeating-itself kind of idea, I suppose. That's why she was so keen on Arling. Seeing herself as a child again, and a young girl—only it was Sylvia and Taffy and Maurice, instead."

"Repeating the pattern," Frances elucidated, feeling proudly that this was indeed an admirable summing-up.

Copper appeared to feel it so as well.

"That's exactly it. You've got it in a nutshell—repeating the pattern. She wants to see herself again, living in her children. I suppose it's natural enough. Still, they won't be children much longer. Sylvia isn't living at home, and soon Taffy won't be. Home'll just be the place they come back to for a year or two longer, and then after that they'll make their own lives. What's the sense of hanging on to Arling?"

"But Claudia ——"

"Yes, I know," he said, impatiently. "But I've danced to Claudia's tune all these years, and I think it's about time I had a say in things. Honestly, don't you agree?"

"Yes, yes. I do," Frances said, solemnly.

She was aware, in a remote kind of way, that she would probably have qualified this statement, in a more normal mood. Two cocktails, taken in the middle of the day after a very light breakfast of five hours earlier, had, she felt certain, impaired her powers of judgment.

A happy confidence enveloped her and seemed to vibrate glowingly between herself and Copper Winsloe.

3

It had been a day of hard work, rushed jobs, and continual irritations. Thank Heaven, thought Claudia, Ingatestone will be back tomorrow.

She had deliberately arranged to do a certain amount of Mrs. Ingatestone's work herself, and this addition to her own multifarious occupations added to the nervous strain under which she laboured.

Her head ached as she presided over the staff conference, and it seemed to her that Sal Oliver was argumentative, Frances Ladislaw half asleep, and the two girls unusually casual and inattentive.

Claudia's self-command enabled her to keep these impressions to herself, but her manner grew more and more curt and peremptory, and as soon as the conference was over she slammed her door viciously and snapped on the red light.

A pile of letters to be signed lay on her desk. She read each one through, making an alteration here and there.

I shall have to stay at Sal's flat tonight, she told herself. I can't face that drive through the traffic and I drive so badly when I'm tired. Claudia knew—it was one

of the facts that she faced most fearlessly and frequently
—that, although she was a careful driver, she was not a
good one. Extra fatigue was always liable to make her
movements rather slower, her judgment a shade less
accurate, than was desirable.

Perhaps it wasn't altogether to be wondered at.

One couldn't do everything—although one might try.

The inter-office telephone bell rang.

"Yes?" said Claudia. She allowed herself to sound
just as exasperated as she felt, at this fresh demand upon
her attention and energy. It was much better that the
office should realize the tension under which she was
living and working; otherwise they might become care-
less and allow unnecessary interruptions.

Claudia's "Yes?" therefore sounded, even to her own
ears, not so very unlike a sharp bark.

"If you please, Mrs. Winsloe, Mr. Winsloe is in the
office. Shall he come up?"

The children, thought Claudia. Which of them is it?
Maurice ——

"Please show him up at once," she directed, and leant
back in her chair.

Copper had never before come to the office except by
appointment.

In the four and a half minutes that elapsed before
Edie knocked at the door, Claudia had lived through a
good deal. With complete composure and presence of
mind she had handed over one or two urgent pieces of
work to Sal Oliver, had commanded Miss Frayle to sign
the remainder of the letters for her, put a telephone call
through to Arling and given various instructions, sent

Edie for a taxi, and stepped into it, directing the driver
to go—where?

Was it Sylvia, or Taffy, or Maurice?

"Come in!"

It was Edie's deprecating knock, but she did not appear. The door opened as though by an invisible agency,
and Copper came in, wearing an unmistakable air of
jauntiness and an unwonted flower in his buttonhole.

Claudia instantly recognized that all her fears had
been without any foundation at all.

"Copper!" she said, sharply. "Is anything wrong with
any of the children?"

"Good God, no! Why should there be?"

Claudia visibly relaxed in her chair.

"I'm sorry—it was silly of me," she said, very sweetly.
"When I heard you were here, quite suddenly, I thought
you might have come to fetch me because one of them
had met with an accident or was ill."

"Well, I haven't."

"I'm so glad."

She looked at him expectantly.

"I say, Claudia, come out and have tea somewhere.
Not now this minute, but when you're ready."

"But, my dear, I'd love it, of course, but I do wish
you'd warned me. I didn't even know you were coming
up to London."

"I know you didn't. As a matter of fact I've got
something to talk to you about. Can you come now?"

She shook her head.

"Not possibly. I've got a woman coming to see me
at four o'clock—that's in ten minutes—and I want to give
Frayle some dictation before she goes—and then Collier

is bringing me some accounts to go through. O Copper, why *didn't* you let me know you were coming?"

"I didn't know you'd be so tied up," he said, gloomily. "You've got to have tea *some*time, haven't you?"

"Not necessarily. If I do it's only a cup that stands on the corner of the table while I work."

"That's the way women always go on," muttered Copper.

"I can't help it, dear, really. You know," said Claudia, mildly and reasonably, "I don't come to the office just for fun, to do nothing."

"I should have thought you could spare half an hour or twenty minutes, I must say."

Claudia sighed.

Then she said, brightly: "Well, I must see what I can do. Sit down and smoke a cigarette, Copper, and perhaps I can reorganize things a little. I suppose you've had lunch?"

"Yes."

He had reverted to his customary monosyllabic way of answering, and Claudia stared at him in some perplexity.

"There's nothing wrong, is there?"

"No," said Copper, without much exultation. "No, there's nothing wrong."

(2)

By half past four it had become possible for Claudia to delegate some of her tasks and complete others. She drew on her hat and coat and rejoined Copper, who had retreated downstairs.

She found him in conversation with Miss Frayle. A peculiar gift for finding out by instinct the proximity of any man, and immediately entering into conversation with him and keeping him entertained thereby, was known in the office to be one of Frayle's leading characteristics.

Even Claudia was aware of it, and rather amused at the graceful creature's pose as she stood balancing a wire basket on one hip, her eyes raised appealingly to Copper's face, her expression one of candid satisfaction in his society.

When Claudia appeared Miss Frayle scarcely moved, yet in some indefinable manner she instantly ceased to be a bewitching houri and became instead a competent young worker.

"Good-bye," said Copper.

"Good-bye, Mr. Winsloe," drawled Miss Frayle, with her best sham-American intonation.

Copper followed his wife into the street.

"Where would you like to go?"

"The nearest place," she said, wearily. "I've had the most frightful rush all day and I'm not nearly through yet. I wonder where they'd serve us quickest."

"Shall we go to the Savoy?"

"Not unless we've come into a fortune, Copper. I think Lyons would be more suitable."

In the end they went to neither of these extremes, but to a small teashop off the Strand.

There Copper told Claudia his news.

She listened attentively, her eyes widening every now and then.

"But, my dear! It's—it's all such a surprise. I had no idea."

"Neither had I until I got Branscombe's letter."

"Why didn't you tell me?"

"I thought I'd like to get something settled first. It's my own show, come to that."

"But naturally. Of course. Only it's so— Tell me, are you committed definitely yet?"

"I don't know what you mean, by 'committed.' They've practically offered me the job, if I can raise the two hundred pounds capital—which I shall eventually get back, of course, in salary—provided the directors pass me; and Branscombe is one of them and was practically told he could appoint anybody he thought suitable."

"Copper, it's all splendid, I'm sure, but—" She hesitated, and then asked him if he would like a second cup of tea.

"Yes, please. What were you going to say?"

"I was only going to ask if you know anything at all about this enterprise—this country-club experiment. Except, of course, what Branscombe has told you."

"Well, isn't that enough?" Copper demanded. "Branscombe has put his own money into it, which is pretty good proof that he thinks it's sound enough—if that's what you're driving at."

"Copper—please! I'm not driving at anything. But naturally I'm anxious. It seems so marvellous—too good to be true, almost."

"You don't sound very delighted."

"I'm afraid I sound tired. I'm so sorry. It's been an

awful day. Never mind that now. Tell me what you're going to do."

"Go up north the day after tomorrow and get the once-over, and then, provided they don't kick me out at sight, look into things a bit. I imagine I shall be wanted for the opening show, when some big bug is coming to make a speech and set the ball rolling."

"I see. And then what?"

"How do you mean? I shall come back, after the opening, to get things settled and tell you what's happened and what sort of offer they've made me—if any."

He smiled rather anxiously.

"I think it's going to be all right. My God! I shall be thankful to have a job of work again!"

"I know, darling. I can so thoroughly understand that. Though I wish it wasn't quite so far away. Still, I suppose it's only temporary."

"Well, I don't know." Copper's voice had roughened. "You must see, Claudia, that if this turned out to be a really big thing—as it very well might—it would be worth almost any sacrifice to keep it."

"Quite," said Claudia, speaking carefully. "I quite see what you mean. At the same time, we've got to consider my position, too, a little bit. I've built up this business at the cost of a great deal of very hard work—harder than most people realize, I think—and a good many sacrifices. And after all, it's been keeping us all for a good many years."

"There's no reason why you should chuck it up entirely, that I can see. I suppose, if necessary, we could move somewhere halfway between your job and mine. Anyhow, there's no need to think of that yet, surely."

"None whatever," she said quickly. "We don't even know whether you'll get the job, if you do apply for it, or how long it would last, or anything."

"I don't understand what you mean. Of course I've applied for it. Upon my soul, Claudia, anybody would think you didn't want me to get it."

"O my dear!" said Claudia, wearily. "Please don't take up that attitude. I'm so sorry if I sounded unsympathetic. It's the last thing I mean to be. But, you see, this has all come on me very suddenly, at the end of a gruelling day. I'm sure I sound very stupid, but it's the last thing I want to be. Why, it would be the most wonderful thing if you could get something to do— even if it only paid your own living expenses."

Copper scowled.

"One less for you to keep," he said, brutally.

Claudia took no notice.

"About this capital," she began. "I do wonder how I could raise it."

"I suppose another mortgage wouldn't be frightfully difficult to arrange. I wish to God I could do it myself, without having to ask you."

Claudia was at once warmly responsive.

"Don't think of that. Anything I *can* do for you, I will. You know that, Copper."

"I thought you might think of it as an investment."

"Yes, I know, but you see Copper—I've got to consider the children, too. I want to do everything I can for you—I do see how much this means to you, I think— We must find out more about it all. I wonder if Adolf Zienszi knows about it."

"They're very keen to get him interested. Branscombe told me."

"I see. Yes, I see," said Claudia, thoughtfully. "I suppose that's why— Yes, I see. Copper, wouldn't you like some more bread-and-butter? You're not eating anything."

"I don't want anything," said Copper, ungraciously. He pushed his chair back and took out a cigarette and lit it, forgetting or omitting to hand the case to his wife first.

(3)

Frances Ladislaw, although less exhilarated than when under the influence of her two cocktails, was, even at the end of the day, sufficiently elated by the remembrance of Copper's good news to ask if the Winsloes would dine with her that night in London. She was much surprised to hear from Claudia that Copper had already gone home and that she herself intended to spend the night at Sal's flat, because she was too tired to drive back to Arling.

"I'm so sorry," said Frances. "What a pity! Well, will you come and have dinner with me, Claudia? Just quietly, and you shall go back to bed as early as you like. You do look dreadfully tired."

Claudia said that was nothing, and accepted the invitation to dinner.

The club of which Frances was a member had moderately comfortable bedrooms upstairs, and superb reception-rooms and a marble staircase downstairs, very indifferent service, and bad cooking.

The members knew this, and bemoaned it quietly amongst themselves, but they took no concerted action. The service, therefore, continued indifferent, the cooking bad, and the cellar abominable.

Neither Claudia nor Frances was perturbed by these failures to minister to their comfort.

They dined, unperceivingly, off dishes made of eggs and scraps of fish, a few chicken bones, and some black coffee.

Afterwards they sat in a remote corner of the enormous smoking-room and talked in low voices about Copper's announcement.

A sensation of puzzled disappointment invaded Frances as she became aware, without quite knowing how, that her friend was less pleased than she had expected her to be.

Claudia was practical and businesslike. Probably she knew what she was talking about when she said they must enquire into it all very, very carefully before risking any money.

"I see," said Frances. "I see what you mean, of course. But wouldn't it be worth risking something—if it is a risk—so that Copper should have something to do—feel that he's working?"

"Yes, of course," said Claudia at once. "That's frightfully important, and I've been thinking about it a great deal. It's been wretched for him, all these years, and bad for his self-respect, though Heaven knows one's had no thought of blaming him, poor Copper."

"It must have been dreadful for him to see you working so hard and not be able to do anything himself. And when he gets this job," said Frances, happily, "you won't have to work so hard any more. It'll all be easier when you needn't feel it all depends on you."

"We mustn't think of that," Claudia said, earnestly. "I'm trying not to let that influence me in any way—I mean the personal consideration. I've managed all these years, and if necessary I can go on till Maurice is grown up."

"But Claudia, Claudia, I'm sure that's all wrong," said Frances, incoherent from mingled grief and astonishment. "You must *want* Copper to take his fair share of responsibility. It's been bad enough, all this time when he couldn't, but now— It does seem to me that you're making a most dreadful mistake if you don't do everything in the world to help him to get it."

Agitated as she was, her eyes met those of Claudia squarely.

Claudia's expression was exceedingly grave, but when she answered, it was in a very gentle voice, without a hint of anger at what Frances herself felt to be her own audacity.

"You think me very ungenerous and unsympathizing about this idea of Copper's, don't you? I suppose it's quite natural you should. I don't see why I should expect you to understand. But you see I've been married to Copper a good many years, Frances. I've seen him let down one responsibility after another. I don't say he can help it; it's partly temperamental, I suppose. But it does mean that I can't feel very enthusiastic about putting very-badly-needed money into a scheme that doesn't sound to me too terribly practical."

"You've just said that we—that you—must enquire into it very carefully. And I quite agree. But until you've enquired into it very carefully, how can you know whether it's practical or not?"

"I can't *know*, of course," Claudia agreed, with perfect equanimity. "It was a silly thing to say. I'm sorry."

So far from being moved by this simple admission, Frances suddenly felt that it would be a great relief to lose her temper, scream at her judiciously-impartial friend, and possibly even return to the methods of the old-fashioned nursery, and slap her.

Horrified and surprised, she actually felt herself colouring with mingled shame and vexation.

Hastily she rushed into speech.

"If the capital is very difficult to find—and I know it must be, with the children costing such a lot—I do wish you'd let me lend it to you. I could really manage it quite easily. I have so few expenses, now, and only myself to think about. I'd love to do it."

"It's sweet of you, and I do appreciate it."

"Then you'll let me."

"Frances dear, if it was really necessary I'd come to you before anyone, indeed I would. But you know I could always get the money from Anna. Adolf settled a small fortune on her, and gives her everything she wants besides. And she's very generous. But it was dear of you to offer."

"I forgot about Anna," said Frances, rather crestfallen. "Still, so long as you can get it somewhere ——"

"I'll get it somewhere, if necessary," Claudia declared. "So far, I've managed without borrowing, and I want never to, if I can help it."

"I think that's wonderful," Frances admitted.

Claudia laughed, the first time she had done so that evening.

"Not wonderful at all. Just common sense," she said, gayly.

For the remainder of the evening they spoke of other things.

Soon after nine o'clock Claudia rose.

"You don't mind my going early? I shall see you tomorrow at the office. By the way, doesn't Ingatestone get back tomorrow?"

"Yes. But I thought I could explain to her about one or two things I've done. If you don't mind."

"Mind! As if you hadn't been a perfect angel, to come all this time and help us out. I'm only too grateful to you, my dear."

"I wish you'd send for me again, if there's anything I can do. I've enjoyed it, you know, and I should be only too glad to help you."

Claudia thanked her again, kissed her affectionately, and said good-night.

Frances, left alone, felt strangely disconcerted.

(4)

At the flat, Sal was out, and Claudia made use of the telephone on her untidy desk, to call up the expensive service-flat where the Zienszis stayed when in London.

She asked to speak to her brother-in-law.

In another moment she heard his quiet, rather nasal tones.

"Yes? Is that you, Claudia?"

"Yes. This is confidential, please, Adolf. Do you know

anything about a man called Branscombe, and a possible job that he's suggested for Copper?"

"Yes. I know all about it."

"Is it sound?"

"As sound as such things ever are, in these days."

"But you mean there's a risk in it?"

"There's risk in everything."

"I know—but ought we—ought he—to put money into it?"

"I think you can quite safely put a little money into it. They've got some very good backing."

"Oh," said Claudia, oddly taken aback.

"Anyway, if I may advise you, get Copper to put in for the job, if he hasn't done so already. It's well worth while."

"I see. Thank you Adolf. I—I suppose it's something he can tackle?"

"I think he ought to do it very well. If you'll forgive me—is that all? There's a man waiting for me downstairs."

"Yes, that's all. Thank you very much. Love to Anna."

"If there's any difficulty about a small investment of capital," said the distant voice, "I think we might be able to adjust that. Anna and I both realize what a splendid thing it would be for all of you, to have Copper land a good job."

She heard the click indicating that he had rung off before she could say anything further.

Claudia turned slowly to the door.

So the investment was a sound one: the job desirable: and the money, if necessary, might be found.

A weight off my shoulders, of course, automatically Claudia told herself, in the very phrase that she would have employed to a listener had she had one.

But before she had turned the door handle she was asking herself doubtfully whether it would not be worse, in the end, for Copper to fail at the job, as she feared that he might, than for him to leave it unattempted.

I *must*, said Claudia to her invisible listener—I *must* look at it all round, as dispassionately as I can, and without taking into account what a relief it would be to me personally, if I didn't have to feel that the whole thing depends on me and nobody else.

4

Copper went off to the midlands, and Claudia prepared herself for three days of intensive work. She wanted to get several things accomplished before Saturday, when she had promised to go down to Maurice's school for a school play. Work was pouring in and she felt extraordinarily tired. The night after her conversation with Copper she slept badly, and woke again to headache.

Sal, eyeing her over the tiny breakfast table, said nothing and poured out a cup of strong coffee.

Sal's flat was a small affair of three rooms, a kitchen and a bath. It looked out onto a broad and quiet square with green trees. She had a daily servant, from whom she obtained excellent service. It was a joke amongst the Winsloes that the friend with whom she shared the flat was a myth. None of them had ever seen her there.

"We each go our own way," said Sal, coolly. "That's why we get on. When Jane's at home for any length of time, I usually go away. That leaves her free to have anybody she likes staying in my room. But most of the time she's away—hotels in the winter, and cruises in the summer."

This singular partnership had persisted for a number of years, and might therefore be accepted as a success.

"That woman makes marvellous coffee," Claudia admitted, gratefully.

"Doesn't she? Have some more. There's plenty here."

"Thank you, I think I shall."

"When do you go down to Eastbourne for Maurice's show?"

"Friday night, if I can, though I can't imagine how I shall get through the work. I may have to put off going till Saturday morning, but I don't want to."

"Ingatestone gets back today, and Frances would stay on till the end of the week."

"I know. I've already arranged it with her. But she can only help downstairs, after all. She can't do my work for me."

"Is there much?"

"A good deal."

They said nothing further.

(2)

In the office, Mrs. Ingatestone was once more in possession of her desk, her files, and her telephone extension.

She had established Diana at a small convalescent home near Bournemouth, had seen her improve almost in the first twenty-four hours; had defiantly sold out a tiny fragment of her tiny capital to defray expenses, and had spent the previous evening in applying to her head the canary-coloured liquid that produced such remarkable results.

The conviction of having rejuvenated her appearance

by this means, almost as much as her ten days' absence from the routine of the office, helped to exhilarate her. Strongest of all was her determination to show Mrs. Winsloe how grateful she was and how ready to set to work.

Miss Frayle and Miss Collier, after their fashion, welcomed their colleague with their customary affectation of indifference, supplemented by various small attentions.

On her desk she found a bunch of sweet-smellin violets, placed there by Frayle, and a little plant growing in a pot—the offering of Collier.

Young Edie, taking round tea at eleven o'clock, shyly indicated that she had selected the biscuits known to be those preferred by Mrs. Ingatestone.

"Miss Frayle's gone off biscuits altogether," she said, confidentially. "And she won't touch milk, even in her tea. Only lemon. She says she's going on a diet."

"Silly girl," said Mrs. Ingatestone, indulgently.

She had before now seen her juniors embark upon diets recommended by the daily press—woman's page— or the friend of a friend, or, in the case of Miss Frayle, a boy whom she had once met in a train and whom she alleged to have been studying dietetics at an American college in the middle west. Mrs. Ingatestone remembered only too well the resultant paper bags filled with tomatoes that had invaded the office, and the smell of oranges against which she had so angrily protested. She remembered clearly the effect of the diet on Frayle's temper. It was a comfort to remember as well that these distressing experiments seldom endured for more than three days.

Mrs. Ingatestone, unmoved by æsthetic considerations, drank her tea and ate her biscuits, listened to Frances Ladislaw explaining various points in connection with her work, and thanked her heartily.

"I really have enjoyed it," Frances said. "I hope you won't find a lot of mistakes. The two girls have been so kind about helping me and telling me anything they could."

"They're nice girls, both of them. What I should call thoroughly kind-hearted, in spite of their silly ways. I often think," said Mrs. Ingatestone, "that it doesn't do to judge by appearances."

Frances agreed that it didn't.

"But I must say," she admitted, "that I *like* their appearance. I can't imagine how they find time to take all that trouble and turn themselves out so beautifully."

"Ah," said Mrs. Ingatestone. "That's now. Wait till they marry—if they ever do. You'd be surprised how quickly that type of girl goes to pieces, once she's *got* a husband. No more perms., or manicures, or bothering about putting on weight. They just let themselves go— slop about in old clothes all the morning at their work, eat sweets and read stories in the afternoon, and worry the poor husband to take them out to the pictures in the evening. Till the baby arrives, of course—that is to say those that make up their minds to have one at all. After that, it's all U P with spending any money or having any more fun. And a woman's looks soon go if she never has any fun.

"Well, I mustn't chatter like this, must I? But I think we're all straight here now. I'm waiting for Mrs. Winsloe to see me."

Edie came in to fetch the tea-things.

"Do you know whether Mrs. Winsloe has got the red light burning?"

"It was on just now," Edie said. "I'll have another look."

She presently put her head round the door.

"Light's just gone off, Mrs. Ingatestone."

"Then I think I'll go up. She may not," said Mrs. Ingatestone, modestly, "have realized that I'm back."

On the stairs she met Miss Frayle, coming down.

"Is Mrs. Winsloe disengaged?"

"Yeah. Christ! what a mass of nerves that woman is!"

"Now, now, now, Frayle!"

"Well, don't say I didn't warn you. God help her child if she goes down to him in this mood! Still, I believe young Maurice is her favourite. He'd be mine, too. Give me a boy every time."

"Is it all right to go in now?"

"As right as it ever will be. As a matter of fact, she asked for you."

"Why didn't you say so before?" demanded Mrs. Ingatestone, bouncing up to Claudia's door and then knocking at it very quietly.

(3)

The day's work proved heavy.

Claudia decided that she could not spare time to go out for lunch, and ordered some sandwiches and coffee to be sent in.

At three o'clock Anna telephoned.

"Have you heard from Copper yet?"

"There hasn't been time. He only went up this morning."

"He might have telegraphed. Darling, aren't you glad about it?"

"Of course I am. If he gets it and if it's all right."

"Of course he'll get it, and of course it's going to be all right. Why shouldn't it be?"

"Why indeed. Did Adolf tell you I rang him up last night? It was a great relief to hear that he knows about the whole thing and thinks it's sound."

"Yes, he does. Adolf's always right about that kind of thing. Claudia, are you staying up in town tonight?"

"Yes. I shan't go back to Arling now till I get back from Eastbourne. I'm going down there on Friday night, if I can possibly get away, for Maurice's school play. Unluckily I've got a frightful rush of work on—so I may have to put off going till Saturday morning. But I don't want to. He'll be disappointed; it means I get so much less time with him."

"Well, look, can you dine with me tonight? Adolf has to go and meet some man somewhere, and I shall be by myself. We could do a play if you liked."

"I'm too tired for a play. Thank you all the same, Anna dear."

"Poor darling!" came Anna's warm, affectionate tones. "I'm so sorry. We won't go anywhere. Just sit and talk quietly."

"I'd love to. What time?"

"Any time you like. Half past seven?"

"Too early. I shan't be through by then."

"O Claudia! What a shame! You could call it a day at six o'clock, surely."

"Not if I'm to get down to Maurice on Friday evening. Could you make it eight fifteen, Anna?"

"All right. I'll expect you then. Don't bother to dress, unless you want to."

"Oh, I keep a change at Sal's flat. Good-bye, darling. Till this evening."

"Good-bye, my dear."

(4)

Anna turned to her husband.

"She sounds frightfully over-strained. She says she'll dine here quietly with me this evening."

"Any news of Copper?"

"She hadn't heard. Of course, he only went up this morning."

There was a pause, and then Anna burst out:

"Of course he'd have telegraphed what's happened if he didn't know—poor wretch!—that she's going to prevent him, by hook or by crook, from taking up this work. He may not *know* that he knows it, but he does, all the same."

Adolf nodded.

He looked sorry.

"You've got to remember that Claudia doesn't know it, either," he suggested. "I'm sure she thinks she's weighing the whole thing quite impartially. She asked me several questions last night."

"Hoping all the time that you'd say it was a bad show and he oughtn't to have anything to do with it! I know. There's one thing, Adolf—we've *got* to back Copper up over this. Make him believe in himself, somehow, and if necessary find him the money."

"All right, sweet. You know I'll do anything you want."

"Darling," said Anna.

Presently he asked:

"Do you suppose Copper's ever thought of leaving his wife?"

"I know he has. It was years ago. He actually suggested a separation to Claudia, and she wouldn't hear of it. She said they must think of the children first, and keep a home together for them."

"Well," said Adolf, quite gravely, "I think he'd have shown more sense if he'd just cleared out."

"I think so, too. But that's exactly the kind of thing that a man like Copper never does. Everything's against him—upbringing and convention and his own lack of resolution. Copper would have been all right as somebody's eldest son, before the war, with an income of five or six thousand a year. But nowadays, with everything in the world upside down, he's not much good. He can't stand up to it."

"He's got to stand up to taking this job," said Adolf, rather grimly, "or he'll hear a few truths about himself from me."

"A few truths about Claudia would be more to the point," cried Anna. "I only hope I shan't tell them to her myself, this evening. No, I won't, poor darling. She's tired to death. I could hear it in her voice. And, anyway, it wouldn't do any good. Telling Claudia home truths is like hurling oneself against a glacier. Everything just slides off, and the impact only hurts oneself. That dreadful, calm, dispassionate way Claudia has of listening, and discussing, and admitting everything—all so fair and analytical and so utterly, utterly false! O Adolf! don't let me talk like this. I do love her. I used to admire her so, and think her so wonderful, when we were little."

"Sure," said Adolf. "You love her. You wouldn't be working yourself up like this if you didn't. There's a great deal that's very attractive about Claudia."

"There is, isn't there? I wish she'd married some man much stronger than herself."

"It might have taken some time to find one," remarked Adolf. "Don't you think now you'd better keep quiet and let me ring down and tell them to send you up some tea or a cocktail or something?"

"I've got my masseuse coming at four. That'll rest me. I'll have a drink or something afterwards. Shall you be back quite early this evening?"

"I shall be through with talking business to Maclean by nine. He's leaving London on the ten-o'clock train. I can go to the Club and get some bridge, or come right back here. Whichever you'd rather."

"I think I'd like you to come back. Somehow we've got to make Claudia see that Copper's got to take this job, even if it means chucking up Arling and starting somewhere else."

Adolf emitted a low whistle.

"Sell Arling? That'd be a bit hard on her, I must say."

"They may not have to. I don't know. I only know that Claudia is *not* going to persuade me, whatever she may do to herself, that there's any reason why that wretched husband of hers shouldn't take his chance of regaining some self-respect at last."

(5)

Now I'm going to be nice and behave *really* well, Anna told herself as her maid held open the door of the bedroom for her and she went down the passage and into the elaborately-modern sitting-room of the flat.

It held a shiny black glass octagonal table, some chromium-plated pieces of furniture that included a radio-gramophone, a number of turquoise-blue and purple cushions, and a single tall, square vase of opalescent glass containing a branch of shell flowers.

The two enormous windows were curtained in an ostentatiously-simple coarse white net.

Above the electric fire, flush to the wall, was a large diamond-shaped clock. The hands were slender oxydized daisies. There were no numerals: only little purple dots in the appropriate places. This room, which also served as dining-room, was rather a difficult one to live up to, Anna always felt.

She wore a very plain black dress, and her pearl necklace, and carried an ivory cigarette-holder, and hoped that she struck no jarring note with her surroundings.

Claudia, when she arrived, was also in black. She looked pale, but greeted Anna with great cheerfulness.

"Darling, this is lovely. I had a sudden idea—I can't think why—that I was going to find mother here. I can't help being glad I haven't. You know what I mean."

"Oh dear, yes, I know what you mean exactly. Poor darling Mummy. She's coming to lunch tomorrow. Have a drink."

"I'd love one."

They drank their cocktails, and talked quietly and without constraint.

"I've got a marvellous dinner for you," said Anna, frankly. "Quite a little tiny one, but lovely. I saw the chef myself. They do things beautifully here."

"Yes, don't they," Claudia agreed, happily.

The years slipped away from them, and they were once again two young girls—sisters dwelling beneath one roof, sharing one environment, and understanding one another with the profound, complete, and effortless intimacy of childhood.

(6)

Never, afterwards, could Anna remember at exactly what stage she found herself saying heatedly to Claudia all those things that she had so definitely resolved not to say.

The remains of the tiny but lovely little dinner had been quietly taken away. They had had coffee, and smoked cigarettes.

Claudia leant back on the divan, that was so much more comfortable than it looked, and Anna extended her graceful length on one of the stainless-steel arm-chairs.

Quite suddenly they were in the midst of it.

It wasn't about Copper, at first.

It was about Taffy.

They had not discussed the matter again since Claudia's promise, given at Arling in August, of thinking it over.

"We've settled to stay here till after Christmas, and

go back to America early in January. What about Taffy?"

"You mean about taking her with you?"

"Of course. What else could I mean?"

Claudia laughed a little.

"I'm sorry. It was a silly way of putting it. I suppose I wasn't really thinking about the words, but the actual question of her going or not. Don't think me ungrateful Anna, because Heaven knows I'm not. It's most wonderful of you—and Adolf, of course—even to have thought of it. But I'm afraid it's 'No.' "

"Why?" said Anna, her voice and her colour both rising, to her own vexation.

"Two or three reasons, my dear. I've thought about this very, very carefully, and tried to view it just as impartially as I possibly could, for Taffy's sake. And I'm pretty sure that I should say exactly the same if she was somebody else's daughter, not mine at all.

"Taffy's not altogether an easy child to understand. You'll agree with me about that, I know. I'm not even sure if, well as you know her, *you* really thoroughly understand her. Wait a minute, please, Anna. I know what you're going to say. You're going to say that it's I who don't understand Taffy. For the sake of the argument, my dear, I'll concede at once that I don't. I don't want to be like poor mother, Heaven knows, always saying that she could read us both like little books. Do you remember how frantic it used to make us?

"But seriously, like most intelligent girls. Taffy is going through a stage of dramatizing herself. She'll outgrow it, of course. But I do feel that the right atmosphere is rather specially important for her. At present she's just one of a number of other schoolgirls of more or less her own age and standing, not specially important in any way. That's exactly what she needs. I may add that her headmistress, to whom I've talked, entirely agrees with me."

"So I should imagine," Anna angrily interpolated. "She isn't going to be such a fool as to suggest that you'd better send one of her most promising girls somewhere else."

"Anna dear, what nonsense! As if one pupil could possibly make any difference in a school of nearly four hundred! Besides, Taffy isn't as brilliant as all that. Nor is Miss Corry that kind of woman. Any advice she gave me was disinterested. And quite apart from her advice, I'd made up my own mind."

"I thought your children were always to be allowed to take their own decisions."

"That's not quite a fair argument, is it? You can bring anything to the *reductio ad absurdum*, I suppose, but it doesn't really mean anything very much. There's no decision for Taffy to take in this case, for the simple reason that she can't possibly know what she's deciding. I can take into account—as she can't—the probable effect upon her, psychologically, of going to America, to an American college, and spending the most important years of her development out there."

"And what," Anna ironically demanded, "*would* the effect be?"

"Anna—Anna darling," said her sister, piteously, "please don't sound so dreadfully vexed. If only you'd believe that I'm trying hard to be perfectly honest over this—perfectly fair to Taffy, and to you, and to myself as well. After all, you'll admit it *would* be easier for me to accept your extraordinarily generous offer and let her go. Selfishly speaking, it would lessen my responsibilities very considerably."

"Then, for Heaven's sake, show a little common sense and let her go."

"But, Anna, there's so much more *to* it than that," Claudia said, still with the same unvarying gentleness. "Can't you understand? Taffy doesn't need a spectacular departure for America, or an American background against which she's going to stand out, simply because she's English. She needs to be one of the herd—to learn that she's quite an ordinary person at present, whatever she may eventually become—and isn't a bit entitled to preferential treatment. Why should she be? Oh, if you knew how difficult it is for me to have to say these things!"

"And supposing you're completely mistaken about what Taffy needs?"

"My dear," said Claudia, with some dignity, "I think I must take the risk of being completely mistaken. Heaven knows I don't think myself infallible. All I can do is try and judge the question as fairly as I can, to the best of my ability. I've given you my reasons. Will you tell me why you think I'm so wrong?"

"It isn't any use."

"Indeed, I'll try and understand," Claudia urged. "I do realize that mothers are usually the very worst judges of their own children. I've always been inclined to distrust my own judgment on that account. But that isn't quite the same thing as knowing what's likely to do them good or harm, is it? Do please tell me your point of view quite frankly."

"I think you're deceiving yourself from start to finish."

Claudia inclined her head, wearing her most characteristic air of intelligent attention.

"Yes? Why do you think so?"

"Because I do!" cried Anna, childishly and furiously. "For God's sake, Claudia, come off this frightful pose and be a human being!"

The whole room seemed for an instant to be shocked into a frozen silence at Anna's uncivilized outbreak. At last Claudia spoke again.

"How difficult you make it to discuss anything at all, when you let yourself get so completely irrational and worked up," she observed, meditatively. "You know, Anna—we've got to face it—you're still utterly incapable of using your judgment dispassionately where I'm concerned, because you're still under the influence of that old, childish resentment. You still think of me—perhaps without even realizing that you do—as the domineering elder sister who bullied you in the nursery. I suppose I've brought it on myself. In fact, I know I have."

"Brought what on yourself?" sullenly demanded Anna.

"Your hostility," said Claudia, sadly. "Your distrust of me, and the fact—I've had to face it and accept it— that I—get on your nerves, as people say. But O Anna! I'd do anything in the world to put things right again between us. Can't you forget what's long past and over? I've admitted everything—that I domineered, and interfered, and tried to run your life for you. But it's all

over now. I couldn't run your life now if I wanted to,
and God knows I don't. Why should there always be
this awful barrier between us *now?*"

"I'll tell you," said Anna, resolutely. "If I tell you
what's really in my mind, will you let me speak without
interrupting me?"

"But of course," Claudia answered, smiling wanly.

"What you think is my resentment at the past doesn't
exist. You distress me beyond words as a human being—
nothing to do with our relation to one another. You
did your very best to spoil my life for me—yes, Claudia,
you did—but you didn't succeed, and that's an end of it.
As you've just said, you've admitted all that and it's
past and over, forgotten, so far as I'm concerned. (It
was partly Mother's fault, anyway, for spoiling you,
and partly mine for being a weak-minded little fool.)
And now you're doing exactly the same thing and, just
as you did when you were a little girl, you're making
yourself believe that all your motives are wise and
rational and sound. *They're not.*

"Shall I tell you why you don't want Copper to take
this chance—the only chance he's had in years? Or why
you bought Arling and insist on staying there when you
can't afford it? Or why you won't let Taffy come to
America with us? You've got a splendid set of reasons
for all of it, I know, but they're not the true reasons.
The true reason is that you like seeing yourself as Atlas
supporting the world. You don't, in your heart, want
Copper to get a job at all. I know you say you do, but
actually you're doing every single thing in your power
to prevent it; and if he does get it, you'll never rest content until you've wrecked it. You bought Arling because

you wanted to see yourself again, in your children—you wanted home to be associated in their minds with you primarily, and your personality. I don't know what you're like in your office, but I can guess. Dramatizing yourself as the world's worker. You talk about Taffy's posing, but what about yours? Aren't you, all day and every day, acting as the perfect, selfless mother, the sole support of them all, the woman who's gallantly working herself to death? I'll grant you that you've taken yourself in, pretty completely; I don't suppose you ever do see anything now, except just what you want to see. And you talk about facing facts and being honest with yourself! My God, Claudia!"

Anna stopped abruptly. She was shaking.

"Have you finished?" Claudia said, icily.

Anna nodded her head.

"Say anything you like, now," she muttered, hoarsely.

"Thank you," Claudia answered, ironically. "I'm not going to defend myself, Anna, from your extraordinary charges. I imagine that the facts of my life can speak for themselves, to anybody who is unprejudiced. But it may interest you to know that you've settled the question of Taffy, once and for ever. If that's your view of me, you're not the person to have charge of my child. I think even you will admit that."

"Poor Taffy! But you never meant to let her go, anyway. She's beginning to see through you, isn't she, and to criticize, and if she gets right away, your influence is pretty well bound to snap altogether. No wonder you won't let her have her freedom."

Claudia, pale and wrathful, gave a twisted smile.

"And yet I let Sylvia go."

"I don't know why you sent Sylvia away. But you knew very well that it was safe to let her go. She's not critical, she's not nearly as clever as you or Taffy. She takes you—she'll always take you—at your own valuation."

"And Maurice. Haven't you anything to say about him? What have I done to Maurice, wicked and unnatural mother that I am?"

"Maurice thinks of nobody but you. He scarcely knows that he's got a father. You've impressed your personality on him, the legend of your self-sacrifice, the way you work for them all. I've seen his poor little face quite pale from worry, at the idea of all you do for them."

"Whereas in reality, according to you, I'm wrecking the lives of my husband and children. May I ask what you think would have happened to them if I hadn't worked as I have done? Or do you think my work has all been pretence too?"

"It hasn't—it hasn't!" cried Anna, despairingly. "I know you work far, far too hard. That's just it. You drive yourself to death, but it's because you like doing it. All the time you're visualizing yourself as you want to appear. You're pretending, Claudia. You're not honest with yourself, ever."

Anna suddenly began to cry wildly.

Claudia, white and rigid, sat motionless and without speaking.

5

In her tiny room in Sal Oliver's flat Claudia lay in bed in the darkness and kept on repeating to herself:

"I must look at this calmly and quite dispassionately. I must—I must."

She found it impossible. Anna's words had hurt her too deeply. That *Anna* should have spoken them!

She doesn't understand, Claudia repeated to herself. It isn't possible for Anna to judge of me, or of my motives, without prejudice. She doesn't know it, but all the time she's influenced by the old feeling that I bullied her when we were little. (And if I did, it was only because I did so adore her and thought I knew what was best for her.)

Anna's got no children. Neither has Frances nor Sal. Yet they all presume to judge of my relations with my children . . . and Copper. They don't know Copper as I know him. What security have I that he'll ever keep this job even if he does get it? Supposing we do give up Arling—my home that was paid for with my money and that I've kept together by my own hard work—and move somewhere else and then he loses his job, as he very well may? What happens to me, to my work, to my children?

Writhing on her pillow, Claudia felt the thoughts tearing round and round in her mind like mice in a cage.

Automatically the familiar phrases sprang to life within her.

"I must be fair. I must face facts. Copper wants this job frightfully, and it's the first real chance of one he's had for years. His salary would help. If I sold Arling there wouldn't be the mortgage to pay off any more—we'd move to a much smaller house. The children won't be at home so much now; the house and garden are not going to mean much longer what they have meant in their lives. I could still do my work, still go on at the office."

Suddenly a fierce indignation seized upon her.

How *dared* Anna speak like that! It would never be possible now to let Taffy go to her. It would be utterly unfair to the child, to expose her to the strain of a divided allegiance.

Anna wouldn't be able to hide what she thinks about me, Claudia told herself, bitterly.

It was a long while before she went to sleep, and her dreams were miserable affairs of drowning in deep waters and seeing shadowy forms in which she vaguely recognized Anna and her husband and children trying unavailingly to throw life-lines that she was never able to grasp.

She continually woke up, often with a violent start, and then dozed again.

When she met Sal at breakfast, Claudia's eyes were dark-ringed and her face pale. She looked every year of her age. Her very hair seemed to have lost its lustre overnight and to fall limp and colourless.

(2)

Would it be any good, Sal wondered, to ask if Claudia wouldn't take the morning off? She didn't look fit to go to the office.

Better wait, perhaps, and find out her mood. She looked far too tired to offer lucid demonstration as to the inability of the office to get on without her for the day.

"How was Anna?" Sal enquired.

"Very well, I think. She and Adolf are going back to America after Christmas."

"Will Taffy go with them?"

"No," said Claudia, speaking carefully. "Taffy isn't going with them. I quite realize that you think I'm wrong about that, but I've gone over the ground very, very thoroughly, and I'm pretty certain that it wouldn't answer. It's Taffy I'm thinking of. Naturally, it would be a great help to me financially to accept. They've made the most generous offers, and one needn't hesitate about that side of it, because Adolf is apparently getting richer every day, and, after all, they haven't anybody to come after them. But Taffy's not like Sylvia. She could very easily lose her head completely and get into some silly muddle over there, that Anna might not be able to cope with at all."

A familiar wave of irritation rushed over Sal.

She forgot all about her compassion for Claudia's exhausted appearance.

"What a very odd reason!" she remarked, coldly. "If you call it a reason at all, that is."

Claudia looked at her without resentment.

"You're quite right," she admitted; "it isn't really a reason, is it?"

She smiled wanly.

"I might have known I shouldn't get that past you, Sal. No. The real fact is that Anna, poor darling, let loose the repressions of years last night and told me a good many things that I'm sure she really felt. The fact that they hurt me terribly hasn't got anything to do with it. I'm trying not to let that influence me in any way. But they did prove to me that, holding the opinion she does of me, Anna couldn't be the right person to have charge of my child."

Sal felt slightly disconcerted.

"I'm sorry," she said, mechanically, and indeed she did feel sorry for the pain and fatigue evident in Claudia's whole bearing.

It was a relief to be able to exclaim, "There's the postman!" and go down the stairs to get the letters.

There were several for Claudia, sent on from Arling, and one from Copper directed to her at the flat. Sal had learnt the day before of his journey to the midlands, and its object.

She went upstairs again and poured out coffee whilst they looked at their letters.

Would Claudia say anything?

Sal found it impossible not to glance across at her.

"Copper's been offered the secretaryship," Claudia said at once, "if he can put up the capital. Two hundred pounds, it is. Of course all the details are still to be settled and it would be six months on trial to begin with, but his friend Clive Branscombe is evidently anxious to have him, and he's backing the whole scheme heavily."

"I hope it will be all right," said Sal, simply. "Will the money be a difficulty?"

"It could be managed, I suppose. Copper says he's coming home tomorrow—Saturday—and we shall have to talk it over. He's forgotten that I shall be at East-bourne till Monday."

"Couldn't you go home on Sunday evening?"

"Perhaps. We'll see: I can't disappoint Maurice."

Sal would not dispute the point.

Presently Claudia looked up again.

"I've got a letter from Sylvia. She really is beginning to like Paris and enjoy her work, and she's making friends with one or two people. There are some Americans to whom Anna gave her an introduction who are being very kind to her. I hope—and I'm beginning to believe—that it's going to be a success and give her just the kind of independence and experience that she needed."

"Don't answer this if you don't want to, of course, but I've sometimes wondered why you changed your plans about Sylvia all of a sudden and sent her to Paris instead of letting her come to London."

"It was her own decision. I think I actually suggested Paris in the very first instance of all—or perhaps Mother did, I'm not sure—but Sylvia decided she'd go there."

Sal nodded, wondering if she was to be told any more.

"You've guessed, probably, that there was rather more to it than that," Claudia said, with a smile. "It was that

Bank Holiday week-end at Arling—do you remember?
—when Andrew Quarrendon was staying with us."

"I remember thinking that Quarrendon was very
much attracted by her."

"Yes. Well, that wouldn't have mattered but, unfor-
tunately he told her so, at the same time giving her to
understand that he had no intention of marrying her.
Sylvia was a little bit in love with him, odd though it
seems, and—it hurt her. That's the whole story, practically. It was much better that she shouldn't take a job
in London where there would have been every possibility of their meeting. The Paris idea wasn't at all a
new one and it was quite simple to send her over there.
I think from the tone of her letters that it's answering
very well."

"Do you ever hear of Quarrendon?"

Claudia shook her head.

"Why should I? You'll grant that I'm not a particularly conventional woman, Sal, but I didn't think Andrew Quarrendon behaved well. It was my own fault,
partly, for not realizing that Sylvia had grown up and
that one ought to be more careful."

"Careful about what?"

Claudia looked up in surprise.

"About letting her run the risk of—of pain and dis-
illusionment," she said.

Sal pushed back her chair.

"Poor Sylvia," she remarked noncommittally.

"She'll get over it. She *is* getting over it," Claudia as-
serted. "Mercifully, things don't leave permanent scars
at her age, as a rule."

Then I wonder why, thought Sal, you came between her and experience. I don't believe Andrew Quarrendon would have done her harm, really, and Claudia, of all people, has penetration enough to have known that.

She did not speak her thought aloud. It would be of no use, and Claudia looked ill and tired.

"I know it's exasperating to be told so, but you don't look terribly fit this morning. Why don't you stay here and I'll ring up from the office and let you know if there's anything urgent?"

Claudia smiled. It was a grateful, charming smile, but her voice held the old note of inflexibility.

"Thank you, my dear, so much. But I think I must go. I'm all right."

"Supposing there's nothing that Ingatestone and I can't deal with, couldn't you come back here and rest until it's time to go down to Eastbourne? That is, if you really are going to Eastbourne this evening."

"I'm certainly going to Eastbourne this evening, and although it's very nice of you, I couldn't ever look myself in the face again," Claudia declared, gayly, "if I did the very thing that I'm always accusing other people of doing—lying down on the job."

Sal shrugged her shoulders.

These were all sentiments that she had heard before, and she wondered why she had deliberately given Claudia so good an opportunity for assailing her ears with them once more.

Without wasting further words she prepared to set out for the office.

(3)

"What a hell of a day it's been!" pensively observed Miss Frayle, flinging down the last sheet of a type-written memorandum.

"Are you doing anything tonight, Frayle?"

" 'Friday night's Amami night.' My two step-ins, three pairs of stockings, and one pyjama get their weekly wash tonight and are dried on the hot-water pipes. A home girl's life is made up of little things."

"An office girl's life is made up of damned hard work and very little fun, if you ask me."

"You never spoke a truer word, Collier. I sometimes think I'll go on the streets, for a rest."

"I bet it wouldn't be as strenuous as this office," Miss Collier grumbled.

"Of course it wouldn't. Trouble is, how does one begin. I must ask Ma Ingatestone."

"She's forgotten, it was all so long ago."

"I say, Collier, could you come to the Symphony Concert one night? They're doing the 'Eroika' next week."

"O.K. I'd love it."

"We shall have to get there early; I can't afford anything but the gallery."

"Oh, neither can I. Standing's frightfully good for taking off weight, though."

"How too marvellous," said Miss Frayle, languidly. "I honestly think, sometimes, that I put on a stone a day."

"I wonder if tea is bad."

Young Edie came in.

"Mrs. I. says I can go off now. Is that O.K. or is there anything I can do for you?"

"O.K. by me, young Edie," said Frayle. "I'm hoping to get home myself within the next twenty-four hours."

"Trot along," Miss Collier benevolently instructed Edie. "How's the great work getting on?"

Edie blushed and giggled.

"I don't get much time for working at it, do I?"

"Well, when it's a best-seller you'll remember us, won't you? I shall want a copy of the first edition, signed and dated."

"O.K. Miss Collier. G'-night."

"Good-night. I say, is it raining?"

"Simply pouring."

"Oh hell!" sighed Miss Collier.

Mrs. Ingatestone came in as Edie went out.

"Mrs. Winsloe will sign the letters now, Miss Frayle. After that we can shut up shop."

Frayle snatched up her papers and skimmed across the room and up the stairs.

She entered the room of her employer decorously.

God! the woman looks all in! she thought.

"Did those chintz patterns go back to the city all right?"

"Yes, Mrs. Winsloe. Edie took them this afternoon."

After that the letters were signed rapidly and in silence.

"That's all, Miss Frayle, thank you. I shan't want you again this evening. I'm going down to Eastbourne to-night and I shan't be here again till Monday morning. If there's anything urgent, though I don't see why there should be, take it in to Miss Oliver and if necessary she can get me on the telephone."

"O.K., Mrs. Winsloe."

"Good-night."

"Good-night," repeated Miss Frayle. And she added to herself, "You look as if you needed it, too."

(4)

The same thought crossed Sal Oliver's mind when Claudia came in to her room to say that she was just going.

Unlike Doris Frayle, Sal spoke it aloud.

"It's a perfectly filthy night, pouring with rain, and the roads will be greasy and the traffic's always bad on a Friday evening. I wish you'd go early tomorrow morning instead. It can't make any real difference to Maurice."

Claudia gave her a slight, grave smile.

"I've never let him down yet, and I'm not going to begin now. I told him I'd come tonight. Then I can take him out tomorrow morning."

Sal was on the point of saying: "You don't look fit to drive a car; for goodness' sake go by train."

But of what use would it be?

Claudia, in the opinion of Sal, would only derive a perverse satisfaction from hearing, and disregarding, such an observation.

(5)

In reality Claudia was much nearer to capitulation than her partner supposed.

She felt far more tired than she could remember having felt for a very long while, and the background to a day of hard work had been the miserable, reiterated recollection of Anna's words of the previous evening.

Whether they were true or untrue, it hurt unbearably that Anna should have spoken them, that Anna should believe them true.

Claudia kept on telling herself over and over again in futile repetition that she must face Anna's accusations, and examine them impartially. But she was so tired, and there was the drive to Eastbourne.

Perhaps, after all, she could remain in London that night, face her problems alone and in the dark, and go to Maurice on the following morning?

A queer little picture kept forming itself before her mind's eye of herself valiantly driving out into the night because she wouldn't fail him. She wouldn't let down her job. . . .

Claudia even smiled a little, recognizing that she was dramatizing the situation.

Not very like me to do that, she thought.

All the time she was putting away papers, leaving everything in order and ready for Monday-morning's work, and finally pulling on her heavy motoring coat and dark béret.

On the threshold she paused and looked round the room. Then she went slowly back to her desk, took up the telephone, and dialled the number of the Zienszis' flat.

Anna's voice answered.

"Yes?"

"It's Claudia speaking, darling. I'm just off to Eastbourne for the week-end and I thought I'd like to say good-night."

"Oh, darling, how sweet of you!" Anna's voice, quick and warm, came back instantly. "I'm so glad you rang up. I was going to write."

"Anna—about yesterday evening—I dare say you were partly right. I'll try and see it—look at it quite straight."

"I oughtn't to have said it. I've been wretched. I think I was horrible. Please, Claudia darling, forgive me."

"There isn't anything to forgive. It's all right, truly."

"You're so generous and good. Thank you for ringing up. Now I shall be much happier."

"So shall I. Let's see if we can meet when I get back."

"Ring me up here on Monday morning. Give my love to Maurice. Have a nice time, Claudie."

"You too, Annie."

It was their childhood's formula.

"Good-night, darling. Thank you for ringing up."

"Good-night, darling Anna."

Claudia hooked up the receiver with a strong feeling of comfort and relief.

She went out to the car.

It was a very dark night and the rain fell steadily.

As she turned towards the river Claudia once more realized that she felt as much tired and shaken as though she were recovering from a long illness. She became aware that she was driving badly, wavering in her decisions, and slightly nervous and unready in all her movements.

I *must* take hold of myself, she thought.

For a moment she envisaged the possibility of taking her car back to the garage and herself returning to Sal's flat for the night. She knew her partner well enough to feel certain that she would meet with no comment.

How silly! As if it mattered whether other people commented or not!

The traffic was heavy and it was only possible to crawl at a snail's pace.

Her thoughts veered round to Copper and the letter that she had received from him that morning.

A very short letter and not an eloquent one, but Copper had made it clear that he had actually accepted the secretaryship of the club and undertaken to find the capital required. No doubt he meant to borrow it. If Claudia didn't offer to lend it to him then Adolf Zienszi would, or perhaps his friend Branscombe.

Anyway, he'll get it, thought Claudia. She conscientiously told herself that to see Copper in a job must be the greatest possible relief. Financially, as well, it would ease the strain upon her.

If she wasn't so tired, she'd be glad.

A thought pricked somewhere at the back of her mind. For a moment she was unable to grasp it.

Arling.

Copper might want them to leave Arling, to go and live somewhere that would give him the chance of getting home for the week-ends at least.

One would have to consider that very carefully of course. Arling was expensive and the mortgage a heavy drain. Still, it was being paid off by degrees and once it was cleared, the house might be regarded as a good investment.

And she loved it so! To see her own children growing up where she had grown up—to make them familiar with everything that was most strongly associated with her own youth . . . it was like an extension of the past into the present, identifying her own childhood with theirs.

What was it that Anna had said?

"You bought Arling because you wanted to see yourself again in your children; you wanted home to be associated in their minds with you primarily. . . ."

How little Anna understood!

Approaching Westminster Bridge, Claudia slowed down again. The traffic was very heavy and the roads greasy and slippery from the rain.

Presently the car was brought to a complete standstill.

She wondered whether Copper would get a new car for himself now. Of course he would. The old Morris was fit for nothing but the scrap-heap.

Perhaps Copper wouldn't succeed in keeping the job. He hadn't, Claudia thought, much staying power, and he'd got into the habit of drinking just a little too much. He ought to realize that it wasn't any too easy, nowadays, to hold down a responsible position. There were so many waiting eagerly to displace the inefficient, the elderly.

Detached phrases with which she would explain this to Copper floated through her mind.

One must face facts.

The close-crowded vehicles began to move again, led by a seemingly endless procession of trams, and Claudia slipped into bottom gear and turned onto the bridge.

Impatience suddenly possessed her and she thought with dismay of the long drive ahead of her, the necessity of unpacking, even the labour of preparing herself for bed. But she'd be all right after a night's sleep. Able to go up to the school and take Maurice out in the morning, before sitting through the play in the afternoon. She wouldn't have disappointed him, even in the smallest degree.

"Aren't you, all day and every day, acting as the perfect mother . . . dramatizing yourself as the world's worker . . ."

Anna's searing, intolerable words flashed into her mind.

With an irrational impulse to move faster, as if by so doing she could escape from her thoughts, Claudia took advantage of the slowing down of the tram ahead, accelerated, and endeavored to pull round it.

A second later she perceived, on the other line, the slow, jerky advance towards her of the second tram.

Startled, she wrenched at her brake, felt the car slew beneath her as it skidded round, heard the long-drawn screech of violently-applied brakes and a man's horrified shout.

The on-coming tram loomed above her, monstrous and menacing.

PART THREE

The Following Spring

*

As the ship ploughed her steady way across the Atlantic
Taffy leant over the side and gazed, fascinated, at the
churning depths far below.

Supposing one of the small children on board were to
fall in, would she have enough courage to spring in
after it? How utterly helpless she'd feel, swimming
about that boundless green waste, with the waves slap-
ping at her relentlessly!

Quickly abandoning that aspect of her fantasy, Taffy
rehearsed instead the comments of the other passengers,
particularly those of the tall boy from Santa Barbara
with whom she had danced the evening before.

He was too young, of course, but she'd quite liked
him, and it was exciting that he should like her so much
—better, apparently, than any of his own compatriots,
although the American girls on board seemed to Taffy
far prettier, more competent, sophisticated, and above
all much, much smarter than herself.

At least, she thought wistfully, it was a mercy that
black and white both suited her sandy colouring so well.

"The slender figure of a young girl in deep mourn-
ing was silhouetted against the sky. Her face was set

towards the New World. Fearlessly she envisaged whatever might await her there."

Could one envisage something if one didn't know what it was?

Perhaps not.

It was pretty exciting, though, to be going to college in America. For two years she wouldn't see England again. When she next saw the white cliffs of England a world of experience would lie behind her.

England would always be home, although Arling was to be sold.

On the whole, Taffy didn't feel that she would regret Arling very much. The new house was smaller and much more modern and could be run with two maids. And His Lordship wasn't there to resent transplantation.

At the thought of her old friend, put painlessly to sleep and buried under the willows at Arling, Taffy felt hot tears pricking at the back of her eyes. She fiercely fought them back and turned quickly in search of distraction.

An American brother and sister, both young, were setting up their portable gramophone on the deck. They smiled at Taffy and invited her to come and listen to their new records.

"D'you know a marvellous one called 'Ice-cream Blues'?" they earnestly enquired.

"No. It sounds too marvellous," Taffy responded, eagerly.

They put on the record and in another moment the heavily-stressed syncopated rhythm of the new tune broke into the afternoon quiet, rousing from somnolence a few well-rugged elderly forms prone in deck-chairs.

Their looks of wrath and dismay passed unperceived.

The young American seized Taffy and began to dance with her, solemnly and with almost professional skill. She followed him expertly, secretly amazed and delighted by her own proficiency, and hoping that people were watching them.

(2)

Anna Zienszi rose from the bridge table, slim and graceful and smiling, her pearls swinging against the soft black-and-white check of her tailored frock.

"Thank you *so* much, partner," she said to the entranced old gentleman with whom she had been playing a highly successful rubber.

She went to her stateroom, powdered her nose and renewed her lipstick, and then proceeded to the Tudor Lounge—a synthetic affair of panelling and gilt mouldings—to write letters.

Her husband sat in a corner there, reading a detective novel.

He looked up and smiled as she stopped beside him.

"How did the bridge go?"

"Very well. I played with the General and we won all the time. I held the most heavenly cards."

"You always do."

"Nearly always," she assented. "Which proves that the proverb, like most proverbs, is utterly wrong."

"Does it, my darling?"

"Of course."

She laid her hand lightly on his for a moment, her eyes shining.

"I thought I'd write some letters. I shan't have a minute in New York."

"You certainly won't. You'll like to show Taffy around a little in New York, won't you?"

"Surely. Adolf, she's having a wonderful time, isn't she? I never saw a girl adapt herself so quickly to new surroundings. Does she ever remind you of Claudia?"

"A little."

"She does me. O Adolf!"

He looked at her, quick to catch the underlying note of pain in her voice.

"She's harder than Claudia, in a way—less vulnerable. And I don't think that fundamentally she's really very like her."

"Nor I. Taffy'll develop into a grand woman one of these days, if she gets enough scope."

"She'll get enough scope, I think." The unspoken "now" was in the air between them. "I shall always be so very, very glad that Claudia telephoned to me that last evening. I don't know how I could ever have borne it but for that, when I think of the things—the dreadful things—I said to her," Anna said, very low.

"Don't you think, perhaps, that the very fact that she did telephone shows she understood—she knew you hadn't said the things because you meant to hurt her?"

"Perhaps. Yes, I think so. When we were children I used to feel that Claudia was wonderful—so tall and clever and knowing so much; I thought she knew everything. We both tried to carry that relationship on into our grown-up life, and of course it wasn't possible."

"Perhaps Claudia never quite saw that," Adolf suggested. "Perhaps she didn't face the fact that it wasn't possible, and so she resented criticism. But affection—which is the thing that matters in the end—was there between you all the time."

Anna nodded.

"That's why she telephoned, that evening," she repeated.

There was a silence.

Then Anna said, "I must write to mother."

"She'll like that."

"Yes. I'm going to be better about writing. Adolf, *make* me send mother a long letter every week. Do you know, Claudia used to write to her once a week, always, when she didn't see her? She'll miss that dreadfully."

"Maybe later on you'd like to have her visit us, if she'd come so far."

Anna laughed.

"She wouldn't. But you're a darling to think of it. I'll write to her and tell her how Taffy gets on, and we'll be coming home again next year or the year after."

"Sure we will, honey. Sooner, if you want to."

"Adolf, have you wirelessed for our reservations yet?"

"Not yet. But I will. I thought you'd like to get in touch with one or two people, maybe, and fix up a little dinner or something, for Taffy's first evening."

"I would. Not the first evening, though—the second. That'll give me time to go and have a facial and get my hair fixed and call up some of my friends. It'll be fun to see Broadway again."

"You like it over there, don't you?" he said, fondly and proudly.

"I love it. Taffy's going to love it, too. Adolf, have you found out anything about that boy from Santa Barbara? The one she's going about with all the time."

"Yeah. He's all right. I know an uncle of his, I believe. Wall Street."

"She's going to be a responsibility!" declared Anna, gayly. "It'll be grand, having a daughter. I like them better all ready-made, grown up," she added, quickly, lest he should think she regretted their childlessness.

"Look, Adolf, let's think up some people now, that we'd like to see in New York. Then you can send off the radios today or tomorrow. They say we'll be in by four o'clock on Tuesday."

He took out a little gold pencil, and found paper on the desk.

"Now let's see," began Anna, earnestly, knitting her brows. "Who is there?"

Absorbed, she gave her whole mind to considering the question.

(3)

To the infinite horror of Mrs. Peel, it was Sal Oliver who appeared in person, in response to an appeal made that morning to London Universal Services.

"This is very good of you," said Mrs. Peel, in disgusted accents, "but I'm afraid I only wanted an inventory made, before letting my flat."

"I know. We quite understood that. But I do sometimes do this kind of thing myself," Sal answered, gently.

To the ears of Mrs. Peel she only sounded a shade less self-assured and objectionable than usual.

"I can help you, of course," she observed grudgingly. "The silver is listed already, and most of the linen. It will only need checking. Won't you take your things off in my room?"

"Thank you very much."

When Sal came back, wearing an overall and without her hat, they did not at once begin work.

Mrs. Peel stood poised above a small table covered with a piece of green baize, on which were ranged small bundles of teaspoons and the like grouped around an enormous fish-slice that looked as though it had never left the retirement of its old-fashioned case lined with red velvet.

She fixed her pale, prominent eyes on Sal, and patted her pompadour with the familiar gesture.

"Do sit down. How are things going at the office?"

"Not too badly," Sal said. "I think sooner or later we shall have to get somebody else in, but not just yet. It won't be very easy to find the right person."

"It would be impossible," said Mrs. Peel, jealously, "ever to find anyone to replace my daughter. Naturally, I know she left everything in order, and of course you'd worked with her for years and knew her methods, but if ever there was anybody who seemed to be indispensable ——"

She broke off and unseeingly fingered one of the little piles of silver.

"I don't think we could ever possibly replace Claudia at the office. She built up the whole business from the beginning, and carried all the responsibility. I only thought, later on, of trying to find some one who could run things when I have to be away, and undertake some of the literary work. We've no one, now, who can do that. All the stuff we get has to be put out, except just routine typing."

Mrs. Peel was not interested in the details of the office administration.

She only wanted to hear that Claudia was missed.

"Are those two girls still with you?"

"Miss Frayle and Miss Collier? Oh yes. And Mrs. Ingatestone. Claudia had a marvellous knack of getting hold of thoroughly good workers. I think she attracted them, somehow."

"She worked too hard," said Mrs. Peel, sombrely. "I shall always feel that she worked herself to death. If she hadn't been so determined not to spare herself ——"

Mrs. Peel paused, shook her head, and applied a handkerchief to her eyes.

After a moment she spoke again.

"I hear that Copper thinks Arling is sold. The agents have had a definite offer."

"I hope it's a good one."

"Whatever it is, I hope he'll take it. None of us could ever bear to live there again," said Mrs. Peel, vehemently. "And I don't know that any of the children ever had very much feeling for the place. It was Claudia who kept it all together. Oh dear!"

Her voice faltered—failed—died away altogether.

Sal Oliver picked up a dessertspoon, looked at it very intently, and observed:

"Copper's job seems to be turning out very satisfactorily."

"So far as one can tell, yes. I've not been up to see them yet. Perhaps when I get back from Italy. Yes," said Mrs. Peel. At the mention of her forthcoming journey, she recovered her equilibrium. There was, she felt, a very great deal to be done, and nobody excepting herself could possibly do it properly.

"Now," she began, "about the inventory. I've let this flat to a lady and her daughter. No children, I said, and no dogs. She's the widow of a naval man, I believe, and the daughter is unmarried. About nineteen. But so long as there are no wet rims of cocktail glasses left about on the furniture."

"Quite," said Sal Oliver.

"I have some *lists* here," said Mrs. Peel. From a small bag she took a key, unlocked with it a drawer, took out more keys, unlocked more drawers, and finally achieved possession of several sheets of notepaper of different colours and sizes closely covered with not very legible writing.

"Having been by myself so long, I've learnt to be very business-like," she said, rather severely, for she felt no certainty that Sal would appreciate this. "I've *had* to be. Now, about the silver I'm leaving. The canteen, which was a wedding present when I married, I'm taking to the bank. I've put a tick against it on the list. We need not do anything about the canteen."

"Is all this silver, or isn't some of it electroplate?" Sal enquired. "Had I better separate them?"

"It's all on the lists," Mrs. Peel repeated. " 'Lowestoft

ware'—oh dear! that must be the china. But I know the list is somewhere amongst these . . ."

She rustled and fumbled and ejaculated, lost to all excepting the urgency of the present.

(4)

Frances Ladislaw had travelled down to Eastbourne for the express purpose of taking Maurice out to tea.

He thought that it was very kind of her. He was pleased to be going out, to get away from the school, and above all to miss a compulsory game of football.

When the parlour maid summoned him to the drawing-room he got up eagerly. Suddenly he remembered.

When he'd been sent for to the drawing-room before, it had always been to find his mother there. But it wouldn't ever be her any more.

Everything was quite different now.

Quite slowly he followed the maid down the passage and almost unwillingly knocked at the door.

Would Frances be standing near the fire talking to Mr. Richards, just as mother used to do?

"Come in!"

Mr. Richards was not in the room at all, nor was there anyone standing by the fire. Indeed, although it was a cold day, the long window was wide open. He saw Frances just outside it and felt terribly shy, remembering that he hadn't seen her since the dreadful thing had happened.

To his surprise and relief he was spared having to greet her.

"Maurice! Come and look at this," she called, just as though they'd only parted half an hour ago.

His curiosity awakened, Maurice ran out and joined her on the path outside.

Frances was gazing intently through a pair of field-glasses.

"I brought them down with me to try," she explained, "and it's wonderful what a long way you can see on a clear day like this. Wouldn't you like to look?"

Maurice would like to very much indeed, and they spent quite a long time adjusting the focus, and gazing at the distant sea and other points of interest.

Then Frances proposed going somewhere for tea.

Maurice hesitated.

"I don't think we'll go anywhere very near the school," said Frances. "Wouldn't it be more interesting to find somewhere quite new? I've got a car outside, you know."

"But won't it tire you to do any more driving, if you've come all the way from London?" Maurice asked.

Mother had always taken him to one of the places in Eastbourne or to her hotel.

"But I'm not driving, myself," Frances explained. "It's a hired car and the man can drive us anywhere we like. I thought we might try Jevington or Pevensey."

"Won't it be too expensive?" he asked.

"Not for this once," Frances assured him. "I'm having one last fling this week, before I go into a very tiny flat I've found in Bloomsbury, where I'm going to live very cheaply indeed."

"Is it anywhere near the office?"

"Not very. But I'm going there sometimes, to do a little work for them when they want me."

"Yes," said Maurice gravely.

He wondered what the office was like now, without his mother who had managed it all.

Arling, he knew, was horrible without her. He was very, very glad that they were not going back there any more, but to live in the new house near Daddy's work.

By and by he asked Frances whether she'd seen it.

Not yet, she said, but Sylvia and Daddy had suggested that she might go there at Easter.

"I do hope you will," said Maurice.

"That's very nice of you. I should like to, very much. And I'm hoping that when I've got into my flat you'll come and spend a day or two with me in London sometime. We could go to the Tower of London or anything you specially wanted to see."

"Thank you very much," said Maurice, gratefully. "I'd like that. There's one thing I do frightfully want to see, although as a matter of fact I've seen it twice already."

"What is it?"

"Well, it's a thing at Madame Tussaud's. I'm afraid it's in the Chamber of Horrors, but you wouldn't have to come inside if you didn't want to. It's a thing they keep behind a curtain, and it's marked 'For Adults Only,' but I've looked behind the curtain each time. There's nothing to stop one."

"Is it something very dreadful?"

"Oh," said Maurice, "it's marvellous. The body of a person with a hook stuck right through him, twirling very slowly round and round at the end of a rope."

"Very well," said Frances. "You shall go and see it if you want to, and I'll wait outside. Now, what about finding somewhere for tea?"

They found a very nice teashop, and spent an agreeable forty minutes there.

It wasn't really a bit like anything Maurice had ever done before because Frances talked to him, a lot of the time, about his father, and said that Daddy was rather lonely and they must do all they could to cheer him up. Could Maurice think of some hobby that Daddy might care about, and perhaps share?

Maurice, although slightly startled by the idea, promised to try and think of something before the Easter holidays. He began to wish that Frances would say something about his mother. She was so nice and sensible, and it seemed dreadful that they shouldn't ever mention Mother, just as if they'd forgotten her altogether. The thought made Maurice feel so miserable that he had great difficulty in not beginning to cry, and he found it impossible to go on talking.

Then when they were in the car again Frances suddenly began to tell him some rather amusing things about when she was a little girl, and then about what she'd done at school. And her two friends, Claudia and Anna, came into that all the time. Somehow, although one knew quite well it was Mother and Aunt Anna, calling them by their names made them seem like people in a story, and yet at the same time took away that awful feeling of not being able to speak about her. So that Maurice laughed, when the adventures were funny ones, and felt happier again.

"When you were a little girl," he abruptly enquired, "did you have a father and a mother?"

"Till I was seventeen. Then my father, of whom I was very fond, died after a week's illness. So you see," said Frances, gently, "I do know a little bit what it's like, although in some ways I think things make one more unhappy when one's very young—your sort of age—than they do later on, perhaps."

"Why?"

"Because older people know that grief passes, in time. It isn't that one forgets, but just that one gets more used to it. And of course," said Frances, looking out of the window all the time, "that's what the people, the ones who've died, would like, isn't it? They wouldn't want one to be unhappy."

"No," said Maurice, in a choked voice.

Frances, still not looking round, said:

"You know, I was very fond of Claudia. So I'd like it if we could sometimes talk about her, you and I. Just when you feel like it, you know."

Then she went on at once to something quite different, and didn't seem to notice it when Maurice had to hunt for a handkerchief.

When she left him at the gates of the school, Frances asked whether he would like to keep the field-glasses.

"I'd love to," Maurice said, "only how shall I get them back to you?"

"I think you might keep them till the holidays, and give them to me when I come to stay."

"May I use them?" said Maurice, awed. "I'll be most frightfully careful. Thank you *very* much."

He felt pleased and excited at the thought of displaying the field-glasses and allowing one or two of his special friends to look through them.

Frances said good-bye to him, gave him a kiss and a box of sweets, and assured him that she had enjoyed their afternoon very much.

"Perhaps we could do it again next term," she suggested.

"Oh yes, please," said Maurice, eagerly.

He went into the changing-room, feeling happier than he had felt for a very long while. A kind of tightness, that had held him in its grip, seemed to have gone.

"Hallo, fool," said a contemporary, amiably.

"Fool yourself," Maurice returned. "Have a sweet?"

(5)

"I'll have one bunch of single daffodils, and one of jonquils, please," said Sylvia.

She paid for the flowers and carried them home.

It was quite a nice little house, she thought, as she went up the three brick steps that led to it. And the garden might be made pretty. There was a walnut tree, and a rather unconvincing little pergola. Beyond the split-chestnut fencing lay a rough field, and the nearest slate roof was at least a quarter of a mile away.

It was a great deal better than Paris, to Sylvia's way of thinking.

She went into the tiny pantry and chose a bowl from the cupboard, then carefully cut the stalks of her flowers and began to arrange them.

Her face was serious and absorbed. Some indefinable change had passed over her, so that, although she was still pretty, the soft, childlike radiance of a few months earlier had left her altogether. She had also grown noticeably thinner.

When the flowers were done Sylvia carried the bowl into the sitting-room. It was an ordinary small room in which some of the furniture from Arling was just beginning to look at home.

The wireless stood in a corner. Sylvia switched it on, listened for a moment to the kind, explanatory tones of an uncle describing elephant life in the jungle, and then turned it off again.

She looked at her watch.

Half past five.

At least an hour before her father would be home.

I could go and help Nelly in the kitchen, thought Sylvia, or do my accounts, or write to Taffy. But she did none of these things. Instead, she sat in an armchair, holding some mending in her lap, but putting in scarcely any stitches.

She felt very old and responsible.

It would always, she supposed, be like this now. Ordering father's meals, and running the house as economically as possible, and meeting new people, who were very kind, but never seemed quite real, and trying to plan ahead for Maurice's holidays.

That was one thing. Maurice was very easily made happy. He only wanted the wireless, and books, and a little grown-up conversation. Much easier than Taffy. All the same, one missed Taffy terribly.

Only everything's so absolutely different now, thought Sylvia.

She wondered, as she had very often wondered,

whether if her mother hadn't been killed they would
have left Arling just the same and come to live up here,
near Daddy's job.

It was marvellous that he should have got a job, and
such a good one. And the people had been very nice,
and found him this little house, and agreed that he should
move into it at once instead of going on living at the
club.

It's queer, she thought, how I always said I'd really
rather stay at home than go and work somewhere.
Though I never imagined it would be like this. Just
Father and me.

He was very kind, nowadays, and scarcely ever impatient. He said Sylvia was a splendid manager. She supposed that he said it to encourage her, for she never
remembered hearing him praise her mother, who had
been so wonderful.

Sylvia lost herself in remembrances that, to her faith-
ful heart, would never be anything but dear and beautiful.

The ringing of the electric bell at the front door
roused her.

The postman, with the second delivery.

"All right, Nelly! I'll go," called Sylvia.

She took two letters from the postman's hands and
hoped vaguely that one of them might be from Frances
Ladislaw, to say that she would come and stay with them
for Easter. Frances was always nice, and father liked her,
and mother had been fond of her.

Sure enough, one of the letters was addressed to her
father in Frances's sloping Edwardian hand that looked
to Sylvia's eyes so old-fashioned.

She glanced at the other and saw that it was addressed to herself and that it was from Andrew Quarrendon.

The colour flooded her face.

She heard from him sometimes, although not often, and the letters never failed to stir her profoundly.

She had not seen him since he had left Arling, in the dawn of an August morning that seemed separated by a whole lifetime from the present.

Sylvia went slowly back to the sitting-room and moved unconsciously towards the desk that had been her mother's. Standing beside it, she very carefully slit open the envelope with a paper-knife, drew out the letter and read it.

It was very short—much shorter than usual.

For the first time, Andrew Quarrendon asked her to see him. Knowing in what that would probably end, he said would she meet him one day very soon in London? The letter finished with the words, "I love you."

Sylvia, dazed, read them over and over again. She knew that she wanted to see him again, to hear his slow, modulated voice, to feel his arms round her, more than anything else in the world.

She thought of her mother.

But of course, Sylvia told herself, she'd have understood. She wouldn't want one to go on always being lonely and unhappy. She'd have said, surely, that the time had come when Sylvia should make her own decision. How often one had heard mother use that very phrase!

Sylvia even smiled a little at the remembrance.

Suddenly and irrationally she felt convinced that her

mother knew about the letter. She knew that Sylvia and
Andrew belonged to one another, that they were bound
by something that was essential to both and that could
no longer be denied. Somewhere, she knew and understood.

Sylvia, wanting to believe this, for the moment did
believe it, so implicitly that she uttered a little low
ejaculation of inarticulate thankfulness, feeling that her
mother heard it.

Then, the tears shining in her eyes and her heart
tremulous with happiness, she wrote her letter to her
lover.

(6)

The work in the Norfolk Street office continued.

No one sat at Claudia's desk, but Sal Oliver had had
her own table brought down to the larger room. Downstairs, the conversation of Miss Frayle and Miss Collier
continued intermittently, between their outbursts of
strenuous industry.

"I found a bit about reducing exercises in the paper
this morning. You can get seven pounds off in ten days,
it says. Not that I think it's true," observed Miss Collier.

"It might be true if one kept it up," Miss Frayle said,
"but one never does. It's quite difficult enough to get out
of bed in the mornings at the ordinary time, without
making it ten minutes earlier so as to lie on the floor and
try and touch the ceiling with your toe or whatever it
is."

"That's what I say."

"The woman Sarah has lost weight, if you ask me."

Miss Frayle by this mode of speech thought to give a great effect of detachment.

"Oh well, she had a bit of a shock last October. We all had, come to that."

"Yeah. Life's a pretty bloody show. Think of those poor kids."

"Well, thank God she didn't know she was leaving them. There couldn't have been time."

For the hundredth time they discussed the details of the accident, for the hundredth time Miss Collier shuddered and looked thoroughly sick, and Miss Frayle's blue eyes grew dark and pitiful at the thought of Claudia's children.

Edie came in with her tray and placed cups of tea on the table.

"Mrs. Ing. wanted some," she explained, "and I thought you might like it, the weather being so damn cold."

"Edie," said Miss Frayle, "if you said what I think you said, leave the room. What young girls are coming to, nowadays!"

Edie giggled.

"No, but, Miss Frayle, really I mean, it *is* something chronic, the cold. Just look at my fingers!"

"Try soap and water, young Edie."

Mrs. Ingatestone bounced in with an open notebook in her hand. Her hair, which had received attention the day before, was the colour of a brass bedstead.

"Good-morning, all," she cried, gayly. "Sorry I couldn't get down before. Miss Frayle, hop along upstairs, dear; she wants you to take down her letters. And there's a child to be met at Waterloo and taken to the dentist at twelve. I'll do that myself. Miss Collier, *she* wants that lease for the house in Hertfordshire. You know—the people home on leave from India. They'll be in, this morning."

"O.K.," said Miss Collier.

"You get back to your telephone, Edie, there's a good girl. If you want something to do, there are plenty of circulars to be got ready."

"What about that novel of yours?" Miss Frayle enquired. "Where the hell's my notebook?"

"Now, now, now!"

"O.K. I've found it."

"Run along now, Edie."

"O.K., Mrs. Ingatestone."

Upstairs, Sal gathered together the threads of the day's work.

It was all going well enough, she thought, and if she could only afford to advertize a bit more it would go better still.

Perhaps something could be done with the weekly papers. She made a note of the idea.

Outside it was dark and very cold.

Miss Frayle's light, decided fingers knocked at the door.

"Come in," said Sal.

In the second's interval between the words and the appearance of her secretary she lost herself in a brief but radiant dream of taking a month's holiday in the summer and going to the south of Spain.

Yes. She'd do that.

Definitely.

"Good-morning, Miss Oliver. Utterly suicidal weather, isn't it?"

"Quite. I think we'd better have the light on, Miss Frayle."

"O.K."

The work went on.

(7)

Copper Winsloe swung himself off the tram, turned up the collar of his mackintosh, and prepared to walk the last half-mile. Betsy followed him, obediently keeping at his heels and eying with some disgust the stream of cars that flashed along the highroad.

Copper was rather glad that he'd given up the idea of a car. The trams were handy, and the exercise good for him. He felt better than he'd felt for years. Soon it would be Easter, although no hint of spring was in the raw atmosphere, nor did the thorny hedges show any glint of green.

The Easter week-end would be a very busy one, with any luck. He'd be at the club all the time.

But if Frances Ladislaw came down she'd arrange something for Sylvia and Maurice so that it wouldn't be too dull for them. Copper felt, regretfully but helplessly, that Sylvia didn't have much of a time nowadays.

Sal Oliver wanted her to go and stay for a bit in London, next time Sal's friend was away and there was room. Well, she must go. It was a shame Taffy should be having all the fun.

There'd soon be young Maurice's public school outfit to think about, too. Copper decided that he ought to see about that himself. After all, he knew more about what kind of things a boy needed than any woman could.

And he'd take Maurice there himself, when the time came.

Copper reached the house and went up the little steps.

He hoped that there would be a letter from Frances Ladislaw. Somehow they'd drifted into a correspondence, and it had become by imperceptible degrees an important thing in his life.

I always liked her, he thought.

Dimly, at the back of his mind, a wistful hope was slowly taking form.

Putting his key into the door, Copper turned it and entered the tiny hall.

There was the letter from Frances, on the table, waiting.

From the sitting-room where the radio stood floated a thin, stuffless, melancholy phrase in a minor key:

> "Good—night—ba-by—
> Sleep—tight—ba-by—"

Rhythm slang and sentiment in the modern pattern combined in an unheeded farewell.

THE END